About the author

Wes Loran is an American author whose stories about the 20th century American fabric are set against the background of real history. The narratives reflect the lives of unsung heroes; men and women who are in essence the giants upon whose shoulders Americans now stand, whether their ancestors stepped on Plymouth Rock or, as Malcolm X famously said, "Plymouth Rock landed on us!" Mr. Loran is working on the second and third books in the trilogy. His wide-ranging experiences during the latter half of the 20th century and early 21st century have afforded him a unique and unapologetic vision of this time as told through the lives of everyday people.

20TH CENTURY AMERICAN: A NOVEL BASED UPON A REAL LIFE LIVED

Wes Loran

20TH CENTURY AMERICAN: A NOVEL BASED UPON A REAL LIFE LIVED

Pegasus

PEGASUS PAPERBACK

© Copyright 2025
Wes Loran

The right of Wes Loran to be identified as author of this work has been
asserted by him in accordance with the Copyright, Designs and Patents
Act 1988

All Rights Reserved

No reproduction, copy or transmission of this publication
may be made without written permission.
No paragraph of this publication may be reproduced,
copied or transmitted save with the written permission of the publisher,
or in accordance with the provisions
of the Copyright Act 1956 (as amended).

This is a work of fiction. Names, characters, businesses, places, events
and incidents are either the products of the author's imagination or used
in a fictitious manner. Any resemblance to actual persons, living or
dead, or actual events is purely coincidental.

Any person who does any unauthorised act in relation to this publication
may be liable to criminal prosecution and civil claims for damage.

A CIP catalogue record for this title is available from the British Library

ISBN-978-1-80468-091-9

*Pegasus is an imprint of
Pegasus Elliot MacKenzie Publishers Ltd.*
www.pegasuspublishers.com

First Published in 2025

**Pegasus
Sheraton House Castle Park
Cambridge CB3 0AX England**

Printed & Bound in Great Britain

Dedication

To the whites and blacks, who banded together in common cause decades before America was ready to accept the effort—the Southern Tenant Farmers' Union.

Acknowledgments

Thank you, Rachel, Scott, Angela, Debbie, Irv, and, most of all, Cathy and Gwen, for your encouragements and criticisms.

And my gratitude for the love and support of Jacqueline and Seth, who suddenly found they had to deal with a writer in the house!

Preface

The town of Paragould, Arkansas was birthed from the commercial coupling of two 19th Century railroad barons; Jay Gould, who owned the St. Louis and Iron Mountain Railroads that later became the Missouri-Pacific Railroad, and JW Paramore, who owned the Texas and St. Louis that became the Cotton Belt Railroad. The cotton-rich fields of Texas, Oklahoma, Arkansas, Louisiana, and Mississippi provided these gentlemen with the opportunity to ship great quantities of the fluffy white gold from the fields to the cotton presses in St. Louis and beyond. The timber stands in the region provided the balance of the incentive as the hardwoods had not yet been depleted to the point of exhaustion. Cotton fed the textile industry from St. Louis to New England, and timber fed the furniture manufacturing, home fittings, and other demands nationwide. There really was no other reason for the town to come into existence except for the junction of the two railroads.

In 1882, this coupling produced Paragould, which itself is a mixing of the family names of the barons. Thus, as though willed from on high by captains of industry, the town was born. Any wealth in the town was never homegrown. The town was a place through which raw materials moved to industry, thus, creating large amounts of capital, and industry trickled goods back to the town and the locals.

The people who supported this flow were unskilled and semi-skilled laborers who periodically moved from place to place and state to state, often illiterate and with several children in tow. Pick the cotton, chop the cotton, fell the trees, and rough-cut the lumber for shipment and work on county road projects when they existed, but go without or starve if you fell through the cracks for even a couple of weeks. If you were a tenant farmer or sharecropper, then you were bound in contractual servitude to the plantation owner: a new form of economic slavery for both blacks and whites. This wasn't Kansas, Nebraska, or Iowa, where virtually every farmer—or their bank—owned the farmable land, and you could decide how best to use the land and pass it on in estate to your children, as long as you paid the mortgage and the taxes.

Thus, the agricultural system in the South was diabolically designed to replace the very low cost of slave labor with the very low cost of exploitation labor of both whites and blacks. It was another definition of servitude. The indignity and suffering of these whites were only eclipsed in severity by that of the blacks, who in addition, were largely disenfranchised from the vote, targeted for violence, barred from organizing, and often paid less and worked harder. The hierarchy for all agricultural workers was this: top of the order was the landowner, next came the tenant farmers bound by onerous contract conditions, followed by the sharecroppers, who by nature of their arrangement, owed the planter constantly and forever, and lowest of the low was the laborer working for 'slave wages' under harsh conditions and without any agreement whatsoever. There were uncounted thousands of day laborers of both races, plus their families in Arkansas in the years 1900 to 1940. The annual number was certainly larger than the number of tenant and sharecropper farmers which stood at about eighty-five thousand in 1940, up from about fifty-six thousand in 1900. However, the change in landowners during that period was less than two percent. Agricultural laborers were largely illiterate or semi-literate, and lived a hand-to-mouth existence while working a million acres or more, mostly in the Delta area of Northeast Arkansas, exactly where Paragould is situated.

Life for the farm laborers in this vast sea of uncertainty was hard, even when families held together, and as is typical of humanity everywhere, it was the children who bore the brunt of the harshness around Paragould in such serial misery, so as to be removed from the middle-class miracle of America in the first sixty years of the 20th Century; as though that miracle only existed on another planet. But there were children, white and black, who through a combination of hope, grit, and determination refused to bow to the misery, drudgery, and their exploitation. They went searching for that 'other' America, and for some satisfying degree of self-actualization. When opportunities were presented by events such as the New Deal, the impending World War II catastrophe, the post-war aftermath of the American economic boom, and the ultimate desegregation of public schools—they got the hell out.

This tale is based upon the real-life story of what happened to one of the five children of just such a white laborer family. His life was that of a 20th century American, not with riches, glamour, fame, and degeneracy as many stories dwell upon. Nevertheless, it is a heroic American story of resilience, perseverance, and talent in the face of incredible hardships. And he was my father.

Chapter 1
The Journey to Nowhere–1926

Charles Dough surveyed the fields before him on the near horizon one morning in early September, 1926. He was lean and tanned standing at 6'1" in a very worn and threadbare cotton shirt and light wool pants. Charles wore no hat today, having forgotten it, and his sandy-colored hair went in several directions. He knew that a headache was the most likely result of spending ten hours in the sun. But cash in hand at the end of the day meant food on the table for pregnant Nellie, six-year-old Dorothy, and three-year-old Charlie. In the years since their marriage in 1918, Nellie had only been able to help in the fields for three seasons due to pregnancies, which put a strain on Charles who worked the cotton fields, the soybean fields, and the sawmill yard occasionally, piecing together just enough money to feed his growing family, and like many of his contemporaries looking forward to cash flow from the labor of his children when they were old enough. But he knew in his heart that at forty-four, he had aged before his time. He walked with stooped shoulders, never once wondering what alternative life there could be for him as he just put one foot in front of the other.

As the work wagons neared the harvesting fields, Charles looked upon his companions for the day, men and women who today were all white. White and black field laborers did the same types of work and Charles had worked in mixed-race work crews, but seldom together per the design of the larger society. Separation was one of the tools that the totally white plantation owners and local authorities used to keep the two races apart, so that it would be nearly impossible for them to unite in any common cause, or so they imagined.

"Gonna be a hot one," he muttered to no one in particular.

"Y'all want head cover, all y'all have to do is ask," responded one woman whose leathery face and lean features spoke of years in the sun with not enough to eat. "Take this cloth and wrap it around your head, boy." Charles started to refuse with a hand gesture, but she went on. "Tell yer Missus to clean it up and you can give it back when yer able. It's the Christian thing to do 'cause anyone can see yer head's gonna fry." Charles thanked her and began to wrap his head.

One of the other two men spoke. "This here's a small town and by now, most of us know that you and yer family got here from somewhere 'bout two months ago, and yer livin' in a shack, north edge o'town. And yer missus is expectin' real soon." He extended his hand. "Name's Jake Willard, and that there's Leedy, who gave you the head cloth," he said with a broad smile, only half endowed with teeth. Leedy nodded in greeting without smiling.

As Charles took Jake's hand and each shook the other's with a firm and neighborly grip, he looked down and not into Jake's eyes. As a man on the move, all his life he was wary of strangers in new places and always wondered what it would be that they would want from him and that he couldn't give. It was his misfortune that he could no longer sense that all some people wanted was to welcome you, no more than that.

"Thanks y'all kindly, and pleased to meet you."

"If yer want to get to know people 'round here, good people, jus' come on down to the Full Gospel Tabernacle Church, jus' up the road from yer house. Sundays, all are welcome and Reverend Walsh is a pretty darn good preacher." Charles promised to bring the family just as soon as Nellie and the new baby were able.

As the wagons neared the fields, some carrying children aged seven to eighteen, Charles took a few minutes to close his eyes and let his mind wander.

His family was everything to him. The joy in his life came from this source. It was Nellie's loving embrace, never complaining about their circumstances, that he looked forward to most when not traveling to work, working, or searching for work. Although he was always tired in the evenings, he indulged the children as best he could and was fascinated by their different behaviors. Dorothy was a pretty, slim, and quiet girl with long, wavy auburn hair. She had just turned six and showed no problems with learning her letters and numbers, but you never knew what she was thinking behind her faraway gaze. Charles Jr., or 'Charlie,' didn't say much at all, and was slow to react to any request. He stared vacantly most of the time and expressed little interest in the world around him. The one thing that seemed to brighten his eyes was when Charles took out his knife and carved pieces of wood into small animals or boats. Watching Nellie with the children made him love her the more for her patience and tender care with a maturity beyond her years. He was a gentleman by nature, and it never occurred to him to question the social norm of his time, and in his level of society of being a widower in his thirties marrying a teenage girl.

Charles had been a farm hand and itinerant laborer for all his life and was self-taught in his letters and writing, though these accomplishments stopped at a third-grade level. He had lost his first wife at a young age to childbirth, along with their stillborn son. But fourteen years had passed since then, when in 1918, at the age of thirty-six, Charles married Nellie who was barely sixteen. They had moved around from Arkansas to Texas, then to Oklahoma, and on to Missouri and Tennessee, where he tried to find better work. But that failed to happen for him though their first two children were born on that journey. Given the combination of rich cotton and soybean fields around Paragould, plus abundant hardwood harvesting and rough-cut lumber in the immediate area—Nellie and Charles decided to settle and make a go of it no matter what, and like human boulders rolling down a hillside, they had finally arrived at their angle of repose for better or worse.

It was under these circumstances that Nellie's mother Cora Belle, who was only four years older than Charles, offered to help with the children, and although Charles did not relish the idea of living in a small and ramshackle house with the domineering and outspoken three-time widow, he faced reality and consented. She was on her way from Tennessee at this moment, trying to make it before the impending birth of their third child. They expected her to arrive tomorrow.

The wagons came to a stop, and suddenly, Charles woke up from his trance and surveyed the cotton fields that held the day's work located eight miles outside of Paragould. The foreman directed the children to the front and the adults after them. There were eighteen souls in all, six to a wagon. Street labor cotton pickers were paid by the pound of cotton picked. The work was arduous, and hands were constantly cut and swollen by the end of the day, treated at home at night. Anyone taller than a ten-year-old would eventually develop severe back problems. The men, taller and stronger as a rule, could pack away more cotton than women and children. They could earn on average a dollar a day at one to two cents per pound. The women generally half that and the children earned twenty to twenty-five cents per day, all working ten hours and a thirty-minute break for a midday meal usually of biscuits, a little bacon, and whatever else could be saved from the prior day. Water was provided by the foreman who had a water boy circulate among the pickers.

The foreman, Mr. Marshall Tibbet, displayed a no-nonsense approach and did not entertain questions of any kind. He was a short man with mild features that belied his fiery temper. It was a temper backed by the full authority of the owner not to pay you if you didn't do exactly as he demanded in the field. Whether through divine order or just a plain ornery nature, Tibbet seemed to view it as his duty not to bestow one whit of geniality or empathy to man, woman, or child in the wagons or in the fields. He saw himself as the frontline guardian of order in a world of potential and even actual chaos, such chaos as blacks and whites finding common cause and common power. He clearly saw that these people standing before him deserved their misery because that is where they had obviously put themselves through their own fault. He held forth in front of the wagons:

"For those of y'all who ain't been here before, this is how it works." He proceeded to herd the children to the first rows, one per row—a row in this case being about two hundred yards. Then, he did the same with the women and finally with the men. Eighteen rows were thus addressed by the slapdash workforce. The adults were all experienced pickers and knew what was expected of them. "You kids, shut your pie holes and keep quiet while you're pickin', and don't speak unless spoken to. Water'll come 'round regular. Everybody! I will weigh your pick when your bag is full, or at the end of the day if it ain't, and I'll make a record. When we get back to town, y'all get paid." He spat a wad of chewing tobacco to emphasize the point. "Now get to work, it's six a.m. and we go home at four-thirty. When you finish a row, come see me and I'll rotate ya to another. Foller these rules, mind you!" And with that, he hoisted his scales, record book, and pack; and parked himself under a poplar as the leaves were still on the tree, that would provide him the shade that he believed he so richly deserved.

"And you kids watch out for black widows. I ain't takin' none of you to town if you're bit." He knew the chances of finding the reclusive and shade-loving spider on the actual cotton plant, baking in the sun, were slim to zero. But he found some humor in putting a scare into the little rascals, and he made an almost imperceptible smile with his thin lips under the shadow of his hat brim, as the smaller children, more susceptible to his baiting, stared with trepidation at the cotton plants. Tibbet was too ignorant and drunk on his own power to realize, that by inhibiting the speed of the children picking from fear of imaginary poisonous spiders, he was decreasing the take for the owners.

Charles began to pick along his row with the speed and thoroughness of a seasoned picker. He aimed to make two dollars today for one hundred pounds of cotton, not unheard of but also not probable. This was a goal rarely met even by the hardiest and most skillful of pickers. Still, he wanted to show something extra for the birth of his newest child. And he looked forward to a few weeks from now when the picking would be over, and there would be a time of work at one of the sawmills for twenty or twenty-five cents an hour for a ten or twelve-hour shift. It was dangerous work, and he had seen his share of horrible disfigurements and amputations in twenty-five years of sawmill experience throughout the states, where he journeyed. But there was something special about wood. He loved the smell of the different species of walnut, cherry, oak, ash, sycamore, and others. Wood held an almost mystical aura that he could sense, and he often wondered where he could go to find out how it got worked into so may fantastic things, to become one of the wood magicians. But right now, he was picking cotton and couldn't think about such things, already having cut two fingers that had to be wrapped as he worked… all because he was distracted by pondering wood, and why he was so drawn to its beauty and its utility as he dreamed of earning much more at the sawmills if only briefly.

The morning wore on to a hot and sticky day, the kind of heat and humidity that draws the water from the body. The water boy constantly circulated, dispensing ladles of water from a common bucket. The lunch break happened at eleven when the sun was high in the late summer sky. People found shade under the wagons or under nearby trees. Charles parked himself on the ground with a small group of men as they took their food out of pouches and packs, their fifty-pound sacks at hand and under watchful eyes.

Jake seemed to want to engage Charles and asked, "When's the Missus due?"

Charles stopped biting at his biscuit and replied through a mouthful, "Any time now." He was worried that Nellie would be alone and deliver before Cora arrived tomorrow, so arrangements had been made for a neighboring mother to check in on Nellie from time to time. They had no automobile, not even a bicycle, and would have to rely upon others for transportation to the hospital so, consequently, Charles had arranged for a midwife to be summoned from a five-minute walk away. The hospital was always a longshot.

"Guess you're excited and a bit worried, bein' out here and all so close to the baby's day. If y'all need any help, anything at all, just get hold of me. We're close by and just round the corner at the end of Webber Street. Last house on the right."

"Thank you kindly, Jake. We'll do that if we need help." Charles couldn't wait to get back to work because he was only a few pounds shy of his first dollar and still had time to close in on the second bag of the day. Two dollars would feed everyone for days and would help a bit with new baby care. Energized by his sense of familial responsibility, Charles sprang up, grabbed his sack and started toward the fields across the road.

Marshall wasn't about to stop him from cutting his lunch break short by fifteen minutes. *Hell,* he thought. *If the fool is so eager, if any of them are so eager, it simply means I bring in more product to the boss. They can work themselves to death on their own initiative if they want. There's plenty more where they come from!*

The next five hours stretched to a psychological eon under the hot afternoon sun. Two people, one man and one woman, collapsed and had to be revived in the shade and given more water. But Charles kept picking at an amazing rate, comforted by the image of Nellie being happy with the money he would bring home. He might even splurge and buy each of the kids a penny bag of rock candy. At the end of the day, at four-thirty p.m., the stop-work whistle was blown, and weighing was then done by Marshall, each amount being entered into the book. This took thirty minutes. When he came to Charles, he whistled, pulled his hat back from his forehead, and remarked, *"Whoa, Charles! You already posted fifty pounds, and now another forty-two! Hell of a day, boy."* That would be $1.84 in his pocket and many times that for the planter. The penny bags of candy would have to wait, well, perhaps one penny bag they could share.

It was six-thirty p.m. when Charles walked up to the ramshackle little house that they now called home. It had a tar roof, sagging walls, and a slowly collapsing covered porch. Three rooms served to provide two bedrooms and a kitchen/eating area. Water was drawn from a pump, and other needs were served by the outhouse a short distance from the house. Electricity had not yet come to this portion of town, but the place had a small stove that burned wood and coal. It was used for cooking and for heat in the winter. The rent was ten dollars a month, paid to one of the landowners who also owned many such shacks around the area.

When he spied a small group of people clustered in front of the house, his pace quickened into a trot and then to an outright run. His worst fears blew through his head like a storm. *Has something happened to Nellie or the baby or both? The baby be of good health?* Charlie, he knew, had been born with an impediment; he was 'slow.' *I can't make enough money,* he thought. *What will I do?* But as quickly as this tide of worries rose, it subsided when he saw the smiles on his new neighbors' faces, and the weariness of the day and of his whole life was instantly shed, as he bounded into the house and was greeted by the midwife. She had been through this at least a hundred times while learning and practicing her craft.

She carried her own wisdom on human behavior to meet the occasion and in these parts, she was an available, welcomed, and cheaper alternative to the doctor or the hospital. If the doctor could be summoned in time, she would defer and render post-natal care as needed. In the 1920s there had been pressure to do away with midwives in Arkansas. However, the establishment soon realized that doctors could not really serve the underserved fully, and they were allowed to continue their service to the community. In rural towns like Paragould, and in the Ozark hill country, midwives were trusted and experienced members of communities, who were often underserved by medical services.

Maddie Harcroft, forty-three years old and a grandmother, had the ability to put mothers, fathers, siblings, friends, and family at ease, and maintained a calm and reassuring demeanor even when difficulties or mortality were involved. Most importantly yet unknowable by her clients, was the fact that local doctors and the hospital respected her judgment, and they had learned to trust that she would never waste their resources and was rarely wrong in her field diagnosis. If she conveyed 'this woman and her baby need help' or 'this baby must be turned' and why she thought that was so, then the medical services responded as quickly as possible.

"Well, have mercy, Daddy! You're about to kill yourself before you say hello to your new son and your lovin' wife. Slow down and go on in, but quiet-like. You can spend a little while with them. But I still have more work to do before I leave y'all to get my supper. Congratulations, Charles, and welcome to the neighborhood!" With that, she gave him a hug and kissed his cheek lightly, then stood aside so that he could enter the bedroom. He responded with a silent, awkward nod. First, he went to the kitchen table and hugged his children, telling them to be patient and he would call them in soon. Then, he entered the room where Nellie and his new son were in bed. The infant born nearly five hours earlier was already nursing in his first feed outside the womb. Nellie's plain and wide-featured face managed a smile, and her long dark brown hair was draped across her shoulders. She appeared tired but happy. At twenty-four years, she was in her peak childbearing years and showed no signs of the difficult and tenuous life she had lived with Charles to that point. Part of her happiness was based upon Charles' promise that they would move around no more.

"You left your hat this mornin', Charlie. I hope you haven't burned your head," she said in a low voice as she eyed him in examination.

"That's all you got to say? Worried about a sunburn?" he faked irritation, then quickly smiled and asked, "How are you, Nellie, and how's our boy?" He could barely contain himself and sat on the bed, kissing Nellie softly on the forehead and gently pulling the light cover from the face of their son, who was quite busy attempting to draw milk, with some success, from his mother's breast. Charles admired the perfectly formed baby who ignored his attention at that moment, fixed on the task at hand the way newborn infants do by holding tight little fists close to their cheeks. He shifted his gaze back and forth a few times between baby and mother.

"I know what you're thinkin', Charlie; another mouth to feed and less space for all of us." He knew she had hit the target. "But we can't stay on the move lookin' for work and raise a family proper. You're a hard worker, so am I, and with Mama here to help with the children, we can do okay. And there's love here, Charlie—real love, and that's a rare treasure we got to be thankful for." Her large blue eyes smiled at him, and for that moment, he felt like he could manage anything to keep the family together and raise good people. But he was also keenly aware of circumstances and carried the burden of growing up as an orphan farm hand in a poverty-stricken area of the country; a burden he constantly fought to shed through his love of Nellie and his children. But he didn't always succeed in the battle within himself. He wished he could have apprenticed somewhere to work with wood, build furniture, or other functional items; but those days and opportunities were long gone, and life had been so lonely in the years between the death of his first wife and child, and his marriage to Nellie.

Sometimes, he just wanted to curl up next to Nellie and forget, to let her warm and loving nature cover him, shield him, and provide a welcome door to another existence. She was, bless her, still young enough to believe in limitless possibilities. He was old enough to know better.

The baby had fallen asleep at the breast, and Nellie gently covered him and adjusted her shift.

"Well, Daddy, what shall we name him?" The name Charles been taken. "How about my Grandpa, Carl?"

"That's a good name, a strong name. I like it, but I never knew your Grandpa. It's good for me though," he said.

"I never knew him either 'cause he passed when I was four. But Mama says he was a good man. What about a middle name? He's got to have a middle name."

Little Carl let Nellie know he wasn't really finished, by puckering his lips and looking for something to suck. Nellie pulled her shift up and silently allowed the baby to re-engage.

Charles thought a moment and he said, "Wesley. It's my middle name, and I want to pass it on. Folks have told me it means 'man from the west fields' in the old tongue, and it seems like a good farmer's name; and besides, the man who started the Methodist Church was named Wesley and you know I favor the Methodists." Nellie had no idea who that was, but she liked the sound of Carl Wesley Dough and nodded in agreement.

She kissed Carl on his head and whispered, "You're gonna be a good man, Carl." Carl responded by clenching his little fists even tighter and increased the pressure on his draw at Nellie's nipple.

Charles said he would like to bring Dorothy and Charlie in for a quick minute before Nellie's rest, and while they were adoringly ogling mother and child, Charles suddenly felt panic and ushered the kids into the kitchen, after telling Nellie to get some rest. The midwife was leaving and promised to return in the morning, assuring Charles that all was in order before she bustled out the door. "Stay here for a few minutes, I'll be right back," he instructed them, and they dutifully sat down to wait. Charles went outside and walked a distance from the house as the sun was setting. As the last rays of the late summer sun adorned the horizon, he stared into space for a few moments, stress lines appearing on his weathered face.

I should be happy for Nellie and the children, I am happy, he thought. But the specter of defeat gnawed at his soul like that sinking feeling in an overmatched boxer, knowing his own fighting spirit to give it his all, but at the same time, realizing that he would bow to the inevitable. *Maybe,* he thought. *If you played by the rules then you went down by the rules.* He wanted to scream at the top of his lungs but held his angst inside for the sake of his family, and to make sure the neighbors didn't ask questions. He would never complain or openly express his hatred for the invisible box that enclosed him, separating him from aspirations. As he clenched his fists, he asked himself how in the hell despite the hard work and the love in his life, he was going to avoid a journey to nowhere.

Lost in his own thoughts, he returned to the house to get supper ready for everyone. Tomorrow, Cora would arrive to help with such matters. His mind settled on little Carl, another mouth to feed. But Charles wasn't going to run, wasn't going to beat his kids or abuse his wife in frustration. He was resolved to do the best he could for his family. The secret he kept inside himself and never shared with anyone, including his beloved Nellie, was that he knew for certain, the arc of his life was set without some outside intervention. There were no open doors for him, but things could be different for the children. They would stay put in Paragould and make it work. The kids would go to school and have opportunities to better themselves so that they could avoid his journey to nowhere. It was what he expected of himself as the father and husband, to turn his dead-end life of hard labor and poverty into a portal through which their children could pass.

Chapter 2
Those Cotton-Pickin' Cotton Pickers, 1933

During the most trying years of the Great Depression, things were looking up in the cotton industry. The drought of 1930–31 was now a memory, as people in Northeast Arkansas returned to the normalcy of hot, humid summer days with intermittent thunderstorms and blazing sun. When combined with the rich soil of the Delta region, these conditions led to a revival of cotton production which meant more work for laborers. Since Carl's birth, one more child had been added, a daughter they named Annabelle, born in 1930. From 1930 to 1934 were probably the worst years for the family. The state and the country were plunged into the Great Depression, the poor certainly at a steeper angle than others. The reemployment of large portions of the nation's workforce under the New Deal was still in the future. So, things looked more promising soon for men like Charles, if you were willing to go to the work camps around the country that were being discussed in Washington and elsewhere. But all of that wasn't here just yet, and timing is literally everything when you're dirt poor.

For Charles, President Roosevelt's much discussed program could be the ticket out of abject poverty, and from what he gleaned from the store radio and newspapers, augmented by porch front discussions with neighbors or at church on the Sundays, when he felt well enough to go, there was the promise of the opportunity for better work and pay. But now at fifty-one years old, the harsh conditions of his life were catching up to him, and he began to experience random and uncontrollable fits of coughing coupled with an increasingly oppressive fatigue after working. As per his dream, Dorothy and Carl went to school and each were getting good reports from their teachers. Charlie, ten years old, wasn't suited for school as it was taught at that time, so he went with Charles to the fields but never to the occasional sawmill work; as Charles considered it an inevitability that Charlie would be injured or worse. The family's fortunes now depended completely upon Charles and Charlie working as much as possible.

Cora had proven to be a much stricter influence on the kids and took to bossing Nellie around, constantly telling her how to manage the children and support Charles, while not really contributing to the actual work of running a household with four children and very limited resources. But Cora saw to it that nobody missed a meal, most importantly Cora. "Mind you, your children will think they're better than you. They need responsibility more than school." Cora would often say. "If your husband was worth his salt, you wouldn't be livin' like this." As for the children, "Put 'em to work, times demand it."

Dorothy was quiet and distant, even from Nellie who lavished her attention upon Annabelle, a perky and inquisitive three-year-old with a head of curly hair that was fiercer in color than her siblings. But Dorothy could not be reached. She had trouble expressing and receiving affection, or to accept closeness to anyone in the family. "You best marry that girl off as soon as you can 'cause she's gonna be trouble, mind you." Cora herself had been married at sixteen and lost three husbands in a row to death. She was a perpetual widow and made the most of it in every way: bitter, demanding, demeaning, and in her own mind, a cunning survivor. Her children were forced out at very early ages.

Then, there was Carl, who at seven, was inquisitive and generally compliant with any request, whether by Nellie, Cora, or Charles. His blond hair from birth had transformed into light brown hair that was growing darker in shade as time passed. His blue eyes always sparkled with his smile and laughter, the most affable of the children. He had started talking about the future, proclaiming in his little boy's voice that he wanted to be a scientist and invent something everybody could use, though, at the time, he had no real idea of how a 'scientist' worked nor any knowledge of the scientific method. Cora, of course, found the boy's head to be full of nonsense and didn't hold back her opinion, as was usual, telling both Nellie and Charles "That kind of dreamin' ain't gonna put food on the table." For Charles, who was out most of the time either working or searching for work, her ranting simply downgraded to background noise. For Nellie, her stock reply was "I'm sure you're right, Momma."

Of course, everyone could see that Charles was in trouble. Hot toddies, mustard plasters, and herbal remedies, all seemed to have little effect except for some temporary relief. As the year wore on, and cotton harvesting demanded pickers, he was faced with the reality that he could no longer guarantee sufficient cash from a day's work, even with Charlie, who was slower at it than most children, who were in turn much slower than the adults. To top it off, Nellie had announced her fifth pregnancy in late August. More mouths to feed.

Cora had silently planned her escape, having taken up with a sixty-year-old widower who owned his own house on the other side of town. At the end of 1933, they were married. He became the fourth of five husbands in her life, and she eventually outlived every one of them to the age of ninety-three.

Charles and Nellie now rented a house with four rooms. They shared one bedroom with Annabelle. Charlie and Dorothy shared a room, and Carl slept on a cot in the main room, where the kitchen and dining area were located. Cora, of course, had her own room before she left for her new husband's house. The house was larger but not higher in quality than their former home, and it also lacked running water and electricity, though electric power was soon coming to their neighborhood. In the last few years, Charles had picked up more higher-paying work at the sawmill, where he never said no to any work request and became known as that 'hardworking, sandy-haired Irishman.' His single biggest fear was that his health would get him booted out of the upcoming mill work. They couldn't survive without it.

One Sunday night in late August, Nellie and Charles lay nestled together in bed, all in the house were asleep except for them. Charles worked up the courage to tell her what was on his mind.

"Nellie, honey, Carl got to help me for a couple of weeks at the cotton pickin'. Just for a couple of weeks till we're done. We need the money and I can't pick fast enough any more to make what we need, even with Charlie. The mill work is at least six weeks away. Don't be mad, he'll just miss a little school and he'll make it up. He's a hard worker and loves his schoolin'."

Nellie turned to face him in the dark. She put her hand on his forehead and smoothed his hair, gently saying "I know it's got to happen for everyone's sake, Charlie. And I don't know what ails you, but I know you can't work like you used to. But you got to promise me that Carl will go back to school. I know that if you promise me, he will."

Nellie had a special place in her heart for Carl. She loved all her children and would have died for any of them. Carl picked up her spirits with his enthusiasm and playful nature, especially if he detected that Nellie needed a laugh or a diversion. And he loved school. She could see that Annie and Carl were kindred spirits. Annie was a feisty and inquisitive three-year-old who laughed a lot. While Dorothy was a mystery and Charlie was challenged, they were her mystery and challenge, and she loved them dearly. And despite the constant struggles to feed, clothe, and house the family, Nellie did not take the road of regret and recrimination in her poverty. She embraced everyone in the family and was content to help them as best she could.

"I promise you that, Nellie. But it would help if your Momma cut lose a bit of her money to help us through a hard patch. I'll be on my feet, and I hope to land more work at the mill.

There's talk of a lot of need for lumber of all kinds next year and after that. Could be a good future for us. Or, I might go for a while to one of the work camps they's talkin' about in Washington. But Cora don't provide no money at all, and you end up doin' all the work around here and now, we have our fifth child on the way. Can you talk to her and see if she can help? After all, I been feedin' her for years now." Nellie and Charles each knew that Cora had money put away in a bank in Memphis from her marriages. She didn't know how much, but Cora never lacked for nice clothes and paid for things like a photographer to take a family portrait in 1930, after Annabelle's birth.

Nellie loved Cora because she was her mother, but she also knew her mother well and placed little confidence in Cora's willingness to part with any of her own money, if someone else could bear the burden.

"Moma's gonna be out of here soon, getting married to old James she is. Probably by the end of the year. So whatever plans we make shouldn't include her. Best for all of us. We'll put Carl back in school at the end of September. Baby's due in March, as the doctor says. You've always been strong, Charlie. We'll get you well and you'll get better work. Folks know you 'round here now and they know your quality. Your boss at the mill wants you there more, and that's lots better than working the fields and cuttin' down trees with a cross-saw. We'll bring no more babies into this world after this one. There's plenty of ways for us to be lovin' with each other that don't result in babies," she smiled at him in the dark.

His answer reflected two sides of the courage/weakness coin. "We'll do our best, Nellie dear, we'll do our best." And with that, he gave her a final hug and rolled over, happy to sound positive to her but a bit ashamed of hiding how his body really felt. It took him two hours to go to sleep, just enough time for three hours of sleep before rising at four a.m. to prepare for the day in the cotton fields. Nellie had kissed him on the shoulder, then rolled over and fallen fast asleep, despite the coughing fit that overcame Charles for a full minute. It briefly woke everyone in the household except Nellie.

Charles and Charlie went to the fields the next morning, picking early-season cotton much as they had done before. But their share of the day's harvest came to $1.28, a disappointing number mainly due to Charles' fatigue. Thus, his resolve was strengthened to enlist little Carl. On a good day with little Carl's help, they could still hit nearly two dollars, whether he was tired or not. But how to break it to him that he would have to wait a few weeks to go to school, after school had started for everyone else? It was rare for the children of field laborers to attend school beyond the first year or two, and Carl and Dorothy were exceptions to the rule. The national public school system and the national network of local Carnegie Libraries were rarely of service to the children of cotton pickers and day labourers, especially if they were black and therefore segregated.

Carl, even at seven, would still have to be told in a way so as to play upon the innocence of a child. He loved his Daddy and his whole family. If Daddy asked him or even told him, he would always do his best, proud to know that he was helping. So that evening, after supper and just before bed, Charles sat him down on the porch as Nellie quietly looked on from the doorway.

"Listen, Carl, there's somethin' that I need your help with, son." He placed his hand on the small shoulder next to him. Carl looked up with wide open eyes.

"What's that, Daddy?"

"Well, you see, just for a little while, a few weeks in fact, Charlie and I need your help working the cotton fields. It's an important job and will help me while I am getting better. Will you do it for me?"

Carl wanted to be big and do what an adult would do. He had a serious look on his face as if he were considering all aspects of the problem. But it took him all of three seconds to answer, "Of course, Daddy, but I don't know how to pick cotton. You'll have to show me. Charlie doesn't talk enough to show me." Then, a light went on in his head. "What about school, it starts in a week, doesn't it?"

"Yes, it does, son. But you're a smart boy and will only have to catch up for two or three weeks, tops. Then, you'll be back to normal." Charles felt horrible and thoroughly ashamed but tried not to let it show. "What do you say?"

"I'll do it, Daddy, I will. Don't worry, I'll help you and Charlie but then I'll go back to school, promise?"

"Yes, I promise. It's just this once. Thank you for helping your daddy." They hugged each other, and Nellie smiled and went back into the kitchen area. Carl never knew his daddy to fail on a promise, even if it took a while to deliver, and promises were rarely made. Promises in his world were never given lightly and always observed unless you died.

"All right, Carl, off to bed. We get an early start and you, Charlie, and I will make some money tomorrow." Carl bounded off the steps and back up them with the energy of a seven-year-old, which made Charles a bit jealous.

The children of this vast population of farm laborers, and occasional timber and mill workers were heavily discriminated against both in and out of school. White or black, they were considered inferior to normal folks who had homes they owned, businesses they ran, or professions they plied. And, most importantly, they had access to money. When such children did attend school, such as those from families that didn't own their farms or worked on the plantation lands, they were roundly teased and bullied, and when they fought back or stood up for themselves, they were generally punished, and/or shunned and made to feel ashamed of who they were. The children of black families in this category didn't even go to school or went to poorly equipped segregated schools, and suffered active and open prejudices, and social and physical brutality from the day they were born. The whites and the blacks in this category were generally referred to as 'poor white trash' or 'them niggers.'

'Ignorant kids of niggers and white trash,' was a common dismissal. In this Jim Crow economy, white or black, you stayed where you belonged, which is to say, to provide a continuous supply of cheap and available labor no matter what the human cost. This, the whites shared with the blacks, who had landed in the same position but had the extra burden of being black in the South, where the Civil War and its aftermath was still a raw issue with many of the locals throughout the region.

Even at his tender age, Carl knew where he stood. But he didn't care. At school, he heard, "I bet your momma and daddy can't even read or write, and that's why you're so dumb. You ain't got no shoes, neither." That much was true, only in winter did Carl wear used or hand-me-down high-top shoes. The soles of his little feet were as tough as rhino hide. Carl, a bit on the small side at this age, wouldn't back down.

"I'm gonna bust you in the nose if you say one more word about my mommy and daddy." Sometimes, a fight ensued, and sometimes, he got the better of it and sometimes the worse. But he never struck the first blow because Daddy wouldn't have a son that acted that way.

"Only fight when you must, Carl. Never fight to take revenge, cause we all got plenty of hurt in this life without having to pick a fight." But then, he would add with a sideways grin, "But if you must fight, fight to win and make the other guy know that even if he wins, he'll get hurt. Fightin's something you don't want to do, Carl, unless your safety or your life depends on it, or those of loved ones."

While little Carl tried to be mindful of Daddy's instructions, he nevertheless learned how to pick a fight and not strike the first blow, just to get one in on the bullies. One afternoon, as he passed a kid named Maynard and his little gang, he recalled with satisfaction the first time he pulled that off.

"You don't belong here, go back to your rathole shack and be a cotton picker like your daddy," shouted Maynard, a hulking fourth grader standing in front of his little band of followers.

"I'm gonna be a scientist, you moron," replied Carl, putting emphasis on the word 'moron.'

"Who you callin' a moron, you little shit?" Maynard strode in a straight line to Carl, his freckled face red with fury and indignation, then took a wide swing, confident in his superior size and strength. Carl ducked under the swing, came up quick as a snake, and landed a fist right on Maynard's nose. Much blood and little real damage ensued, which gave Carl a brief opportunity to land a couple of harmless body blows to the briefly stunned and much larger Maynard. But it wasn't in Carl's nature to want to hurt people and he started to back off. Maynard regrouped and pushed Carl's hands down, and proceeded to drive him to the ground… the worst place to be in a fight, especially fighting somebody bigger and stronger than you. Shouts of encouragement came from Maynard's gang, but the amount of blood now staining his new clothes dismayed him, and with one punch to a pinned down Carl, he managed to make him see stars but got up and stumbled away. As if he could recover it, he was trying comically in his cupped hands to catch the blood pouring from his nostrils, while the pain in his nose started throbbing. Carl lay defeated on the ground, dizzy and smiling with a head full of pain. But Maynard never bothered him again.

Yet, blood was on Maynard, whose father was the assistant manager of the train yard. Carl was punished by having to write a hundred times on the chalkboard, *"I promise not to fight again, and I am sorry I hit Maynard."* The teacher hadn't bothered to give him a grammatically correct sentence. He also received the switch on his hands. Nellie was roundly chastised by the school principal for raising a little ruffian. But Nellie knew he was a good-natured child with a strong sense of right and wrong. She understood that what he really wanted from the other kids was for them to like him. She listened patiently, keenly aware that Carl's record in academics would not obviate the principal's prejudice against her economic class. "Don't worry, we'll make sure everything is all right." And she bid the principal good day.

The next day, Carl needed to consult with someone he trusted. "Why do some kids have to be so mean, is it jus' cause they got money, Mamma?" he asked Nellie while handing her clothes to hang on the line.

"People can be mean for lots of reasons, not just because they think they're better than you. Sometimes, it's because they want something that you have, and the only way they think they can get it is to be mean, ornery, and tricky. It's a sort of revenge if you follow my meaning." Carl nodded his understanding. "And if they can't get it themselves, then they want to take it from you because they think that'll make them feel better, but not all people are like that." Nellie had seen and experienced all kinds of meanness in her life, not the least of which came from her mother in a passive-aggressive style.

"What do I have that anybody'd want? I got nothin' to speak of."

"Well, Carl, you have a family that loves you. You also have a curious mind and do good in school. You're also a nice boy, always friendly to people, even those you don't know. Trust me, even people with money often don't have those things. Kids are no different." Carl thought upon her last words and started to say something, but Nellie cut him off. "We're done here, my sweet boy. Time to go inside." And she left him to ponder her answers. And ponder he did.

Three months after the fight with Maynard, on the first Monday in September, Carl accompanied his father and Charlie to his first day in the fields. In his mind, this was an adventure, something new that he had only heard about from others, but now he had the chance to make some money for the family, and Daddy promised to give him five cents to spend at the general store near their house in honor of his first day of work. Charles would have given him five dollars if he had it to give. He was so proud of how little Carl had stepped up to help, and he carried a bit of guilt about the guile of playing on his sickliness and

Carl's love for him. But the money was sorely needed by all.

Carl and Charlie fell asleep on the long ride into the countryside and to the fields being picked that day. He had arisen, eaten a breakfast of eggs and biscuits, and literally jumped up and down the entire walk to the trucks assembled to take the pickers to the fields. But once he was seated, he fell fast asleep against his father's shoulder, not even stirring when Charles broke into a fit of coughing, which he tried to stifle with his hanky, one of which he now always carried with him. A few years back, he had come by some cotton overalls and had enough pockets to hide hankies.

When they arrived at the work fields just before six a.m., he woke Carl and Charlie and told them to wake up and get ready. Carl immediately became animated and expressed his eagerness to get to work, ignorant of the type of day that lay ahead, yet certain he would return to school in two or three weeks. He looked at Charlie, who just stared as he usually did, then at Charles, who was trying to take deep, slow breaths in his struggle to maintain normality and mindful of the need to give Carl confidence.

The trucks came to a noisy halt and the work boss motioned to everyone to get out of the trucks, but before he could speak, a shrill and boyish voice yelled out enthusiastically,

"C'mon you cotton pickin' cotton pickers, let's get to work!"

Charles was mortified, had never seen anything like it in all his years in the fields, and he feared some form of rebuke or retribution from the work boss, who was not known for his sense of humor. For being cut off by a child, he could have benched Carl with no work and no pay for the day, and blacklisted him from his work crews. He let out a deep and throaty laugh and yelled out, "Son of a bitch! This boy's got the right attitude ladies and gents, boys and girls. Wouldn't hurt any of y'all to adopt it." But then, he looked straight at Carl and said in an even tone, somewhat menacing to a seven-year-old, "But now it's time to get to work, so there'll be no more yellin' out. If anyone does any yellin', it'll be me," and he emphasized the last word.

Little Carl didn't know what to make of it, but his daddy whispered, "Don't talk, Carl, don't say a thing." Then, the work boss proceeded with a speech very much like Marshall Tibbet seven years earlier, and echoed by countless field work bosses in the history of cotton picking since the Civil War ended. Before that, such speeches weren't necessary for slaves. They had plenty of oppression and incentive to toe the line, when singing was the only expression allowed, and then only with the permission of the overseer.

But Carl got the message, and already he didn't like picking cotton nearly as well as being in school. Petulance was an emotional expression that was totally alien to Carl. Quiet resolve, even at this young age, was his answer to such prejudice and restriction. Still, on a certain level, it hurt his feelings. He resolved to show this boss that he was the best damn seven-year-old cotton picker he ever saw. By the end of that day, he had picked over thirty pounds of cotton, cut both hands multiple times, and his energy even wore off on Charlie, who managed an unprecedented twenty-eight pounds. Charles, who had to stop for coughing fits, still managed to pick one hundred and ten pounds, so the day's income happily met his expectations.

"How did I do, Daddy?" he asked on the truck home. "I'm gonna pick as much cotton as I can before I go back to school." His bravado belied his deep apprehension about being able to do just that.

Charles was so proud of his son, of both his sons in fact. "You did great, Carl, you both did great today," he said, as he looked at Charlie with a smile. Charlie managed a small smile of his own and looked at Carl, whom he clearly enjoyed having along as company. "And so, here's a nickel, Carl. Now, you share some of this with your brother, as he earned it, too. Don't expect this every day, now. Family needs the money, so we all have enough." Carl's hands hurt and as his father explained to him how to avoid cuts, which would always happen at some level no matter the precautions, he listened and promised to take it to heart. Right now, he wanted his Mamma to tend to his cuts and swelling. But it was all going to be okay in Carl's eyes, because he got to help his daddy and be with him and Charlie, got to make some money for the family, some store treats for Charlie and him, and most importantly, to Carl, he would go back to school soon. The threats of bullies seemed to fade away in importance.

When the work trucks arrived at the edge of town, the weary company of cotton pickers slowly slid off the truck beds where many had fallen asleep, including Carl and

Charlie. Their tallies had been done in the field and the work boss led them to the paymaster, who also possessed a 1911 model Colt .45 sidearm. When their names were called, the workers presented themselves to the paymaster, who then doled out the correct amount for each worker with the children's money handed to the parent they accompanied. Three strangers watched these proceedings from the evening shade of a nearby building, and patiently waited until the field boss dismissed the entire crew.

The odd thing about them, was the fact that two were white and one was African American, and all wore shirts and ties. As they quickly strode toward the group, one of the white men raised his hand and shouted out to the group, "Folks, just a minute of your time, please! Y'all most likely want to hear what we have to say." Most in the crowd looked uncertain, but also unwilling to pass on something that might benefit them, and they were wary of snake oil salesmen.

"My name is Harry Mitchell from Tyronza, as you know not far from here, and these men are Mr. Clay East, business owner, and Mr. E.B. McKinney, tenant farmer."

"You got no legitimate business here, fellas. These people don't want to hear the Commie bullshit you're peddlin'. Go on home now, all of ya. There's plenty of folks who can work for us besides you, and they won't give the time of day to the likes of these." He paused slightly. "Men." The work boss said this last word slowly, as his gaze fell upon the only black, E.B. McKinney. The paymaster puffed up his chest and made sure he presented his holstered sidearm in the direction of the crowd.

Mitchell ignored the two and continued to address the workers, only a small number of which had dissolved into the evening. The rest, including Charles and his sons, stayed in place.

"We're forming a union soon and it's gonna be named The Southern Tenant Farmer's Union, and it'll go far beyond Arkansas to many other states, where the likes of us need to work together. We're raising up all of us, tenant farmers, sharecroppers, and laborers like yourselves. All will benefit from our joint efforts!" Mitchell went on in a louder voice,

"They can't silence us, this is a free country, and we all have the right to speak our mind, public and private. FDR set up the AAA, and part of what it does is pay landowners not to farm, and people like us are supposed to get part of the money 'cause we lost our farming rights. But they never share what the law intended for them to share."

The paymaster and field boss made a menacing move toward the union organizers, but Mitchell continued, knowing he needed to end his address very soon. "If you want to learn more about how we can all work together to improve our lot, then come to the Baptist Church grounds in town here on Sunday afternoon, at about three p.m. All are welcome." The other two men tipped their hats to the crowd, and the three walked away, ignoring the insults that the two plantation men hurled at them, as the crowd dispersed to their homes.

"Daddy, who are those men?" asked Carl, as he grabbed Charles' hand and took Charlies' hand in the other for the walk home. "And why did the Boss and the moneyman cuss at them?"

Charles kept walking a slow and steady pace, and it was a good twenty seconds before he answered Carl. "Listen to me, son. They're with the Southern Tenants Farmers Union, just getting' off the ground. We and our brothers and sisters in the fields, and the tenant farmers on plantation land, are worked hard and paid very little and always in debt to the people we work for. Always been that way. Now, we can keep goin' as powerless people and hope to God that at least one of our children gets an education to open up another type of life, a better life. But that kind of opportunity don't grow on trees to be picked like ripe fruit. It's real hard." He wanted to go on but fell into a coughing fit, and when Carl started to speak, he waived him off and after half a minute he was able to speak again.

"As I was sayin', son, it's hard and you know what it's like to love school. What happens if you don't have it? Well, these men may or may not succeed to help us get better wages and conditions, instead of all the money winding up in the hands of the planters, even money from Washington they's supposed to share with us but never do. So, if we work together, our chances are better than not. I *want* to hear what they have to say, *but I can't.*"

"Because they have colored folks with them, Daddy? We don't have nothin' to do with them."

For the first time during the walk, Charles stopped and turned to his boy, and his tone became deadly serious. "Now you listen to me. And you remember what I say. The people keepin' us down are the same people as are keepin' them down, havin' us all doing the same work, and even those as are tenant farmers and sharecroppers, black or white, all getting' put under the thumbs of others in the same ways. Years past, I've picked and chopped cotton with Negroes and met plenty of good men and women working side by side. Of course, we should work together, 'cause we got similar problems and need respect for our work and our families, white and black. Makes me a bit scared because you're too young to realize it, but when whites and blacks work together to achieve something good, there's plenty of men in this part of the world who will do anything, and I mean ANYTHING," he emphasized. "To keep that from happening. Do you understand?" Carl conjured up the image of the purser's pistol and the man's belligerent attitude. His young and excitable mind got the point.

After a few moments of contemplation, Carl posed the question, "It could be dangerous, Daddy?" Carl at his age could only imagine an undefined foreboding presence in the background, and though he didn't really know what it was, it was dangerous.

"It *will* be dangerous. That's why we ain't goin' to that meeting on Sunday. Maybe if I didn't feel so poorly it would be different."

"That's okay, Daddy. I know you ain't a coward, you just need us to be safe, right?"

Charles pulled Carl away from Charlie's grip and hugged him to his hip, and not wanting Charlie to feel bad, he pulled him in as well. "Let's get home and see what Momma made for supper." Nobody argued with that.

Later that month, after Carl's last Friday of cotton picking, the three of them took a Saturday afternoon walk to Spencer's General Store, three miles away and outside of town. It wasn't their normal store, but they all felt like an outing and with a bit of money in their pockets they set out, intending to be home by four p.m. Nellie had begun to show, and Cora was at the house, so this little luxury trip was fine with everyone. Charles promised to find some 'good whitlin' wood' in the tree stands along the road to make something for each child except Dorothy, who considered herself too old for such things. It was a slow walk because Charles was tired, but he didn't want to disappoint his sons. He figured if he paced them properly, his coughing and wheezing would be at a minimum. Carl was excited to be returning to school and proud to have helped until his father had higher-paying mill work. He and Charlie were hoping to score a Coca-Cola and a candy bar, in total a ten-cent splurge, and the first of its kind in their lives. Carl noticed that Daddy didn't say much and looked straight ahead. It was Daddy's birthday the next day, and this trip with his sons was his birthday present to himself.

After a two-hour walk including a couple of stops to identify the best tree branches for whitling wood to be picked up on the way back, they approached the store. Two black Fords were parked in front of the store, which of itself would have been unusual since people living on farms in the area walked or rode a bicycle or horse to this store most of the time. Very few owned cars. Carl noticed that there were several people in each car, and Charles noticed that the suspensions hung unusually low, indicating a lot of weight. The cars were dusty and the windshields dirty. They had apparently been driven on country roads for quite a while.

Spencer's General Store had no gas pump, so they weren't here for that. As Charles and his sons climbed the two steps of the porch, Carl glanced at the first car where he saw the window rolled down and a pretty woman with a cold, hard stare looked right back at him without smiling. Charles noticed that the men in both cars kept looking about as if expecting something.

The exact moment that Charles opened the door, he went into a coughing fit so violent that he lost his balance and fell into the man coming out the door. The man was tall and fairly handsome, and wearing a dusty, blue pin-striped suit. He had dead eyes as he instinctively pulled a revolver from the shoulder holster beneath his suitcoat and pointed it at Charles, who stooped in coughing agony at his feet. The man's visit to the store for Coca-Cola and directions was about to turn into something else.

"CLYDE BARROW, YOU STOP THAT RIGHT NOW! THAT MAN DON'T MEAN YOU NO HARM, AND HIS BOYS ARE LOOKIN'," Bonnie Parker yelled at the top of her voice. Two of the other four men started to get out of the car, but Barrow waived them off. He put his pistol back into its holster and looked hard at Charles, who was beginning to cough up blood for the first time ever.

"Please, Mister, don't hurt my daddy! He's sick as can be and we don't mean you no harm."

Carl didn't know who these people were, but the instant appearance of the gun had frightened him. Unbeknown to him, the Barrow gang was notorious for killing anyone who got in their way, civilian or law. They were a well-armed gang of sociopaths and had successfully robbed the Plattville Armory in Illinois in August, and were now making their way to Texas and to their ultimate fatal destiny even now being orchestrated by a retired Texas Ranger. They had enough weaponry and ordnance, including a BAR, to level the entire wooden store building.

Barrow looked straight at the boys, eyes showing no emotion, as he said in his Texas drawl,

"Your daddy's gonna die, boys. Take care of him as best you can." After a brief moment, Barrow added with a light sneer, "Cotton pickin' cotton pickers." And with that, he flipped a silver dollar toward Carl who was too paralyzed to catch it, stunned by Barrow's use of his own phrase and by the imminent danger to Daddy. As it rolled on the floor of the plank porch and settled in place, Barrow smiled a cruel smile and walked to the front car.

"Jesus Christ, Clyde," complained Bonnie, who was recovering from a leg wound. "You almost orphaned those boys right in front of their eyes for no reason." Without another word, the cars thundered down the road, away from Paragould, and into the country southwest of town. Dust flew in clouds as they drove on. Carl picked up the silver dollar. He would give it to Momma with the lie that he had found it. He and Charlie helped their daddy up and into the store. Mr. Spencer, a graying man of medium height and build with a pair of wire spectacles, went over to help but insisted that Charles sit on the porch and have some water as he didn't want 'no flu' in his store. For Charles, coughing up blood was a new and very unwelcome development.

When he caught his breath, he told the boys, "Looks like we'll be a bit late getting back. But we'll pick up the whitlin' wood no matter. Now, here's a dime. Go and get yourselves each a coke and candy bar." Carl quietly handed him the silver dollar, and Charles smiled then closed his eyes to rest a bit. But the boys, even Charlie, were too rattled to enjoy their treat. It took three hours and frequent stops to walk home, but Charles made good on his promise to collect some suitable carving wood.

Nellie, while busy with Annabelle and Dorothy, had been frequently checking the front yard and peering down the road to see if her man and boys were coming. Concern led to worry, and after five p.m., it became fear. But shortly before five-thirty p.m. she greeted them on the porch, relieved but apprehensive because of the look on Daddy's pale face. Charles had warned the boys not to ever discuss what happened at the store with the Barrow Gang, it would only make her worry more. They never told her. After instructing Dorothy and Cora to take care of the boys and their supper, Nellie took Charles into their room, closed the door, and then helped him gently onto the bed without a word spoken. She propped his head up on two pillows and stroked his head softly as he steadily wheezed into the still air.

Nellie looked at him, connected with his eyes, and an age of the earth passed between them in a few short moments as they finished their gaze, each with a slight smile on their face. They instinctively knew that Charles was on a long decline to death, or at best, a permanent incapacitation. His working days would soon be drawing to a close, and quick access to effective treatment of any type of pulmonary disorder was not in the cards for him in the world in which they lived.

"Nellie Dear, I'll work at the mill as long as I can. What about Cora? She can help, I know it." He coughed again, bringing up a little blood, not as much as at the store but enough to notice.

"We'll talk with Momma in the morning, it's Sunday tomorrow and you're not fit for church, but I'll talk to her before we leave for Sunday service." Nellie knew in her heart that would be a difficult discussion, and the results would be uncertain. But Momma just had to listen.

Charles went to sleep after Cora brewed a hot toddy, and Nellie made sure he drank it.

Chapter 3
Calamity, 1934–1935

Daddy passed away at home on Pekin Road on March 1, 1934. The newspaper stated pneumonia as the cause of death resulting from an incurable infection but it was an uncertain diagnosis. Nellie was due in two weeks, and even though Charles' death was not a surprise she found herself fearful of a miscarriage or early birth, which, in her circumstances would likely have doomed the child and possibly her. She needed her mother to support her emotionally and provide for the children until she could get back on her feet and figure something out.

But Cora had already put plans for her personal survival in place and announced that despite Charles's decline from last year, she had proceeded to remarry and with '*A wife's place is with her husband,*' and she dismissed Nellie's pleas except to promise a release of some of her sequestered money to 'tide you over.' But tide Nellie and the children over to what? In Cora's mind, the only rational course was for Nellie to remarry as soon as possible, after the new baby arrived, and damn the observed convention of letting a suitable time pass between a spouse's demise and the survivor's remarriage. Everyone understood survival. Each time Cora brought it up, Nellie would cast her eyes upward without moving her head and say,

"Not now, Mama, I got enough on my plate." To which, Cora always replied, "You also have children to worry about."

The funeral took place on a cold and windy afternoon, with services at the house and burial at the Shiloh Cemetery in a simple grave, with no marker other than a wooden cross that would ultimately dissolve with decay and rot, so that his descendants would never be able to tell where he was buried. Nellie, Cora, and all of the children were present as Reverend Guy Walsh of the Full Gospel Tabernacle officiated. A handful of Charles' fellow laborers attended in quiet respect, and the manager of the mill where Charles had worked sporadically for years sent the only flowers of the day, along with twenty dollars raised from the mill workers and management 'to help the family along in this time of grief.'

Nellie and the children had done their weeping for many weeks before Charles' passing and were silent in vigil over Daddy's pine coffin, donated by the church. At the end of the brief eulogy, which the Reverend Walsh padded with many biblical references and prayers, and a promise that Charles had gone to his reward, Nellie stepped up with her belly swollen with nine months of pregnancy and bent to kiss the coffin. "You were a good man, Charlie, and did your best, I love you," she whispered. When she stood up straight and backed away, all of the children gave her a group hug that was spontaneous and brief. Cora didn't move and maintained a serious face throughout.

There was no wake, but the midwife Maddie who was now in her fifties and graying, brought a vanilla cake and some chicken and beans. "To hold y'all over 'til you can do for yourself," she said over her shoulder as she walked out of the house. "I'll see you soon, Nellie dear, and we'll welcome your new baby!"

Nellie was exhausted and bade her family goodnight. Then, she fell into a deep sleep in her bed, too tired to care what Cora was telling the children, and not caring for the moment what lay in store in the future, nor what lay on the road behind her. Later that night, Dorothy, Charlie, Carl, and Annabelle slipped quietly into the boys' room after Cora had gone to sleep. Cora had not been a great comfort to the children, and had given them a short speech before turning them all to bed at an early hour.

"Now your daddy's gone and Mamma's about to have another baby, I'll be leavin' soon now as I'm married. And I'll be leavin' your Mamma a bit of money to tide y'all over for a bit, but it won't last long. You're all gonna have to help your Mamma and just remember, that this family needs money and food before schoolin', so make sure you all find a way to help her with that, and the new baby. Dorothy, I'm gonna introduce you to a nice young man named Worlick who's looking for a young wife. You'd be advised to convince him it should be you if you don't want to end up on the street someday. The rest of you find a way to help your Momma 'cause she'll have a new little brother or sister very soon. It's up to you and Charlie, Carl. I think school's out of the question but that's really up to your mother. Now, y'all kiss Granny goodnight and get to bed!"

And with a royal aire, she offered a cheek. Each of the children dutifully planted a light kiss on it before going off to bed.

Cora was deep in survival mode and wouldn't let anything stand in the way of her escape. *Well,* she thought. *I've done what I can do… the rest is in God's hands.* But as events would show, placing the remaining family's fate in the hands of God wasn't going to help anyone but Cora.

Carl lay in bed with his stomach in knots. Daddy was gone forever. He had loved Daddy and Daddy had loved him, he well remembered. Hadn't he been promised to stay in school where his teacher constantly praised his hard-won results, especially in math for which he showed a great aptitude? But now, with only two and a half years behind him, his school days were in danger. And he knew it.

Promises were never broken unless you died. Daddy had died. Dorothy had already left school this last year to help with Daddy's comforts in his illness and to assist Nellie with the household. Nobody seemed to notice Cora always finding an excuse to avoid any heavy work.

In Charles's final months, Carl helped with as much as he could and did his schoolwork by the light of a kerosene lamp after everyone went to bed. As things deteriorated over Christmas and New Year, while school was out, Carl wandered around town offering his services for anything that could bring in a little money; sweeping and cleaning, running errands and other spot jobs, but there were others offering the same services, older and stronger, and Carl spent more time looking for work than actually doing any work. But he never gave up and accepted less money than others when given work, because he was too young to know about worker pride, self-respect, and value for services. It was easy for his employers to take advantage of him.

And it was because with a child's sincerity he wanted to help his family. He was allowed to return to school after the mid-year break only because the dying Charles wouldn't have any talk of him leaving school. With very little money coming in, the family was reduced to beans and potatoes and whatever catfish, perch, and crawdads could be caught in nearby ponds, creeks, and lakes, once or twice a week. Winter fishing in this region was spotty at best.

On a cold and frosty day in January, when Carl was headed out the door for a return to school, Cora had walked into the bedroom where Charles lay ailing. Nellie was busy with Annabelle and helping Carl get ready. "You ought not to be so stubborn!" she berated Charles. "This family needs money now more than ever. Carl and Charlie should be scouring the town for work, bringin' in anything they're capable of makin' happen. People's future depends on it."

"Listen here, Cora, I been quiet for a long time. But school is Carl's future and his future is through school. And I promised him 'cause he took his little hands and picked cotton when his daddy needed him, chopped cotton and done odd jobs for extra money." Charles started to cough but went on. "You know I can't work now, nobody'd have me as I am. Why do you think this family is in such danger? *Cause I ain't been nothin' but a wanderin' laborer all my life* with no special skill at anything, and you're the only family here who has some money, which I'm sure you earned one way or the other." Cora harumphed and acted indignant at this remark. "But I don't see you passing any of it on for Nellie and the children's sake. I don't want that ever to happen to Carl," he said emphatically just before he went into a violent spate of coughing, resulting in a bit of blood staining the cloth that he brought to his mouth. But the look in his eyes was determined and signaled the end of the discussion. "As long as I live, he goes to school. I don't care if we have to catch rats and eat wild greens! When he grows up, he ain't never gonna have to rely upon someone like you. Don't trouble me with this no more, Cora." And with that, he rolled over, with his back to her, signaling that the discussion was over. But Cora had to have the last word.

Just before he was to walk out the door for school, Carl, and indeed the entire household heard the exchange between Cora and Charles, which resulted in Cora huffing and shaking her head from side to side as she busily stepped past Carl as if he wasn't there and left the house for some fresh air. She yelled out while walking away, "Your family will see that your pride and spitefulness will lead to a bad end for all." *Your family, too,* he thought.

Under different family circumstances, Carl could have been comforted by Daddy's dying position on the critical importance of his education, but it had the opposite effect… he was frightened. It was clear that Daddy wasn't going to live long and could never work again. He loved his mother and her gentle ways, but she was heavily pregnant, tired, and had her hands full with Charlie and Annabelle. He realized even at his young age, that there would be little she could do to keep him in school. Dorothy had already left school the year before. All he saw in his young mind ahead of him was work all the time to support his family, especially Annabelle and the as-yet-unborn baby.

The day before Daddy passed, he asked for Carl to come into the bedroom alone. His effort to speak was constantly accompanied by wheezing and many pauses, but he had something he had to say. "Carl, son… I am so sorry that I… I won't be able to see you finish high school"—coughing fit—"and apologize to you for… leaving you to work so young… I know"—coughing fit—"… you will find a way to make… your mark, son. I believe in you." More coughing and wheezing.

Carl, seven years old, stood by the bed with his eyes open wide, fingers nervously grasping his hands in different combinations. He listened to every word Daddy spoke, waiting patiently during the coughing and the wheezing. Then, as Daddy finished, Carl abruptly cast his head into Charles' side and cried out through his tears, "Don't worry, Daddy, it ain't your fault. I will always love you, Daddy." Charles weakly placed his hand on Carl's head. After several minutes, with no further response from his father, Carl slowly got up and left the room, not breaking into a run until he had walked past everyone and out the door. Then, he ran and ran, not really paying attention to where, until he threw himself down under a poplar tree and cried into the earth as only a sad and wounded child can cry. Great sobs from the depths. For the loss of Daddy. For the loss of school. For the loss of his freedom.

Carl was like a weathervane of the family, the winds that moved through him generated feelings of anxiety mixed with a determination to take care of his family, and always underlying it all was the immense hole that Daddy's death put in his life.

Later that month, after Daddy's passing, little Martha Nell Dough was born on a cold and windy March night. She favored her mother in looks, with a broad, plain face and widely spaced eyes but with her hair favoring Daddy's and Annabelle's in color. But Cora had made herself scarce, retreating into the confines of her new marriage and fending off questions from her husband about the welfare of her daughter and children, and he knew enough not to press her on the matter. The children hardly knew anything of her after that.

Martha's birth seemed to be the cosmic signal for calamity to rain down upon the remaining Dough family.

The money from Cora and the post-funereal kindness of others had nearly evaporated by May, and Nellie was face to face with living off the generosity of others or starving. This couldn't last, she knew, and little Carl and impaired Charles would not be able to make much money, if any, before the mid to late-summer field work. It broke her heart to have to tell Carl that school, for the time being, was out of the question. Everything was falling apart with little Martha Nell and Annabelle needing constant attention. Cora was nowhere to be found, as if she had no family to care for. Dorothy, who at nearly fifteen should have been a great help to Nellie, was nearly useless for work in her constant trancelike state, wherein her mind played out the drama of whether or not to get married as had been recommended. She was stunned by the circumstances of her family and fantasized about having someone marry her, put a roof over her head, food on the table, and provide love forever. After all, she was still a child.

As much as Nellie despised her mother for the abandonment, she focused on what her mother had said was the only way to survive outside of church charity; get married again, and soon. Nellie detested the idea, was repulsed by the thought with Charles so recently put into the ground and still a vivid memory, with his five children a constant reminder for Nellie of the love they had shared throughout hardship and deprivation. *It's the children,* she thought. *The welfare of the children comes first.* Even at thirty-two, she was beginning to tire easily and knew that her ability to catch a husband with five children in tow, and being constantly fatigued, was suspect. But she discretely put the word out through neighbors and church members that she was open to remarrying even at this early date but told the children nothing of her plans.

Winter would be coming in five months or so. "How do I save them all?" she asked herself.

"I'll start with the youngest and work my way up to them as can better take care of themselves, 'cause it's a rare man in this world who could and would take in so many." Nellie could not foresee the decidedly mixed results of her decision.

Martha Nell:

Martha was the most promising for adoption; an infant and a clean slate that needy potential parents would find appealing. So, Nellie worked through the church and the County to see how Martha could be adopted, not fostered, once she was finished with breast milk at six months, a little early but necessary. She was a quiet baby, with all her pink toes and fingers, and hair more ginger than Annabelle's; Nellie was going to hurt but she was resolved to give her baby a better chance in life. After two months of searching, the adoption authorities presented Nellie with the Hodges, who lived more than eighty miles away and owned and ran a dry goods store. They had no children and were looking to adopt two or three eventually. In early September, the Hodges took Martha away, and though they raised her with an adopted brother so that she had 'family' and afforded her access to education, she made poor life decisions and ended up marrying an abusive and alcoholic husband, although she finally settled into a peaceful life in Southern California with her children. Most important was the fact that her children adored her to the end of her life.

Annabelle:

Even at just four years old, Annabelle was not high on the desirability lists of the day for adoption. The authorities and the church pastor advised to put her into a foster home, where there were other children, since foster care wasn't permanent. But if things worked out, sometimes foster parents adopted the child. This sounded promising to Nellie, so she put Annabelle on the foster home list, and the feisty little girl was eased into her new situation.

Nellie enlisted eight-year-old Carl, to whom Annabelle was very attached, to help convince Annie that it was going to be a great adventure that Nellie and her brothers and sisters would be part of.

"It'll be fun, Annie," Carl cheered as he hugged her on her way out the door. "And I'll come to visit and play with you as often as possible, you wait and see!" But Annie wasn't having it.

"I wanna be with you and Mama!" Tears began to roll down her red cheeks and crying was right behind. She spoke through inhalations during her cry. "You promise to visit me, Carl! Keep your promise!" This order was given as strongly as a four-year-old can give a command.

"I promise, Annie, I promise. I swear it. Momma says it is only for a while until things get better, and I know they will, Annie." But in a rare display of utter anger, when Annie was out of sight with Momma walking her to her new home, Carl ran around the house and screamed, and let out the fiercest war cry his little body could summon as he kicked and punched the side of the house, and beat it with his fists until his hands were more swollen than if he'd picked cotton for three days in a row.

The Nooner family, who were somewhat well off in town, took her into their care and promised to give her the love and attention every child needs. They did not fulfill their commitment in that regard, but Annabelle's energetic personality was not dimmed at that point, primarily because, she trusted Carl to look out for her and he could 'visit all the time.' She was the only one of the Dough children who graduated from high school, after eventually being placed with a truly caring family after several years with the Nooners.

Carl and Charles:

Nellie was going to hold onto the boys. Nobody would adopt them and nobody would accept Charles' condition unless it was a clergy's family. Carl was exuberant, attentive, and loving, and Nellie sensed they would need each other, and that Carl would be a more welcome attachment for a new husband. She would have to put her foot down with any new man concerning Charles, and Carl could go back to school most likely, she thought. When Nellie did remarry, the boys would go with her. But Carl never went back to school and Charles eventually found his way to the pastor's house.

Dorothy Mae:

A twenty-six-year-old young man named Worlick fancied Dorothy and made a show of wooing her and appealing to Nellie for Dorothy's hand in marriage, even at the tender age of just-turned fifteen. Dorothy was scared. She was old enough to know that all sorts of doors were closing on her, now that Daddy was no longer here, and she paid attention to what Nellie was doing to save her children. Nor did she wish to live with a stepfather, and Worlick was handsome and bright. He was very attentive to Dorothy, bringing her flowers and candy, and taking long walks with her without so much as trying to kiss her—even on the cheek. And, he was a nephew of Silas, the man that came calling on Nellie, hoping to win her hand. Dorothy gave in and begged Momma for her approval, and in her own body and mind, she had already felt the stirrings of passion for Worlick. They were married in the Church of Christ in October, a month before Silas and Nellie were married. Carl was the only one who seemed apprehensive about it all. There was something about the smile that Worlick made when he thought no adults were looking… possibly dangerous. He made Carl vaguely uneasy. The same applied to Silas, a man in his forties who said absolutely nothing to the children and very little to Nellie, even though he was asking her to join him in life.

Nellie's plan had come to fruition, her children were saved for the time being. It was too early for her to realize how badly things could go. Later that year, Nellie married Silas and Carl and Charlie went with her into his house. But it wasn't long before Nellie's life was turned inside out.

Dorothy and Worlick never came to visit, and on the two occasions over the next six months that Nellie did see Dorothy, the girl was decidedly unhappy and downcast as well as silent.

Dorothy did a good job of hiding the bruises inflicted by Worlick's 'persuasion.' Silas and Nellie began to argue about Dorothy and Worlick, then about Charlie and his condition, and finally about Carl. At first, Carl thought he would be able to go back to school.

But when Nellie raised the issue with Silas, he simply said, "Boy's got to work. Money don't grow on trees, and if your boys are gonna stay in my house and eat my food, then they have to earn their keep." Nellie and Silas argued about the boys, about Dorothy, about money, and about Charles, and the arguments got to the point where Silas slapped her in front of Carl, at which the little boy flew into Silas like a wolverine flying into a grizzly bear.

"Don't you hurt my Momma!"

Silas roughly pushed Carl to the floor and said, "Listen, you little son of a bitch, you never tell me what to do under my roof."

"I'm warnin' you, Mr. Hafford, don't ever hit my Momma again or you'll pay." Carl knew there wasn't much he could do to Silas, and his tears of frustration clouded his eyes.

But Nellie stepped in and tried to calm Silas down. "Silas, dear, we been arguing lots lately, and I know it's mostly my fault. Let's start again and I promise not to bother you with my children's problems." She looked carefully at Silas for a sign of contrition but saw only a steely glare.

After a few seconds, he said, "I'd like that, Nellie." And she took him by the hand and led him to the door. "Let me talk to Carl, dear, I'll join you in a moment."

Silas responded, "But I won't stand for any backtalk from your boy, and I'll let him off the hook… this time."

After Silas left the room, Nellie quickly put her arms around Carl. "I'm so sorry, my little man. I love you so much. We have to be careful because winter is here and nobody can afford to be without a home or warmth. Stay strong for me and please stay out of Silas's way. I promise you, I will make things better for you, just be patient darlin'." And with that, she kissed him and left the room. Not once did Nellie ever complain about the burden she carried for her children, sleeping with a man she didn't like, and constantly maneuvering to keep Carl and Charles out of harm's way. Shame lurked behind her curtain of resolve and the love for her children. She fervently hoped that Charles and the angels were looking the other way.

Carl, in his anger and frustration about school, about Daddy, and about the constant pressure to work, began to seek the company of other boys in and around town. He got to know some of the nearby farm boys as well, and learned to smoke from discarded cigarette and cigar butts. Carl learned to avoid trouble when he could, and visited Annabelle as often as possible, where he was a different boy. He went where he wanted to go, found whatever work he could, and hung out with other truants in the woods and along the waterways.

In his visits to Annie, he was never allowed inside the Nooner home, only on the front porch.

When he was 'home' he doted on his mother and stayed out of Silas's way, dutifully giving her most of the money he earned from odd jobs, cotton picking, and chopping over the next two years, but he sometimes kept enough to go to a movie or buy something sweet to eat. Sometimes, when school was out for the day, he hung out behind a house or shrub and observed the comings and goings of the students, but after a time, he gave that up because the pressure to work increased, and because in his disconnect he pretended not to care anymore about school.

Slowly, ever so slowly as the next two years passed by, Nellie became ill more and more often. Silas, who worked for the railroad, married Nellie because he wanted a woman to cook, clean, do laundry, run errands, and make herself available to him when he needed her to perform her wifely duties in bed. As Silas's wish list became more and more difficult for Nellie to meet, he turned even more inward and silent. He considered that he had made a bad investment as though he had bought a horse without examining its teeth or gums. As her health deteriorated further in 1936, she found enough strength to go to Pastor Ellis, the Baptist preacher, and his wife, Doris, to convince them to take Charles on out of Christian charity. Charlie, ever compliant, accompanied his mother and enjoyed a fried chicken lunch.

The Ellis' had just received a new baby boy into their family to add to their three-year-old daughter, and while they wanted to help, they were not in a position to do so. Nellie was too weak to go elsewhere and resigned herself to giving Charlie over to Dorothy and Worlick.

She had no idea what was going on in that house, but at least Dorothy was family.

Carl wandered in from working odd jobs, and from his running with the other boys and asked Nellie, "Where's Charlie? I brought him some candy."

Nellie clutched Carl closely, almost smothering him with the intensity of her hug. "It's just you and me now, Carl. Charlie is better off with Dorothy. You can visit him there. They'll love him as God's creature and take care of him." She began to cry deep sobs as she clutched the only child remaining with her, now nearly ten and showing a tough veneer on the outside but very tender on the inside. He was, she had realized years before, the most sensitive of her children.

"I'll take care of you, Momma." But his bravado covered fear, fear of losing her, the mother he loved so dearly. She only hugged him tighter, but her sobbing stopped.

Carl never went to church after Nellie became bedridden. But he visited Charlie and Annabelle every week. Silas was indifferent to Carl as long as he stayed out of his way and kept silent. In late 1937, Nellie required constant care, her breathing was labored, and she barely had enough strength to move from the bed. The doctor told Silas that he needed to make her comfortable, because it was not at all likely she would recover. His sister, Margaret, came over every day for a couple of hours to prepare food and clean, but for Carl, the reality was that he needed to take to the streets and fields more often, learning things often incorrectly since he learned mostly from other feral boys. He was fatherless and mostly motherless. Already an orphan in situation, if not in fact.

One still late-summer night, a few months before Nellie passed away, the sky full of stars with no moon to dim them, Carl lay in the grass beside a soybean field with his friend, Cheeks, who was two years older and much larger. Both boys were barefoot and dressed in hand-me-down pants and shirts. Their hair was tousled and unkempt, Carl's was brown and bushy, and Cheeks' blonde locks hung limp. As they stared up into the void with the earthly illusion that the stars hung there twinkling, they chewed on stalks of wild grass, apparently deep in their own thoughts. They'd caught a 'mess' of crawdads that day, with a bit of bacon tied to strings and had proceeded to boil them in an old coffee can that served its purpose but needed constant refilling because it leaked a bit. The crawdad tails were most excellent, eaten with bread and a little vinegar that had been liberated from Silas's kitchen.

After a time, Carl spoke up. "Ya know, Cheeks, someday, I'm gonna finish school and find out what's up there. Ya think there might be other people livin' somewhere up there?"

After a few moments of serious consideration, Cheeks wrinkled his brow and replied, "Sure as hell there is, and they'll be a damn sight better off than we are! How you gonna' find out, Carl? Ain't nobody done it before."

"Well, I was readin' in the Gazette that scientists, astronomers as they's called, have seen other planets that go round our Sun, like us, only at different distances and they don't know what's on them yet. That's what I want to be, a scientist… to know things and find things out."

"*Aw,* you just want to be like Buck Rogers or Flash Gordon and fly around in a rocket ship savin' people all the time. You ain't that handsome, nor that smart!" He laughed and poked Carl in the side. "Like you would be a space adventurer, ya can't even spell Buck Rogers!" he laughed, and the boys played a bit of tickle but when the laughter died down, Carl looked up again and became serious.

"I ain't gonna stay in this pigsty when I grow up, Cheeks, not even if you're here, and if you're smart then you'll get out too. I'm gonna get my education somehow and make my mark with somethin' to do with puttin' men up there to find out, maybe even me."

"Earth to Spaceboy… time to go home." Cheeks became a bit uncomfortable with his friend's statement and felt guilty for staying out so late without checking in with his sickly widowed mother. They quietly got up and began the walk under the stars back into town.

But a few months later, after Carl turned ten and Nellie needed constant care, Silas turned Carl out to live with Worlick, Dorothy, and Charlie. Whether Silas knew what he was putting Carl into or not, thus began the final brief but tragic period of Carl's young life.

Chapter 4
Dee 1929–1944

Under a clear and starry sky, with the moon a waning crescent, a fourth daughter was born to the Nation family on the evening of May 5, 1929. She was delivered without professional assistance, even though the midwife was summoned, as the distance was too great to cover in time. The midwife, Margaret, had been busy with a difficult delivery and Loran 'Jack' Nation, Dafnie's father, had driven his rickety used Model T along country roads as fast as the vehicle allowed. He found her and brought her to the farm in time for Margaret to tend to the post-natal needs of mother and baby. Paragould was over twenty miles away, and nearby Delaplane was a wide spot in the road. There was no telephone, nor electricity yet on the farm. Her mother, Ima, had already delivered three healthy girls prior to Dafnie, and self-administered each birth including cutting the umbilical, washing the baby, and wrapping her in clean cloth—all of which Jack prepared for her before he left to fetch the midwife. Edna, Gay, and Leoma (Lee), all waited on their mother as directed and were thus introduced to the mysteries of childbirth at very early ages.

The Nations were each the descendants of people whose lineage since William the Conqueror took very different paths, ultimately resulting in Jack and Ima. Most had done very well for themselves in France, England, and the Colonies. but their wealth and education dissipated with the increase in progeny, in marriages and circumstances. In America, this process ultimately led to these two being of very humble status in their world… tenant farmers in Northern Arkansas by way of Illinois, Tennessee, and Kentucky; beholden to the plantation owner and in perpetual debt. They were two economic status notches up the ladder from the Doughs, but comforts were nevertheless painfully scarce.

Ima's ancestors were the Blakes and Bryants from England, and Jack's included an unfortunate boy nicknamed by posterity *'Servant John Boy Nation,'* sold into indentured servitude to the Colonies in America. Sir Ricard de Blakeland assisted Duke William in the subjugation of England. His great-great grandson, Sir Robert de Blakeland, was the initial Member of the House of Lords for Wiltshire in the 13th Century. As the centuries rolled on, the de Blakelands became the Blakes of Wiltshire. Members of their family migrated to the American Colonies in the 17th Century and eventually Frances Blake and Francis Thierry, who had recently fled to America from France in 1790, were married and the Bryants from Tennessee and the Blakes from Ohio and Kentucky produced Ima. She was from a middleclass family of the time and was educated beyond high school. Laconic Jack was educated to year eight and kept his thoughts to himself except for Ima. He was a man of few words, and his sole reading was the occasional newspaper he was able to obtain.

Jack Nation was six feet of rail thin man and of extremely tough fiber. His family had lived in the border state of Kentucky when the Civil War erupted, and some migrated to Illinois and supported the Union, while others migrated to Tennessee and supported the Confederacy.

Jack's part of the family was the former, with several serving in the Grand Army of the Republic. If he had known it at the time, the irony would not have been lost on him that his direct ancestor, Servant John Boy Nation, was essentially a white slave when he was kidnapped at the age of twelve in 1707 from his home in Somerset, England, and sold to a wealthy merchant/landowner in the Carolinas. Eventually, he gained his freedom and prospered as a merchant and businessman. He never owned slaves and was not a planter. But he saw opportunity in commerce and real estate and pursued his fortune with fierce determination. Never again would he, nor any of his family, be subjected to the humility of indentured servitude. His sons fought for the British as Colonial Officers in the French and Indian War, as the colonists called it. It was a titanic struggle between those two imperial powers for dominance in North America and the Caribbean.

After the American Declaration of Independence in 1776, John Boy's sons became officers in Washington's Continental Army. Later, as fate would dictate, some members of Jack's family suffered the lot of many after the Civil War having been sucked into a downward spiral of economic degradation for those who refused to go West and face its risks, or who were not otherwise connected by family to some degree of wealth and education.

But Jack was able to gain tenant farmer status in the years after serving in Blackjack Pershing's American Expeditionary Force in France and received a small financial gift and the Model T from Ima's family after marrying Ima. They never really approved of Jack because they did not see ambition in him, but Ima knew her mind. He had a mule, forty acres owned by someone else, a shack of a house, and borrowed every year against his share of the proceeds of crop sales from corn, soybeans, and alfalfa. Jack arose at four a.m. every morning except Sunday, and went to bed at eight-thirty every night, and he never complained about or questioned the justice of his life, except to wonder why Providence had not seen fit to award him a son after four daughters.

Ima Gwendolyn Bryant had married Jack at seventeen while he was still in the Army, and recently returned from France. She was a small and perky woman with a good sense of humor and kept the home clean and well-ordered while Jack worked the fields and ran errands into Paragould or Pocahontas. She was also educated and loved to read, which became more difficult as she took on the increased duties of mother and farm wife.

She was very attentive to her daughters, which partially made up for Jack's disinterest in them. She convinced herself that his disengagement as a father to the girls was primarily due to long hours with no help on the farm. Jack loved Ima but his expression of emotion went no further than her. She knew that he was attentive and tender with her, but outside of his interactions with Ima people thought Jack had his nerves removed after the war. They had made only one trip to Memphis to see their families since their marriage.

The Nations and the Doughs represented the array of mingling of cultures and interplay of fortunes, that only America in the 18th and 19th centuries could produce; sometimes for the better and sometimes for the worse. For those people like Charles and Nellie, and Jack and Ima, their lives reflected bad luck, limited choices, and lack of opportunity. Or perhaps, all three elements were in play somewhere in their ancestries. It was up to them to endure all and try to do better in their Twentieth Century.

Dafnie's life until age four was a typical farm toddler's life; learning to feed chickens and explore the area around the house and shed, where the plough mule and tools were kept. Edna, Gay, and Lee were her older sisters. They doted on her and Ima regularly read to her and told her stories about her distant and long-dead ancestors. By the time she was four years old, it was clear to everyone that Dafnie was very intelligent and was already learning to read from her mother. She was a pretty girl with auburn hair and piercing gray eyes and was never far from the sort of trouble that inquisitive pre-schoolers will get into. By the time Ima became pregnant when Dafnie turned four, her sisters had begun to leave her alone as they didn't share her love of reading and learning to write and were much older, preferring to be tomboys in the nearby woods and creeks and always discussing getting married someday; particularly boy-crazy Edna. They knew that Dee was different and no longer felt like tending to her as before.

"Besides," observed Edna, when the girls were cooling off at the creek on a hot summer day,

"We had enough schoolin' at Evenin' Shade… boring!" Lee and Gay laughed heartily and expressed their agreement. But Dee hung around Momma all the time, now that she was pregnant. Jack silently hoped it would be a boy and saved his tenderness for Ima, but to the uninformed, which included just about everybody except Ima, it would appear that he just didn't care. Often, Dee would stand in front of Jack's rocking chair when he was in it, hoping to be noticed—to receive some praise or a kind word. She waited in vain until one day she just gave up. About the only response she ever got was "Don't you have something to do, Dee-Dee? Your Momma probably needs some help." The truth would have been hard for Dee and her sisters to understand, even had it been explained to them.

Jack had a deep-seated belief that he didn't deserve to be alive, and should have died like so many of his mates at the battle of Chateau-Thierry in the summer of 1918, at the same time as Belleau Wood. Since these were the first offensives using the American forces of Army and Marines in the war, casualties were high, but the offensives had some success in breaking through German lines.

When her time came in April, Jack was in the field preparing for the planting. The pain was excruciating for Ima, and her little body constantly tensed as the contractions intensified. Edna ran shouting to Jack at the beginning of labor, and she knew that something was wrong. Jack had prepared things as before and had no clue as to the trouble that Ima and the baby were in. But he ran hard to the house, quickly told Ima to hold on while he fetched the doctor or midwife, and then drove straight to nearby Delaplane where there was a phone available at the country store. He called the doctor in Paragould.

"This is Doc Ames. What can I do for you?"

"This is Jack Nation, Doc. We got problems with my wife's delivery and there ain't no midwife close by. Ima's had four girls and never had a problem, but she been in labor for eight hours and in terrible pain. I think somethin's wrong, real wrong. Can you drive right away to County Road sixteen east of Delaplane, we're number six, third farm on the left. Please come!"

"Where are you now, Jack?"

"At the country store in Delaplane."

"Wait there and we'll go to your place together, I'll follow in my car. And please calm yourself... I'll be there as soon as possible. With that, he hung up and Jack was left for the better part of an hour to wait for Dr. Ames, who simply honked his horn when he drove up and proceeded to follow Jack for the ten-minute drive to the farm. As the two cars approached the farmhouse, Gay and Dee jumped up and down screaming for the men to come quickly.

Little Dee would never forget the doctor's entrance, determined and in charge, but stopping to pat her on the head and say in a low and steady tone, "Don't worry, little one, it'll be all right." This reassured her, but eventually led to a misplaced mistrust of doctors that lasted all her life.

Nearly ten hours of intense struggle and pain had wracked poor Ima's little body. It was clear to the doctor in moments that this was a breach birth, and try as he did, he could not turn the baby. He knew that without access to the hospital in Paragould, it was likely that one or the other of the mother or baby would be lost, possibly both. After nearly half an hour trying to turn the baby in the womb, while Ima passed out once, Dr. Ames went outside to confer with Jack, who had been ordered to keep the girls except Edna out of the bedroom. He told the girls to go outdoors while he talked to Jack.

"I am sorry tell you, Jack, that I can't turn the baby who is positioned to come out feet first instead of headfirst. If Ima's labor continues as is, then she and the baby will die. I don't have time or resources to get her to the hospital in Paragould, where I could perform a Caesarean section and the odds of both mother and baby surviving would be decent. But given the time and place, I can let both go, or try to save the baby and do what I can for the mother. It involves cutting the baby out of the womb, and I only have chloroform here as anaesthetic, which is only going to offer some comfort to Ima. I need your permission to try and save the baby and do what I can for Ima. She will never survive the trip to the hospital in Paragould. I'm sorry. Your decision, Jack."

Jack was shell-shocked. Possible life without Ima, possible life with a son, possible life with neither... all of these were swirling in his head like a plague of rabid bats each yelling, "Pick me!" And what of the girls? He clenched his jaw and stared into the wall.

"Jack! I need a decision from you now! There isn't time to wait." Dee had parked herself just outside the door and heard everything.

Then, Jack in his distress made a decision that would have consequences for all. "Listen Doc, I ain't got a good choice, but save the baby… and save my wife if you can, please! God knows I don't want to lose them both."

Dr. Ames ordered the girls to bring clean towels or rags and more hot water, and then dismissed them all. Ima's screaming subsided with the application of the chloroform, but diminished to heavy groans and then silence. After fifteen minutes, Dr. Ames opened the door and slowly motioned Jack into the bedroom, telling the girls to wait outside, then closed the door behind Jack. Jack already knew in his heart that Ima was dead, but he only realized that the baby was dead as well, when he saw the small bundle completely wrapped in cloths, bloodied by the procedure. Ima was peaceful on the bed, her eyes covered by the doctor, and much blood on the bedding.

"I did everything I could with the limited resources I had, Jack. Things were too far gone. If I had been a few hours earlier, chances to turn the baby in the womb would have been better. But there was one other complication against us. In addition to the breach position, the baby was strangled by the umbilical cord so that he was starved for oxygen. If that hadn't happened, then I would have had a better chance to save him."

"You said, 'he.' Was it a boy, then?" Jack's voice broke as he asked this.

"Yes, he was. I'm so sorry, Jack. I've got to get back to Paragould as I am scheduled to be in the hospital early tomorrow. I'll let myself out. Be with your children now, Jack, you're going to have to be strong for the girls. Do you have someone to come and help with arrangements for the funerals and to help with the girls?"

"One of my sisters can help us for a while. The girls will manage the cleaning up and laundry, and I'll drive over to see Rev. Jackson in Delaplane tomorrow, as he'll help with funeral arrangements. But I can't talk like this anymore now. I know you did your best to save them." Jack looked down at his feet, despondent and lost.

Dr. Ames knew he should go. "Don't worry about settling with me… just take care of your family and come and see me when you are able. We can talk then." With that, he left and did not look at the girls as he walked brusquely to his car, eager to escape the scene. Jack came out of the bedroom and told his girls that their mother and baby brother were both dead, and that nothing could have been done for them. He was in agony inside but tried to hold it together for the girls.

"Get your things." The four girls stared at him, unable to move. For once, Jack found the courage to show empathy and the words to attempt a more involved response. "You'll have to stay at Aunt Leedy's for a few days while I take care of things around here and prepare for the funerals. I'm not gonna let you see Momma and the little one right now until the service in a few days. Just remember your Momma as she was, a good and beautiful mother to all of you, who loved each of you and would have loved your brother just as much as I know you would have. Now, please get goin', I got lots to tend to."

He said no more until they all arrived at Leedy's place a half hour drive away. Each of the girls had been crying on and off, clutching each other during the ride. But little Dee was the only one who showed anger. Her dark brows remained furrowed, and finally, just before they arrived at Leedy's, she yelled out through her tears, "You didn't love Momma, you let her die. I heard you tell the doctor to cut the baby out of Momma. You killed her, Daddy! You killed her!"

Jack said nothing, but he felt everything. Dee never forgave him in her heart for the loss of Ima and her little brother. Her early childhood impression was her lasting impression, rightly or wrongly. She didn't know it at the time, but her child's anger at Jack would be stoked further by his ignorance of her ultimate plight, and this bitter attitude toward her father would shape her life and the lives of her children. As with so many families, there are those who never fully understand each other and some who never wish to.

Shortly after the funerals, Jack had to work the fields to take care of his family. The girls needed parenting, but between the sorrow and bitterness that Jack carried in him, and the demands of working the farm by himself, he became even more distant from his daughters and even less communicative than before Ima's and the baby's deaths. Leedy and Flossy, his sisters, each came by once a week to clean, launder, and prepare food, while Edna at fourteen and Lee at eleven kept things going otherwise. But a new visitor came to the farm to 'look out' for the younger girls, Gay and Dafnie. He was Basil, Jack's younger brother, taller by two inches than Jack and wiry of build like Jack. Basil always wore a hat so that the brim shaded his eyes, no matter the condition of sunlight or rain. You could never really know what was going on under Basil's wide brim hat.

The contrast between the two brothers could not have been more marked. Jack was a hard worker and responsible tenant farmer, whereas Basil always got others to do his work if it was at all possible. He primarily lived off his sisters and their husbands. Jack never made excuses. Basil constantly blamed others or fate for his lack of money and work. Jack was strait-laced and moral. Basil was a pedophile, and nobody had figured that out yet. In a time and culture that celebrated the marriages of teenage girls with older men, the societal goalposts on the definition of pedophilia were differently placed.

But no mistake, Basil was a pedophile under any and all definitions, since he lusted after sexual contact with small children. And he hid his proclivity very well by choosing his victims carefully over the years and nurturing trust and then fear in the shadowy places of their young lives to keep them quiet. He was content to destroy their childhoods and had never tested himself by taking a young life. Violent rape and assault were not his style. His tools were emotional seduction, guilt, and fear of punishment, and many young children in the poor farming areas of

Northeast Arkansas had thus been violated by him. This was a society where children were to be seen and not heard. Rich picking fields for such as he.

Over time, he found it was easier with family than with strangers. Jack would have killed him if he had known, and some might say that his lack of meaningful communication with his daughters was ultimately his way of absolving himself of such knowledge. Dee certainly thought so, and the blame she heaped upon Jack grew over the years as a result.

Before Ima's passing, Dee had been a happy and curious young girl. She wasn't content to learn the alphabet and spell basic words like 'dog' and 'look.' She asked to read more, not waiting to be told that she would learn soon enough in school. And when Ima presented her with early reading at ages three and four, Dee always asked questions about what she was reading whether a simple nursery rhyme like Jack and Jill, or a child's story like Hansel and Gretel.

"Why didn't the witch eat other food? How can you build a house made of candy and cake, Momma? Wouldn't it melt in the sun?" There was no end to her questions and curiosity, and Ima patiently tried to answer Dee every time, or promise to find the answer if she didn't know it.

Her auburn hair, fair complexion, and gray eyes made Dee a pretty girl in the eyes of many and made her the envy of her plain-looking sisters. When Basil started to come around, it was once a week for a while, then twice a week, and finally three times per week, whenever he could arrange it, when Jack was in the fields or off on a trip to town. He quickly narrowed his focus upon Dee, and saw that Gay was eager to spend time with her older sisters so it was not difficult to convince her to do so. Things were easier for Basil when school was on, because Dee was home alone and under strict orders from Jack not to go outside while he was in the fields or gone on an errand. It would be another year before Dee started school. To a five-year old that is a very long time.

Basil groomed Dee for his crime shortly after Ima died. He did this by visiting when adults were around during May to August, and when they weren't around. Basil gravitated to his niece, and often hugged her and expressed his intense feelings of the loss of Ima and the baby. He told her stories that cast Ima in the most positive light, knowing how much Dee had loved her mother and spent large swaths of time with her. His expression of loss was a lie, of course, because in life, he and Ima barely spoke. She couldn't abide his presence when all he did was ask for something: food, money, or some favor. But Dee was glad that an adult member of the family paid attention to her, Lord knew that Jack did not. And her sisters went on to other self-preservation concerns within a month of the funerals.

"I know that you miss your Momma, Dee-dee." Basil would say as he hugged Dee close, and put her on his lap for a rock in the rocker. I miss her too, very much." And Basil would fake crying, burying his head in his hands.

"I'm sorry, Uncle Basil. Don't cry!" And then, Dee would start to cry, and when she gently cupped Basil's face with her little hands, he practically swooned. He resolved to continue reading with Dee and answer her questions as best he could, to draw her out and trust him further.

When the older girls went to school a few months later, Basil made his move. By that time, Dee looked forward to his visits as a bright spot in her life. Basil had laid the groundwork for developing a trusting relationship and a shared grief. He was clever enough to know that Dee's life was limited; no school as yet, abandonment by her sisters, and emotionally abandoned by Jack. She was lonely and craved attention. And he gave that to her. His next step was to convince Dee that they would do anything for each other. Once he was confident with that aspect, Basil went to work convincing Dee that no matter how fearful it might be, he was an adult and had needs that only she could help him with. When she asked him what that was, he showed her and told her that only she could help him, and that nobody else would understand. Basil didn't commit fornication with Dee at that point, but he coaxed her to handle him as he directed, and this became a constant feature of his visits as long as they were alone. But he was clever and experienced in the ways of violating children her age, so when she said she didn't want to do it anymore, "Please, Uncle Basil, I don't want to," he threatened her with exposure to Jack, who would surely punish her severely, and of course she believed that quite probable.

Then, he softened the blow. "This will be our little secret, so your daddy never has to know that you did."

Dee withdrew from everyone, even her sisters. Basil knew this would happen, and was content that he was not in danger of being discovered. But Dee had become a shy and unfriendly girl, withdrawn from the happiness afforded by everyday life and finding no joy in anything. When she went to school, she was known as strange by her peers and 'anti-social' by the school staff. Her childhood had ended long ago, killed by a combination of Basil's evil intent and Jack's voluntary absence. And her sisters paid no attention. Nobody put two and two together. Dee transformed from a gregarious, bright pre-schooler, to a bitter, angry, and withdrawn child. She trusted nobody. She saw herself worthy of nobody, and was in the world but not part of it.

Basil continued to molest Dee, including forced intercourse from age eight, until he moved away to Memphis when she was twelve. But Dee was obsessed with one thing; getting out of where she was. At the end of year eight in school, when she turned fourteen, she left home to find work in Paragould, and lived with Edna and her husband Alvin, who had a good job operating road maintenance equipment for the state. Within Dee, there swirled a toxic blend of shame, fear, rage, and low self-esteem; a girl who had suffered in silence the crimes of assault, abuse, and neglect by adult men in her life from a very young age.

She had to get out, and get a new life, at any cost. But she knew she couldn't do it alone. For the next move to the Great Escape, there had to be a partner.

Chapter 5
Annabelle's Christmas, 1937

On Christmas Eve, 1937, you could tell it was not going to be a White Christmas. After dark, the few streetlights in the small town of Paragould provided an opportunity for shadows to play in and out of the buildings. Their dim glow mingled with the slow and steady reduction of illumination passing through the windows of houses and businesses as daily life wound down to a dark and freezing night. It was nine p.m. and the gray haze of the day had produced a starless night. The Arctic air mass from Canada had slowly spread like a peaceful yet deathly blanket over the Midwest and into the South, forcing the poor and the rural to endure around their wood-burning stoves or with no heat at all. Albeit many even prayed for a bit of snow.

People with means lived in the neighborhood behind the Vandervort Hotel near the edge of downtown. Those were the folks whose homes boasted Christmas trees and a few decorations, where children received presents, and whose fathers held the few jobs that entailed some work other than hard labor, or owned businesses that allowed them to approach the national income average of one thousand and six hundred dollars per year. But in this neighborhood, a raid was afoot that night. The pillager flitted from shadow to shadow, doing his best not to be seen, waiting patiently before his next move. Discovery meant a beating, or worse.

A thin boy of average height, with bright blue eyes and brown hair, slowly emerged from the shadows beside the hotel, wearing a very worn knit hat that was too large for him, and an old hand-me-down brown wool coat two sizes too large for him. His right shoe had the stitching coming loose at the sole, and he knew that he couldn't outrun anyone without tearing his shoe apart. The only noise he made was the sound of hunger coming from his gut.

He was always hungry, always cold this time of year.

Eleven-year-old Carl was on a mission. He wasn't looking to steal, but if he had to, then he would, because he had made a promise to his mother, Nellie, on her deathbed three weeks earlier and his sense of purpose was all-consuming during this holiday time of year. Daddy Charles had long since passed of pneumonia and a weak heart at fifty-two, leaving Nellie no choice but to re-marry if she wanted to hold on to her children. But her new husband, Silas, had simply given her up to her own sickness and then death, figuring it had been a bad deal to marry the widow. So, after the re-marriage strategy of holding her children failed, some say that she indeed died of a broken spirit, as much as the pneumonia that was the official reason for the end of her young life.

The promise that youngest son, Carl, had made to Mother Nellie was that he would take care of his younger sisters, and since four-year-old Martha Nell had been adopted elsewhere in her infancy and beyond his help, that left Annabelle who was now seven. He had never had more than an orange or a beating for Christmas, but his heart was full of the need to serve a deep well of love and devotion, and since Mother was gone, he focused those emotions and his sense of responsibility on Annabelle. The fear of another beating from his brother-in-law, and the anxiety of possibly not being able to help his younger sister, each weighed on him. But he had plucked up enough courage to overcome both fears. Courage and determination did not shout out loudly from Carl as they did from most; they quietly flowed like water finding its way over, under, or through the most difficult of obstacles.

"If I see that you gone out tonight, you're really gonna catch it!" Worlick had warned him.

"Ain't nothing for you, but Santy don't care anyways," he said through a toothy grin. Worlick loved to taunt and control his young brother-in-law, and Carl being so much younger and smaller, there wasn't a whole lot that he could do where Worlick was concerned, except to evade him whenever possible. The strange relationship that his older sister Dorothy had with Worlick, who was twelve years her senior, angered him. She had been a fifteen-year-old bride and now was a seventeen-year-old wife/prostitute.

He really believed that someday, Worlick would kill him, and there was nothing Dorothy, Charles, or the police could or would do about it. The folks at the church knew of the situation, quietly looked down their righteous noses and whispered "What a pity…" before turning away. Since Daddy's death, Carl had been turned out of school to work in the fields or at any job his brother-in-law deemed suitable. Worlick figured he had it pretty good; a very young wife to 'break in' as he put it, and her brothers earning enough between them to keep food on the table and a roof overhead, with his comforts being served above all others. He was a man of much cunning and little imagination.

What then little ten-year-old Carl had been forced to do with men that Worlick 'introduced' him to, had destroyed his remaining childhood during the last year, as surely as the deaths of his parents and the cynical distribution of his siblings by a society abysmally ill-equipped to help. As far as Carl was concerned, he became an orphan long before the sickly Nellie passed. At that moment, Worlick completely took over the lives of Dorothy, Charles, and Carl.

Carl hated him and imagined all kinds of horrible endings to Worlick's life, which of course, his gentle nature never would have allowed him to execute. Maybe.

Carl hated him even more after Mother died in early December of 1937. His defiance was growing over the years as he would disappear into the streets and creeks, ponds, and woods by himself or with other boys. They would play cowboys and Indians, Flash Gordon, and WWI Doughboys in the trenches. Many of them had more normal lives, living with family or foster parents and going to school at least until year eight, sometimes until high school graduation. Carl took to smoking, mostly cigarette butts found on the ground but sometimes a full cigarette if he was lucky. It helped with the constant lack of food and smoking was a habit he carried with him all his life.

Over the last four years since Daddy had died, he had found the best part of his life in the wandering packs of boys, his escape from the realities of his life with his sister and her husband, and the uneven stream of men who came to see them. Carl continued seasonal work in the cotton and soybean fields and Worlick gained additional income from the boy's work. The consequences of going off alone always involved a beating and some form of deprivation and humiliation served up by Worlick without a peep of protest from Dorothy. Carl, however, defiantly persisted. Worlick was the king, enforcer, and grand pimp of his castle, and that was just how he wanted it.

As he crouched in the shadows waiting for the right time to move unseen, Carl remembered the first time that he rode the flatbed trucks to a cotton-picking job after coming to live with Worlick. It was with a large crew of predominately African American families. He felt a bit nervous like a fish out of water, but his social nature was evident to the adults one of whom asked him questions. Mainly, she wanted to know where his parents were to which he replied,

"They've passed away, Ma'am." The woman clutched a small girl of only three or four years old to her side, while her husband got out of the truck with their son, perhaps a year or two older than Carl.

She was a full-figured woman about thirty, and her husband was much taller, well over six feet with a lean build, and it struck Carl that the man's clothes flapped around his body just like Daddy's had done. "I'm Maddy Graham, Mrs. Graham to you, son. This here's Belinda, and my son is Jason. Elijah, say hello to this young man, an orphan by the sound of it." Her husband nodded toward Carl and said, "I'm surely the Mr. in the Mr. and Mrs. Graham, Carl. But I ain't so formal. You can call me Elijah. Jason let's get ready. Help your Momma with Bel. Time to go to work. Carl, you can work alongside Jason if you want." Maddy put Bel under a tree for shade. The little girl was under strict orders not to move until Maddy or Elijah came to get her. They left her a small cloth doll and walked on to their positions.

Carl remembered how accepting of him the Grahams were right off the bat. He played with the children on the lunch break, and after the workday was done, they went their separate ways. As he walked away and waved goodbye, he called out, "Hope to see y'all again!"

They all waved in return, and Maddy whispered to Elijah, "Lordy, I don't know who's worse off us 'cause who we are, or him as is 'poor white trash' without parents or school."

"In this world, I'm bettin' it's us, Mother," replied Elijah. "But at least, we have a family. I reckon he'll end up in jail or dead before he's twenty. Nice boy, though." With that, the Grahams turned and walked away into their own futures. Carl never heard any of this, so his memory only went as far as them waving goodbye.

Tonight's Christmas Eve episode was a risky foray, but this one Carl did alone. Annabelle was in year two of school, and her foster parents, the Nooners, wanted nothing more to do with her as they had really wanted her youngest sister infant Martha at the time. They had to 'settle' for Annabelle at age four. The Nooners never abused Annabelle physically. But they never let her forget that she was second choice, and 'really not suitable for this household' as Mrs. Nooner put it to her on many occasions. They considered themselves good Christian people and fed her, housed her, and sent her to school. Apparently, Jesus didn't require more than that. Annabelle anxiously awaited the infrequent and brief visits of Carl, and had been spared watching Mother Nellie during her long journey toward her death. So, Carl and Annabelle loved each other intensely as brother and sister may often do, when no love is coming from where else as it should.

The Nooners were looking for another home for Annabelle and Carl prayed that it would be found in town. When he came to visit her, he was never allowed inside, not even in winter, as if he would contaminate their home with the germs of his unfortunate existence. They embraced on the porch or at the back door, and Annabelle was never allowed to roam farther with Carl than that.

"I want to go with you!" she would sob with tears running down her freckled cheeks, clutching her brother in desperate affection as he tried to leave and had his chin buried in her curly brown hair. "I love you! I love you! Why can't you live here?" Carl was not free to tell her why. Some secrets had to stay secrets.

"It'll be fine, Annie, fine. I love you, too. I will come back and bring you something good!

We'll be together, I promise." And he meant it, but as soon as he walked away, his young mind realized that he could not make that promise a reality. But this Christmas, he was going to make sure that Annie had a Christmas, a gift from her brother, and something to brighten her existence in the Nooner house, something to give her hope that things would get better.

In his mind, Carl had already plotted several ways to escape his life but really couldn't figure out how to make any of them happen as he had no money, could only perform basic reading and writing, and had no adult he could trust to look out for him.

One of his buddies, Cheeks—he once dropped his pants and mooned a shopkeeper—who was already thirteen had been beaten into a coma by a railroad Bull, and was now pretty much a vegetable being taken care of by the Presbyterian Church preacher and his family. Riding the rails was free but very risky for anyone, especially for a young boy.

Carl well-remembered the day he had met Cheeks, who had then just turned twelve. Cheeks' real name was Tyler Bryant, and he was large for his age, and at twelve, could have been mistaken for a sixteen-year-old. Tall and solid, he was also quick-witted and 'fast at the mouth.'

Some older boys had allowed Carl to tag along to a nearby creek on a hot and sticky August afternoon. Being much smaller and not knowing how to swim Carl was a natural target of the older boys. Ry, the ringleader at age sixteen, asked "Ain't you never been swimmin' before?"

Carl shook his head no, and thus, summary judgment was passed on him. He was unceremoniously thrown into a creek pool over his head, and was soon in trouble as he failed to relax, thrashing wildly for something to grab. The older boys laughed hard: all except one. Carl was starting to gulp water when a pair of hands grabbed him, as Tyler pulled him from the swimming hole. As Carl gasped for breath, crawling slowly up the mud bank, Tyler turned on the gang of three.

"Y'all ought to know better! Coulda killed him!" He gave a steely stare to Ry, but George, one of Ry's followers and aged fourteen, stepped in front of Tyler.

"Maybe, we oughtta do you something special, woman." He turned for a nod of approval from Ry. As he turned around, Tyler hit him square in the face, so hard that George collapsed on his ass, oozing blood from all those capillaries around his broken nose. Tyler picked up a heavy stick.

George was down, two to go. "We're leavin'. Any of you shit-brains wanna try to stop us?"

"Plenty of time and ways to get to you," Ry menaced. But he let them go, with Tyler half carrying Carl and saying, "Be all right, boy. You need some swimmin' lessons." After that, Tyler indeed spent a bit of time teaching Carl to swim in the creek and in a nearby pond, careful not to be near any cottonmouths, who tended to be very aggressive poisonous snakes. As Christmas 1936 approached, and Tyler had a bit of money in his pocket, he tried to negotiate a better price on a hat for his widowed mother, but the shopkeeper wouldn't budge, so Tyler mooned him in front of a lot of people, and for that, he gained the nickname 'Cheeks.' In 1938, he hopped a freight car for Tennessee, meaning to come back right away, but as he was returning on another empty freight car, he ran into a rail cop who only meant to hurt him a bit and scare him, but Cheeks' head got in the way of a nasty baton blow and it cracked his skull. Cheeks disappeared that day but someone else who looked just like him took his place in Reverend Small's household, someone who could barely feed himself…

As Carl silently rounded the back corner of the hotel, he crept to the rubbish and garbage bins. Everything was mixed together: food scraps, metal, paper, glass, and grease from the kitchen. He had no gloves. Undaunted, he plunged his hands into the mess and felt around for anything that might be salvageable, but after nearly twenty minutes, he admitted defeat and moved on. He headed northwest from the center of town to the Oak Heights neighborhood hoping to find better luck in cleaner trash. But this would take some stealth, because the houses were not close together, and any discovery would find him treated harshly like an adult burglar.

"Gotta get back before anyone wakes up," he said to himself. His plan was to bring a present to Annie on Christmas morning at all costs, but first, he had to find one. Most of the homes were of brick, sharply gabled, and with normal to small windows. The lights were already turned out and it was approaching ten p.m. At the second house, he discovered a hard form with his hands and arms buried to the elbows in waste. He slowly and gingerly pulled it out of the mess, and saw in the dark that it was a doll-figurine about eight inches high and intact but badly marred by stains and sludge. White. Why did it have to be white? The worst color to clean. But he had to try. A nearby dog began to bark, and Carl knew he had to get out of there fast before discovery… it was only a matter of moments before someone would turn on the lights and come out to determine the reason for the sentry barking. He ran for the trees, hobbling on one foot because of the damaged sole, and made it to the trees for cover just as the lights in the house were turned on.

A tall, thin man in long pants, suspenders, and a long-john shirt stepped out with a lamp, looking around. He sniffed the quiet and cold air, and seeing nothing, he cursed the dog under his breath for disturbing his peace and quiet on Christmas Eve, then turned and went inside. Carl remained still as a mouse for five minutes more and then made his way back to the hotel, shivering all the way. How to clean this doll up in time? It occurred to Carl that the kitchen was in clean-up mode at the hotel, so he walked to the back of the hotel at the delivery entrance and knocked quietly.

The African American kitchen hand came to the door. He was about sixty with graying hair and a piercing gaze that immediately startled Carl. "We ain't got no extra edibles tonight, kid," and he started to close the door, but Carl worked up the courage to say, "Please Mr., I got this doll for my sister and I gotta clean it up for her Christmas, but I ain't got nothin' to use. I don't want any food. Just some hot water and a bit of salt if you can." Maynard looked him up and down, and then noticed the little ceramic doll which was as dirty as the inside of a pig's mouth. After a few moments of appraisal, Maynard simply said, "Wait here," and closed the door.

After what seemed to Carl a freezing eternity, but in fact no more than two minutes, Maynard opened the door and set a bowl of steaming water and a small bottle brush on the ground, with a small bowl of sand. "Sand be better than salt. We're out of here at eleven p.m. so be done by then." Before Carl could say thank you, Maynard turned abruptly and closed the door, off to his own concerns about finishing work and getting home for Christmas.

Carl's hands immediately went to work with the water, brush, and sand. The brush helped to clean the crevices and folds, his hands with sand grit and a rag cleaned the smoother surfaces, but he had to be careful not to scratch the doll. Carl had never had a Christmas present other than a piece of fruit, and possessed no toys except what he made from wood and bits of rubbish.

Daddy's whittled toys were long gone. But the elation he felt about this filthy and unremarkable ceramic doll was as great as if it had been a very large piece of gold he had extracted from the rubble and waste. Slowly, the original surface of the doll emerged, though not totally in the cracks and folds. Carl had run out of time.

Maynard opened the door at eleven p.m. Just as he said he would. "You got to go now, kid. Hand me the bowls and the brush and be on your way." Carl did as he was told and said,

"Merry Christmas, Mr., and thank you so much."

"Merry Christmas, kid. And get that to your sister directly tomorrow morning." Something passed through Maynard's gaze, as if this incident had evoked a true memory of his own. He slowly closed the door quietly, so as not to let anyone hear. With a soft click, he was gone. Carl never saw Maynard nor spoke to him again. He never forgot.

Annie's Christmas Present

When he returned to the ramshackle tar and wood house on stone blocks that was the home of Worlick, he found to his relief that Worlick was sound asleep and snoring, after having consumed enough bourbon to dull his senses. Dorothy didn't sleep much. She was awake but didn't raise her head when Carl entered the small house. The other bedroom was occupied by Charles and Carl, and Charles was also asleep. Charles was 'slow' in the vernacular of the day. He would, in later years, be called 'retarded' and when that went out of fashion, he would end his life as 'probably autistic' requiring special needs. He was an easy mark for Worlick, who was, at that time, in his life a psychological, social, and economic apex predator in the small town. Most people steered clear of him once they knew him, except for the mill workers, railroad men, and others, who needed Dorothy's wan beauty for a few minutes to an hour, or Carl's childhood innocence to meet their own predatory needs. Charles was simply no fun for such as these, but he could pick and chop cotton and wield a broom as well as anyone, and therefore was useful to Worlick, and therefore, he had a place to sleep and food to sustain him.

Worlick hadn't 'found Jesus'—was he ever lost? in his life yet, and he felt no need for repentance or remorse. Yet, in a town full of Baptists, Pentecostals, Church of Christ Doomsdayers, and other evangelicals, it was only a matter of time before Worlick, with Dorothy in tow, would seek redemption and be forgiven for the son of a bitch that he was so that they could fit in with normal society. Forgiven by God and Jesus, but not by Carl. Ever.

The pot belly stove had burned firewood all day and evening, and the warmth had spread throughout the little four-room house so that when Carl settled into his sleeping cot he didn't need his coat in addition to the single wool blanket, no sheets. But he knew from experience that by early morning, the heat plume would be gone, and if he wasn't covered properly, then he would awake shaking to the bone with cold, unable to feel his feet or his fingertips. Charles slept in his cot nearby, oblivious to all and covered well. Worlick and Dorothy had sheets and ample blankets and body heat to resist the creeping, biting cold of the late night.

Extra wood had been burned this day, but only because it was Christmas Eve. Two stockings were pinned on the wall in the greeting room, each bulging with a piece of fruit, most likely an orange or an apple. Extra wood burn and a piece of fruit, such was the celebration of Christmas at Worlick's house. Carl knew from the past Christmas, that it was unlikely anyone would come to visit Dorothy or him. And if they did so, the only Christmas music likely to be heard in that event would be grunting and groaning from the visitors.

Carl pulled the doll from his coat lining and examined it with pride. The cleaning was the best he could do with the little time he had and the meagre cleaning supplies, though generously provided by Maynard with more kindness in his heart than he made visible to Carl. He hardly slept that night, not in anticipation of Christmas at his home, but in anticipation of the joy he might bring to Annie, and therefore, also to Mother Nellie in heaven. The vision outside the hospital on the moment of her death was as real to him as the sun shining, an angel conjured from the low-hanging and overcast sky, and the lights of the hospital, that for a moment, appeared to his child's eyes as confirmation that his mother was going to a better place. Like many illusions that people have in childhood, it sustained his soul for the rest of his life and provided some measure of meaning to Nellie's death.

Christmas morning saw a dark, gray dawn. Most people really wanted to see some snow instead. But it was not to be. By seven a.m., Worlick had drunk a cup of ranch coffee made by Dorothy, and had fired up the stove from the coals left over from the night before. Carl needed to pee, and the outhouse was twenty-five yards away from the house, so he had to get dressed. In doing so, he slipped and the doll fell to the floor, landing with a thump but undamaged, because it had fallen on part of the wool blanket.

"What the hell you got there, young'un?" Worlick's tone was threatening, and he would brook no attempt to lie about it. He rushed in just ahead of Dorothy, and they both saw the doll on the floor on top of the blanket.

"You playin' with dolls now, little girl? Where did you fetch that from? Did you steal it? Had to have stolen it, cause you ain't got no money!" Worlick was clearly pleased with the situation, another chance to humiliate Carl.

"I found it in the trash, look, it's been cleaned but has garbage marks on it!" Carl had a pleading tone in his voice. In a split second, his head exploded with pain as Worlick cuffed him hard across the left ear, knocking him to the floor. But Carl didn't cry. He just stared at Worlick. It would have gone to the worse for him if Dorothy, completely out of character, hadn't spoken up behind Worlick.

"Honey, please, it's Christmas, please let's not have such words. Carl, what have you done?"

She ventured a gentle hand on Worlick's muscular forearm, strange form for a man who did no physical work. She half-expected a shove or a blow. Worlick stared menacingly at the boy. "Tell us what you are up to, or I swear I will beat it out of you, boy!"

But Carl just stared back at Worlick, he wasn't about to back down, and suddenly, was ready to absorb any punishment for bringing the truth out. "Annabelle needs a Christmas present. She don't get any where she lives, and with Momma havin' passed just now, I thought it would be best for her to receive something from me, and of course, from y'all, so I went through enough garbage and trash until I found her," he pointed at the doll. "I jus' want to give it to her this mornin'. Please let me do that and I promise on my Momma, that I'll work twice as hard here and, in the fields, come spring and help with more money."

Now it was transactional, something Worlick could accept. More work, more money… better for Worlick. "What do you say, Honey?" asked Dorothy in a timid voice. By now, Charles was fully awake but totally uninterested in what was going on. He just stared at them all.

In trying to show wisdom and justice on his terms like the king he perceived himself to be, Worlick straightened his frame, looked down at Carl, and said as if passing judgment in a firm and even tone, "I will forget your sass in goin' out without permission just this once, and allow you to see your sister with the doll because it's Christmas, but the payment is that you will fulfill your promise to me as made right here in front of witnesses, or so help me, God, I will work you to death and you will not see your twelfth birthday. Do you agree?"

Carl replied solemnly, "Yes, sir, I agree."

"And we thank you for this Christmas," Dorothy said to Worlick.

"Be quiet and get my breakfast, woman. And Carl, be back here by ten o'clock or else." That was Worlick's final word on the subject. Carl got ready to go and visit Anna Belle at eight-thirty a.m. that morning.

As Carl went up the gravel path to the Nooner house, he smiled with satisfaction. He had realized a new weapon against his physically superior enemy: greed. It would buy him time to figure out a way to get free.

Mrs. Nooner saw Carl coming, holding something wrapped in cloth. "Anna Belle, your brother is here! Come meet him at the front porch. Don't be too long with him." The Nooners had provided a tree and presents for their children and would go to church later, but Anna Belle was excluded from the present opening and was given an orange, peeled, and sliced to eat, which she did not turn down. The Nooners were looking to unload Anna Belle at the earliest opportunity, and if all else failed, she could go to an orphanage. It wasn't that she was a problem child, everybody liked her including her teacher. It was just that she didn't fit into their plans which really had included an infant for ultimate adoption. Someone they could mold from the start. Annabelle was feisty with a mind of her own. They, of course in their self-righteousness, were totally oblivious to the fact that they were inflicting emotional abuse upon a small girl, that had begun when she was age four.

Carl was excited by the anticipation of Annie's reaction to his present, and a little apprehensive because he recognized the doll's failings as a toy. Annie opened the door and said, "Mama Nooner says I can't be too long. Merry Christmas, Carl! I drew you a picture!" and she handed him a folded piece of paper.

"If you don't mind, lil' sister, I will look at it when I am alone, and thank you so much!" He carefully put the paper in his coat pocket and noticed Annie staring at the parcel in his hands.

"This is for you, lovely Annie. Merry Christmas." He handed it over to her small hands, and was surprised at the strength with which she clutched the present and took it from him.

"Ohhh, Carl! My big brother, what have you got for me?" and with that, she quickly unwrapped the doll and without really examining it she jumped up and down and kept saying,

"A doll! A doll..." over and over until Carl gently grabbed her by the shoulder to keep her from jumping.

"It's the best I could find, and I hope you like it."

"Her name is Mary, Carl, she is Mary, and she and I will have many adventures together. She's the most beautiful doll in the world because you gave her to me, and she is mine. Santy couldn't have done better!" Grasping

Mary in her right hand, Annie gave Carl a big hug with a kiss on the cheek. "When are you coming to get me so we can live together with Dorothy and Charles?"

"Someday soon," he lied. "I'm working on it, Annie. We'll move to a bigger house so there will be enough space for you. Be patient, please. They aren't hurting you, are they, or making you do stuff you don't want to do? You'd tell me, right?" The thought of Annie living in the same house as Worlick made Carl's stomach turn.

"No, they jus' pretty much ignore me." As Carl heard this, he thought about how wonderful it would be to be ignored at home.

From inside the house, Mrs. Nooner called to Annie, "Time to say goodbye, Annie. We have to get ready for church service." She didn't even have the courtesy to say hello to Carl, as if he didn't exist. Carl smiled with satisfaction as he walked away. It had been a good Christmas all things considered. Worlick had been placated, Dorothy had, for once in her own way, stood up for her brother, and Annie, lovely little Annie with the curly hair and rosy cheeks, really loved the doll. But most of all, as he smiled to himself and tears started to roll down his cheeks, the kind that just flowed without the sounds of crying, he had kept his word to Mother Nellie and would keep doing so no matter what stood in the way.

Annie loved the doll, not because she loved the doll, but because she loved the brother who brought it to her. Even at seven, she understood that he had found it and cleaned it, but that didn't matter ever to her. Mary was in her possession for the rest of her life, and was indeed passed on to her grown daughters seventy years later, when she passed. Carl never knew that, but he always remembered the joy on Annie's face the moment that she took Mary into her hands. He couldn't know it, but the optimism that was sparked in Annabelle's psyche by this act of Christmas kindness was rewarded in very unexpected ways, when she finally left the Nooners and landed in the supportive household of the Jacksons, who would eventually become mom and dad to her.

Carl had just enough time to walk back home and was halfway there, when he pulled the drawing that Annie had made him from his coat pocket and unfolded it for a look. It took him a moment to absorb the contents, and after a few moments, he realized that he was looking at a house with smoke coming out of the chimney, flowers popping outside, the sun in the sky with rays projecting, and a little stick girl with a dress, and a taller stick boy with overalls holding hands. Nobody else was in the picture. The thing that stunned Carl, was that the picture was drawn in dark lead, no colors, just black lines for form. Even so, the message was clear that this is how Annie sees happiness. But then, there was what looked like a bush away from the house and he noticed two eyes staring from the bush. That sight made Carl a bit dizzy, and he put the drawing away and finished a quick walk the rest of the way home. It was a mystery he never forgot but never solved.

Chapter 6
Sometimes, It's Good Just to Be Lucky—
1940/41

At the age of nearly fourteen, Carl had had enough of life under Worlick's roof, even if he wasn't there all that much anymore, mostly to bring money from his eclectic labors. He knew that there was no future for him there, nothing but misery and exploitation, and he just as surely knew how badly he wanted to kill Worlick. In his fantasy, he would then free Dorothy and Charles. But it was only a fantasy that he knew he would never bring to reality. After living most of his time the last two years running with the pack of displaced and unfortunate boys, Carl knew he would never back down from a fight that someone brought to him, but he also knew he would seek to avoid one if at all possible. He decided to strike out on his own, and to look in on Annabelle as often as possible with her new family. At the same time, he wanted to get somewhere in life. Anywhere but where he was.

Worlick, of course, was not having it. But Carl was lucky that Worlick was a frequent and sleepy drunk, and thereby the boy found freedom and escape. Worlick threatened and sometimes beat Carl, but as time wore on to the middle of his thirteenth year, Carl spent fewer and fewer nights in Worlick's house, often preferring to ply odd jobs and sleep where he could. In a town as small as Paragould at that time, virtually everyone knew Carl and saw him as deserving of odd jobs, and sometimes a bit of charity because he was honest and a hard worker. He would sweep and clean, carry out errands, pick cotton, chop cotton, tend to animals, split firewood, and generally apply himself to anything that needed doing and was within his ability to do. Sometimes, he got paid in hot meals, which was just fine with him. He was too young for the mill or the railroads, but he was able to secure spot work in the farms surrounding the town. There was always food to be taken from the creeks, rivers, and ponds. And whenever fortune smiled, there was the occasional movie. And of course, Carl never failed to bring something to Annabelle, dear little Annie who was killing it at school, and who never tired of his visits.

One night in July, just shy of his fourteenth birthday, Carl came to Worlick's house with something in his hands; an old baseball bat with a couple of chunks of wood missing and a splinter or two showing. The business end of two four-inch carpenter's nails protruded from the thick end of the bat. Carl had filed the heads off and driven the nails an inch into the ash wood. He quickly hid it under his blanket before Worlick returned home from another bout of cards and drinking. Charles was sitting on the small front porch sporting a listless expression and staring into the gathering twilight, picking out fireflies as their intermittent glows speckled the air. Carl came up and sat down beside Charlie, putting his arm around the older boy's shoulders.

"Listen, Charlie, I won't be comin' round here anymore, but I'll be watching out for you, and I'll talk to the reverend and his wife about takin' you in. I love you." He gave Charlie a squeeze, and slowly walked into the house. Dorothy was away near the rail station, with a man set up by Worlick. Carl didn't feel like saying anything to Dorothy that he hadn't already said. Many times, he had asked her to leave with Charlie and him, but her fear of Worlick was greater than any desire she had to leave. Bruises and light concussions had convinced her. She rightfully believed that their lives would be in danger from such a move, and Paragould was a very small town.

Dorothy arrived at midnight, and Worlick came home an hour later. He took the cash from Dorothy and yelled at Charlie to stay in bed. He took a look at Carl, who feigned sleep but was quite awake, with his right hand closed tightly on the bat that was hidden from Worlick's view. "I'll deal with you in the morning, ya little bastard," he rumbled, and then staggered off to bed.

After two hours of deep snoring and no movement from Worlick, Carl arose silently from his bed. He was primed like a coil of tensed spring, and knew that he had one chance to make sure that Worlick didn't follow him anywhere after this night. He moved slowly, in total silence, and controlled his breathing at a slow and soft pace through his mouth, in order to remain silent. He knew that he had to control his rage at his brother-in-law, and resist the temptation to bash his head in. When he reached the bed where Worlick and Dorothy lay sound asleep, he slowly placed the bat in Worlick's face so that one of the nails was an inch from Worlick's right eye. Carl poked Worlick on the chest with the other hand and quickly recovered a two-handed grip on his bat, careful not to stick the man in the eye, yet. Worlick slowly opened his eyes from his deep sleep and immediately saw the nail menacing his right eye in the dim light.

His voice trembled in the dark. "Who are you and what do you want? Did I wrong you in some way?"

He was greeted by a familiar voice, but one that had turned into a low growl. "You fucker! You even move one inch and this nail is gonna go right into your eye, and into your brain. Just try me!"

"Well, what do you want from me? As soon as you move away from this bed, I'm gonna beat you to death with that bat."

"You dumbass. You gonna' be blind so if you think your eye and your brain is worth it, and you think you can take this bat away from me in the dark and half blind before I do worse to you, then go ahead, fucker!" Carl gave his most convincing and controlled projection of menace, and Worlick got the point.

"Is this what I get for taking you in, feeding you, and putting a roof over your sorry head, you sneaky little shit?"

"Here's how this goes, Worlick. I am leaving this shit hole of a house for good now, and you're not going to take it out on Dorothy, or Charlie, who will be taken from you soon enough. You will not try to follow me or track me down. If you do anything to harm them or come after me, I will catch you asleep and bash your skull in, do you hear me? You do your part, then you'll never hear from me again. Now, shut up and blink once if you understand!"

Worlick knew he had been temporarily outfoxed and wasn't ready to part with an eye or worse. Dorothy moved slightly but still appeared to be out cold, facing the opposite direction.

Worlick blinked once.

"Close your eyes. It's dark outside and I have this to fuck you up in case you're thinkin' of runnin' after me." With that, Worlick closed his eyes. Carl knew that Worlick would never cause Dorothy to wake up, only to find the two in a struggle with an uncertain result for Worlick. He had figured out just as well that Worlick was at heart a coward like most bullies.

When Carl backed out of the room and into the darkness, Dorothy smiled a smile that Worlick never saw, and she didn't open her eyes until she awoke in the morning.

Carl made his way into the nearby woods outside of town, constantly checking to see if Worlick was following out of the house, but he never saw him do so. When he believed he was safe, about a mile away from the house, he slowly sat down under an oak tree, shaking with fear, and sending the mixed sounds of soft laughter and muffled crying into the night. After a few minutes to catch his breath, he went to the lumber yard, as he had many times over the last three years in good weather, to sleep the rest of the night between the stacks. Somehow, the smell of freshly sawed wood comforted him. He drew a half-crumpled cigarette and book of matches from his pocket and lit up, no longer afraid of being found by Worlick.

Carl drew on the cigarette deeply, at just shy of fourteen he was used to smoking deep in his lungs.

"What the hell are you gonna do now?" he asked himself out loud. He couldn't go back to school, had no foster care, and no place to live. But he did have faith that he would be all right. "Well, whatever comes and whatever you do, you dumb son-of-a-bitch, Daddy's watchin' and he'll be really upset if you just give up." Carl stared up at the night sky, a tapestry filled with a mixture of clouds and stars on a moonless night. Exhausted, he fell into a deep sleep in a sitting position with his back supported by a stack of rough-cut lumber. He awoke to the movement of the stack and the deep growl of Simon, the yard foreman. "What the hell, boy! You ain't got no business sleeping here, Carl. Now, get out of the yard, and next time I won't be so easy on ya." Simon, like nearly everyone in Paragould and surroundings, knew Carl, and like most people, he respected the boy for his hard work and trustworthiness, but he also harbored a belief that any time now he would turn into a low-end criminal like most such boys would, because his unfortunate position usually led to such an end no matter how promising the beginning. The way of the world. No family, no place, no money, and no prospects; just jail or worse.

Carl stood up and stretched to the sky. "Mornin' Mr. Perkins. I promise I won't do it again. I'll be on my way, sir, careful as you please." Carl knew that if Simon had ever really meant him harm, he would have certainly felt it by now.

For the next eight months after his fourteenth birthday, Carl developed into what could only be described as the town working vagabond. He did odd jobs for people and small businesses in return for a place to sleep and often food in the bargain. Winter was the most difficult, but a few houses were willing to take him in 'on the back porch' because it was commonly known in Paragould that he was reliable and no thief. He still lived part of his life running with the feral boys, but that eventually gave way to no time with them as their thoughts and scheming turned too dark for his liking. He then simply stayed away. They called him a fool for working like this when more money could be made in other ways. Who did he think he was? But Carl preferred the gratitude and adulation of the mainstream folks, and ultimately swam only in those waters.

One morning, in May 1941, with $3.80 cents in his pockets, half a pack of cigarettes and some matches, plus the clothes on his back and an old pocketknife, he woke up and decided as soon as his eyes opened; that he was going to make a plan to escape this town and make a better life.

He then made a decision that would change his life, though he didn't know it at the time. He figured that if he had a big breakfast, which would set him back just under two dollars, that would see him through the day, and there would be enough left over for another meal the next morning. There were at least two places that would pay him fifty cents to clean the store premises, and perhaps he could convince an elderly person or couple to pay him to split wood for the fire or stove. This reminded him that winter was only a couple of months away and he needed to find shelter soon, maybe somebody's covered porch or barn. After relieving himself and washing his face and hands at the mill, he started out for Bill Katty's General Store and Café in central Paragould, to have himself the biggest breakfast available, the first step in his plan. The second step was to figure out how to save enough money to leave for California.

When Carl arrived in front of the café, it was seven thirty, too early for anyone but farmers coming to town and a few sleepless souls. There were two automobiles, a flat-bed truck, and a horsedrawn farm wagon in front. Carl boldly went through the swinging front door and immediately drew the attention of Betty, Bill's wife and the waitress. She zeroed in on the boy, whom of course she knew, and warned him, "This isn't a home for charity, Carl. If you want a bit of somethin' then go and see Alvin at the back." Carl knew Alvin, the African-American cook, and he knew that what he could buy in a full breakfast far outweighed what Alvin would cough up from the kitchen, which might be a biscuit with a bit of bacon in it.

Carl, emboldened by his new sense of freedom, squared his shoulders and stood as tall as he could, "Now listen Mrs. Katty, I respectfully ask to be seated because I can pay for a full breakfast this morning, and I want one." She frowned and then he quickly remembered his place. "Please, may I be seated, Mrs. Katty?"

"You may not! But you may have all the breakfast your money can buy sittin' at the back of the building." Carl's shoulders drooped.

At the corner table at the front of the café, there sat a man and a woman in the middle of their meal, whispering something to each other. The man cleared his throat and said, "Now listen here, Betty, Gurdy and I are invitin' this young man to have breakfast with us 'cause we have business to discuss with him. Y'all don't mind do ya?"

Betty's eyebrows arched in surprise and bemusement. She slowly responded, "Well, I guess not, Grant. You and Gurdy know your business I suppose. Go ahead, Carl, and have a seat with the Wilsons! I'll take your order directly." With that, she rushed back into the kitchen.

"Come on, Carl. Take a seat," Grant smiled a wide smile. Carl took them in for only a second as he knew of them but didn't know them. They were big people, both tall and Gurdy hefty, with wide faces that radiated kindness and understanding as far as he could tell. Grant wore his faded blue overalls, and Gurdy wore a flower print shift with a light sweater of sky blue.

The Wilsons were an anomaly as Arkansas farmers went, because they owned and farmed a quarter-section of land, or one hundred and sixty acres, nearly half of which was devoted to hardwood production. The other half was farmed in rotating crops. Working the property was hard, especially since all ploughing, furrowing, and tilling had until recently been done with horses hooked up. And while the farm yet relied upon well water, electricity had been provided courtesy of the Tennessee Valley Authority, one of the most successful and impactful of Franklin Roosevelt's New Deal programs. Grant and his son, Edward, spent a lot of time during winter the last two years grinding and filing the various blades and edges of the equipment. And they made sure that their two plough horses were well-tended throughout the year, even though they had acquired a small tractor recently.

Gurdy ran the farmhouse and the farmyard animals, including Mickey the Blue-tick hound, who was most useful when flushing cottontails and quail during a hunt. The Wilsons never went hungry while planting and harvesting nine months a year on average, and considered themselves more fortunate than most, which they were. They were humble and never put on airs. And they were kindly, if a bit stern. Most consequentially for Carl, their farm was their own.

Carl took his seat with the Wilsons and never took his eyes off them. "Don't worry, boy, just figure out what you want to eat, and it'll be on us. We get to town once a month for farm business, and always like to start the day with a late breakfast here!" It was not yet eight in the morning, but Grant could be forgiven for calling it 'late' since breakfast for his son Eddie and him was routinely at five a.m., after feeding the animals every day but Sunday.

"Sir, please, don't take this the wrong way, but why would you be buyin' whatever I want to eat for breakfast? I was ready to pay for my own. But I always heard 'never look a gift horse in the mouth.'" He immediately regretted that he had been so inartful with these two kindly souls, and yet, experience had taught him to suspect people before accepting them. Grant and Gurdy let it pass and Gurdy replied.

"Carl," she said in a friendly tone. "You have no proper place to live, and by the looks of you, there are often gaps in your feeding schedule, to put it mildly." *That much was true,* he thought. "Everyone in these parts knows at least something about the hardships of the Dough family, just as sure as most people know you're a good boy, who is likely to go bad if things go on like this for you."

Carl thought he was in for a lecture on how to fly straight, which was sometimes the price of the charity he seldom received. He really had no idea why else these people would buy him a breakfast big enough to fuel his young body through a whole day.

"I'll just come out and say it," blurted Grant. "We're inviting you to come and stay with us. We could use the extra help cause our son, Eddie, has finished high school, great marks mind you, and doesn't really want a life of farming. He's got ideas he wants to be a naval aviator and fly dive bombers or some such thing. So, he wants to join the Navy right after graduating from the Rolla School of Mines in a few years." He paused. "They's war in Europe for sure, but old Franklin D. will keep us out of it, and we don't see who else we'd be fightin'. But he'll be away for a long time, and we could use the help 'cause I ain't getting any younger."

He paused and then laughed a deep and genuine laugh, "Or thinner!" and he slapped his pot belly—made more conspicuous by his thin frame—with both hands, a tall man who otherwise showed no extra weight.

Carl smiled a nervous smile, afraid to laugh at Grant's self-criticism. And to be accurate, he just couldn't believe someone would offer to take him in on a permanent basis.

"Would you like that, Carl?" asked Gurdy. Gurdy had a reputation as one of the best bakers in the county, and the idea excited Carl. Steady work, nice people, good food, and a chance to learn something. He could only consider with wonder what it would be like to live in the same house with an older boy, who had actually finished high school. Maybe there was going to be learning in his future. But the reality was bittersweet after Grant added, "You'll be up every mornin', rain or shine, except Sundays, Christmas, New Year's, Easter, the 4th of July, and your birthday, at four-thirty, breakfast at five, whatever I tell you to do until lunch at twelve, which is sometimes in the house and sometimes in the fields, depending. You got your own room in the house, and room and board plus ten dollars a month to start. We'll take care of any medical expenses within reason, and hope you don't have any. You can visit your brother and sisters if you wish, on Sundays or other off days. Sometimes I like to go fishin' in the river, mostly on a Saturday night. We think we're good Christians, but we don't go to church. Gurdy disappears with some of her friends, or has them over to our place, and they get up to God knows what."

"God knows but you never will, you old fuddy-duddy," she replied.

He rambled on, "Probably some farmwife witchery, like how to put a spell on your husband so his mind is so fogged he can't see what you're really up to. What you have been puttin' in those pies and cakes?"

Gurdy answered, "Love, Granty my dear, love!" With that, she took his hand in hers, nearly equal in size to his big paws. Carl could see there was real love between these two. And going fishing with Grant in the river on Saturday night sounded very exciting to him. He never went night fishing, or in fact, never went anywhere at night without one or more of his feral companions. When he was alone in the dark, he conjured visions of being attacked by Worlick and killed. The dark, alone, was not where he wanted to have Worlick track him down. He would be safe on the Wilsons' farm, he was certain.

"I'll do it, Mr. and Mrs. Wilson! I will live and work on your farm and try my best to earn your trust. I'm a hard worker, you'll see." He said this just as Betty approached the table with Carl's full breakfast on a tray: scrambled eggs, two pork chops fried, a pile of hot grits with a pat of butter on top, two buttermilk biscuits covered in gravy from the pork chop drippings, and a glass of orange juice.

"That's a lot of food for a boy your size, Carl," said Gurdy.

"I can finish it, Mrs. Wilson," replied Carl in a determined tone of voice. I won't waste a thing!" And with that, he tore into the meal with gusto and said with a mouthful of biscuits and gravy, "I don't want to hold ya back none, but my Momma always told me not to eat too fast or my stomach will tell me when too fast is too fast."

"We'll wait, Carl, take your time, son."

And Carl thought, *'Sometimes, it's good to just be lucky.'* But he kept that thought to himself.

Chapter 7
So Near to Heaven, Yet so Far From Paradise—May, 1940 to November, 1941

The Wilsons were prodigious readers. They only listened to the radio once or twice a week, though Eddie seemed to be transfixed whenever national or international news was presented. He eagerly listened for news of the war in Europe, and the conflicts the Brits and Aussies were having with the Nazis in Europe, and Africa and the Japanese Empire in the Pacific and throughout Asia. He was the only child of Grant and Gurdy, but he wasn't spoiled, nor did he lack empathy for others. While his parents were generally kind and loving people, who considered themselves to be lucky enough to have a profitable and working farm, and a smart, handsome, and gentle soul for a son—when any conversation turned to the mention of African Americans, Eddie would usually only nod in agreement upon their disparaging remarks, and use of the 'N' word so as not to disrespect his parents. But such talk made Carl want to leave the room. He had worked for years with African American cotton pickers, played with the children as time allowed in the fields, and was always treated well by them. And, of course, he never forgot Christmas Eve 1937. Also, his daddy had warned him that there were those white folk who would do ANYTHING to keep whites and blacks from joining in common cause, and he knew in his heart that Daddy had spoken the truth which had been borne out over the years by reports of lynchings, beatings, homes burned to the ground, and other inflictions of terror upon the members of the Southern Tenant Farmers Union. Carl had been too young to understand the depth of courage and conviction that the union members and organizers possessed. But in his boy's mind, he held them in esteem as an abstract thing that sounded good.

Eddie really didn't like to think about such things at eighteen. His life was farm work, studying so he could graduate to ultimately become a pilot on an aircraft carrier, and engaging in heavy petting with Maggie Snell, whom he dreamed of marrying after what he envisioned, would be a dazzling career as a naval aviator. Well, maybe earlier. Eddie was now six feet tall, with dark brown hair and piercing green eyes, and showed no signs of the obesity that had always been a feature of his mother's appearance. He was solidly built, not athletic in stature, but strong from so much farm work. His wide and toothy smile was genuine and conveyed a friendly nature. But he was stubborn once his mind was made up and could not be moved, even by his parents whom he adored. To him, the arrival of Carl to the household was no threat, in fact, he welcomed him because he knew he would be 'flying the coop' soon to pursue his dreams, and it would be good to have Carl on the farm to help his aging parents. So, when Carl arrived that day, Eddie was eager to show him around the farm, and it was an eagerness at least partly borne of pride in the place, because Eddie knew that the signature of his own hands was on it.

Eddie had always had a passion for flight and dreamed of being able to pilot a plane from the deck of an aircraft carrier. But under current conditions, it would be impossible without first getting a college degree or by attending Annapolis. The Naval Academy was not an option for him, but a college degree was, and he had his sights set on the Rolla School of Mines at Missouri University of Science and Technology. With his parents' permission and the endorsement of his high school science teacher, he had already turned in his application and he was accepted into the Freshman Class of 1940. Most of the world was already at war, and he knew in his young heart that it was only a matter of time before America would send its young men to war. Better to be up in the air and doing what you love than slogging through the mud or enduring being stuck in a submarine sardine can. Like everyone else at his age, he had no idea where risk really lay, and in fact, didn't care much to think about it.

"Eddie, Carl here is going to be with us for a while at least, to help with the farm and to see that Momma isn't overly worked. He's a good boy who has come upon bad luck with his parents being dead, and his brothers and sisters scattered. And he's a hard worker. Give him a tour of the place and let him know which jobs need doin' and when." With that, Grant sauntered off to the house.

Carl said nothing. There was just a bit of apprehension clouding out his gregarious nature.

Eddie mistook this for shyness and kindly put a hand on Carl's shoulder as he said, "I'm sorry for your bad fortune, Carl, but you have come to the right place for peace, honest work, and two people who only know how to care about whomever they take to. And looks like they've taken to you." Then, he looked the fourteen-year-old in the eye, and said as he slightly increased the pressure of his hand on Carl's shoulder, "Never misplace their trust or do anything that would harm them, and we'll be the best of friends, Carl. Understand?"

Carl replied with sincerity, and not out of any fear, "Of course not Eddie, my momma and daddy taught me better than that. 'Never get ahead with your boot print on someone else's back.' Daddy told me when we worked the fields together. And I aim to be true to that. I loved my daddy very much."

This was enough to cause Eddie to let go of Carl's shoulder as he could see the truth in Carl's speech. "Well, let's get on with the tour, Hombre," he said in his best John Wayne voice, which didn't sound much like John Wayne, yet, still managed a smile from Carl. With both boys at ease, the tour began.

Carl learned all about the plough horses, already partially replaced by a small tractor, but retained as members of the farm family. He learned which chores needed doing before breakfast, and the cycle of farming, which Grant would help him execute. The farm was newly planted in spring, and the soybeans, corn, and cotton were all coming along in early summer. Grant didn't farm cotton, preferring to make money on food crops of mostly soy-beans, corn, and lettuce. Eighty acres of first and second-growth trees supplied firewood and some occasional cash, and fishing was handy in the small river that flowed north on the east flank of the farm, where Grant and Eddie loved to set up with a small fire and their fishing poles for some night fishing for catfish, bream, and perch when Saturday evenings with good weather allowed. The Wilsons had a sizable private farm for the region, and Grant had shrewdly guessed what and when to plant food crops. Their economic situation was, therefore, better than most, and certainly better than tenant farmers and most small land holders. Eddie would have to work part-time at Rolla, but they could afford to help him.

Eddie gave Carl a tour of the house and showed him his own bedroom adorned with hanging models of airplanes of all types and a picture of Maggie, a pretty girl with blonde hair and a lovely smile, prominently displayed on his desk. Something Carl didn't expect was the two sets of bookshelves filled with hardback and paperback books of all kinds. "You read all of them?" he asked Eddie.

"Sure have," replied Eddie. "And then some." Carl felt ashamed because he barely stumbled through the local newspaper, and comic books were about as complicated as his reading got. He then showed Carl his room, always a guest room reserved for family and friends, and now his own room. It wasn't much, but had the comforts of a single bed, nightstand, chest of drawers, and a wall clock that had to be wound from time to time. Carl was dazed, and he let his emotions get the best of him. His eyes glazed over as he said softly, "Ain't never had my own room, ever."

Eddie tried to lighten it up. "We'll have to teach you not to use a double negative, Carl." He didn't mean anything by it, but the impact on Carl was instant shame. He clearly didn't know what a double negative was, and seemed to be too terrified to ask. There was a short, awkward silence and Eddie blurted, "Well, let's get you some clothes and shoes, Carl, cause Momma has kept nearly everything I wore during my life! Race ya to the barn!" And off they went, running through the house and blasting out the creaky screen door in the kitchen, where Gurdy was busy preparing dinner. She looked up as they sped past and smiled.

***

The following three months, until Eddie left for Rolla, were the happiest of Carl's young life. Eddie and Grant were patient teachers on the things that Carl had to learn, never scolding him when he made a mistake and always gently correcting him. Carl responded to this nurturing environment without mistrust or apprehension. He seemed to fit right in. He loved working on the farm and helping the family, as well as he loved night fishing with Grant and Eddie.

Eddie's stories about high school life held Carl's attention, and often left him fantasizing about his dream life at school. Carl never stopped asking questions about things… how the tractor worked, why the different crops needed some things the same, and some things differently. He asked about flying, and listened with complete attention when Eddie described lift and pitch, and yaw and the physics of a dive. And best of all, in most evenings after dinner and before bed, Gurdy would sit with him as he progressed in his reading, vocabulary and language, night after night as if she were teaching her own son. He was even more awed by Eddie's desire to climb to the stratosphere, and the fact that his faux older brother was going to a technical college. Even with the demands of working a sizable farm, Carl found time to begin reading on his own and practicing arithmetic.

Carl was starved for family, for stability, for caring. When Eddie finally left in early September for Rolla, Carl felt like he really lost a big brother. "See you in November, Carl! Take good care of my parents and don't catch all the fish in the river… save some for me!" Grant and Gurdy took Eddie to the railroad station in Paragould to send him on his way by train and bus to Rolla.

When he walked into the house to be alone for a few hours, it hit him. *'I'm a big brother, too!'* he remembered. He needed to see Annie, sweet Annie, who would be wondering what happened to him. She was ten years old now, happy with her foster family, and adopted by them, with the emotional neglect of the Nooners already forgotten. She was also happy at school and seemed to thrive as a social animal, but she missed Carl when he was gone for too long, and he hadn't seen her for nearly six months! He also needed to check in on Charlie, and the reverend and his wife. He was hard on himself for not being consistent in fulfilling his promise to his dying mother, and perhaps, feeling a bit guilty for the positive changes in his life. Dorothy was not on the list, nor did he allow himself to think about her and about Worlick. *Might as well be dead,* he thought. Margaret was on another planet and had never been a part of his life.

The memories of the terrible experiences as a young boy at the hands of Worlick and his clients had been deeply repressed, obscured daily by the struggle for survival, where until now he had been constantly subjected to the opinions of others that he simply wasn't on the same level as them, and did not deserve more than what he got and would never likely get more from life. His natural curiosity and desire to please, combined with his will to accomplish something beyond picking cotton or sweeping floors, found unwitting support from the Wilsons who simply were doing what this lovely part of their nature compelled them to do, which was to nurture him and let him find his way. But for Grant, the dark side of his nature emerged whenever the topic included those he labeled 'Niggers' and 'Yankees' and 'Poor White Trash.'

The next day was Sunday, and Grant and Gurdy seemed determined to stay at home that Saturday night. "Mr. and Mrs. Wilson, tomorrow being church and all, I was thinking that it's time I check in on my little sister and my brother Charlie in his new home in town. It will only be an hour's walk from the church, so I was wonderin' if it is okay with you that I take off and visit them?" Grant was fiddling with the radio and looked up. "Tell you what, Carl, I'll drive you to your sister's place and pick you up at the reverend's house three hours later to come back here.

That way, you can see both Annie and Charlie. That okay with you?"

"Couldn't be more okay, Mr. Wilson." Carl couldn't believe his good fortune.

"Well, you're part of our family now, Carl," said Gurdy, as she peered over her spectacles.

"And none of this Mr. Wilson or Mrs. Wilson! We're your mom and dad now. Won't do to call us by our family names!" Carl ran to her and put his arms around her neck, burying his face in her shoulder. He said nothing except the words 'Mom' and 'Dad.' Then, he ran into the hall and into his room, embarrassed by his spontaneous display of affection. At barely fifteen, he was still child enough to be overwhelmed by sudden emotion despite all of the evildoings and misfortunes that had permeated his young life.

Grant looked at Gurdy with a smile and whispered, "Well, you done it now, Momma."

To which, she replied as she arched her brow, "And you haven't?"

"Well, I guess we're both guilty. But there's no adoption gonna happen. He's a good boy and we will treat him like family. But he is not family, Mother. He's proven to us and to Eddie that he belongs here with us, and we're good for him and he for us." With that, he returned to the radio so that they could listen to their Saturday evening shows.

As time wore on, there was affection, if not love, from the Wilsons, and if young Carl misread the situation, could he have been blamed? Until nearly his fifteenth year, he had not known 'family' since Daddy passed away. Even Annie and Charlie had that before now. But he had known what it was like to be alone in the world, to hunger for parents and siblings and friends built around a home life. Everything from Gurdy's pineapple upside down cake and pecan pies, to Grant's patient instructions on catching fish at different times of the year and in varying water conditions, all spelled love to Carl, and in fact, by the second year with the Wilsons, he had truly grown to love them and to see Eddie as an older brother. Of course, Eddie was fully engaged with his college studies and his long-distance relationship with Maggie. But he never failed to treat Carl like a younger brother whom he trusted completely.

The November frost was on the ground and Carl's spirits were riding high. He was growing strong on farm work and growing on down-home cooking, and his mind was exercised every evening not spent fishing with Grant in his sessions with Gurdy. She had managed to tease him forward from level two reading and writing to level four in a few months, as well as in history and the news of the day. Her tutoring in math was quite easy for her, as Carl picked up maths very quickly, and by the end of the year, was poised to tackle Eddie's high school books involving algebra and geometry, but at that point, he was on his own since Gurdy's knowledge of maths stopped at the use of basics. Carl applied himself with gusto to long division, multiplication tables, and problem solving, to seek percentages and probability. He began to move on to basic Algebra and Plane Geometry. On such a frosty morning, he took the bicycle for the long ride to town, as Grant had given him the day off, to visit Annie and look in on Charlie, and to scour the stores for presents he could afford.

That evening after dinner, Carl went to bed early as it had been a long day and tomorrow meant work on the farm. As a result, he missed hearing the conversation between Grant and Gurdy.

"We ought to get him back in school, Grant," she said one evening after their evening radio entertainment. "He's a bright boy and is learning fast. He could have a future with something, and I don't think it's farm work… not meaning any disrespect, mind you."

"Well, Gurdy my dear, Carl is a blessing that the storms of life blew into our arms. We need him and he needs us. You know that I'd have to hire a farmhand now with my health and all, and yours, too. But Carl brings us support and warmth and we bring him family, stability and…" he said as he looked directly at Gurdy, "Education. Ten years ago, I would have agreed to send him to school, but now with Eddie charting his life off this farm, this is the best arrangement for all of us."

"What you say is practical, for him and for us, but someday he is gonna want to spread his wings, and I don't want him thinkin' that we held him back."

"Gurdy, you'd have to blow that boy off this farm with dynamite." And with that, he arose from his massive rocker and left the room to get ready for bed. The conversation was over.

Gurdy murmured softly as she completed her row of knitting, "That's what I'm afraid of, you big lummox!"

As Grant and Gurdy discussed Carl, he lay on his bed with the door closed and mused on the last time he had seen the Nooners. He wondered at the difference between the Wilsons and the Nooners. It had been August, 1938, and he had dropped in on the Nooner house to visit Annie and bring her some candy. Rumor was, that she was about to leave the Nooners at last.

Instead of finding the usual perky girl who would always be ready to run to him and give him a hug, he saw her sitting on the porch steps holding back more tears as it was clear she had been crying. He ran up to her and sat down beside her, putting his arm around her.

"Why can't I live with you?" she asked, while holding back more tears. "I hate it here anyway, and now they're getting rid of me! I don't know what I've done for them to kick me out of home."

"Listen, my little Annie, who by the way is not so little anymore. I'm saving my money and someday we're gonna be together again. But I can't give you school and everything that goes with a normal life… not that this has been normal for you. Where will the welfare folks put you?" He didn't use the word orphanage, which conjured up all sorts of terrible images in the minds of children of that time. But he was worried.

"I really don't know. Talk is that I'm to be put into another foster home, I heard the name Jackson, but I don't know if that's what's gonna happen, Carl."

"Here, I brought you some sweets, Annie." She placed one of the hard rock candies in her mouth and began sucking on it slowly, deep in thought. The then ten-year-old stuck out her chin and said with pride, "I'm not a little kid anymore, Carl. I know I am only ten, but I ain't gonna be pushed around like some rag doll. What should I do?"

"Tell you what. Give this new family some time, a month or two, and if it looks like they're not right for you, I'll figure something out, Annie. I promise." He squeezed her tightly and they simply sat there, arm in arm, and for a time the problems of the world disappeared as they embraced in a peace that had been rare in Annabelle's short life. Finally, Carl got up and knocked on the door of the Nooner house.

"What are you doing, Carl?" Annie expressed some degree of worry on her face. She hadn't realized that her brother had grown into a young man, weathered by life beyond his years.

"Don't worry," he replied, "I'm just a messenger. And don't say anything, please."

Mr. Nooner, a balding middle-aged man wearing a cotton shirt and blue jeans, answered the door. "What do you want, Carl?" His tone of voice held no warmth.

"Hello, Mr. Nooner. I simply wanted to deliver a message to you. First, thank you for taking her in, feeding and clothing her, and making sure she went to school. But you have not made her part of your family, always looking down on her."

Nooner looked hard at Annie and replied in a rough tone to Carl, "What I do in my house is none of your business, especially coming from a wild urchin like you. And, I don't need your thanks, I need you to get your pathetic ass off my property and as for…" he was interrupted by a loud and even-toned voice from Carl.

"You listen to me! I am keeping my eye on Annie, and you will see to it that she goes to her new foster family without a problem. I love her dearly and there is no telling what I will do if things have gone badly for her. I've dealt with worse than you, sir, believe me." With that, he kissed Anna Belle on the head, turned on his heel, and strode onto the street without another word. Nooner stared at Carl's backside, and Annie was speechless and stayed sitting on the porch steps for a few moments before going inside. Then, Nooner closed his front door quietly without further word.

Carl, on the other hand, trembled with a mixture of excitement and anxiety, but he kept his gait even and never looked back. He meant what he said, any report from Annie that she had been further mistreated, and he would exact revenge of some kind when Mr. Nooner least expected it, and anyhow, he believed that Nooner had got the point.

A bit later, he visited Charlie for an hour and had a cup of coffee with the Reverend and his wife before returning to the Wilsons' house. *'I'm never gonna let any of these sons-of-bitches keep us down, Annie.'*

Now, one year later as Carl returned to the Wilson farm, the Dough children's circumstances had changed for the better, and Carl wondered if Momma and Daddy in heaven were happy for them. He was sure they were.

Chapter 8
The Spoiling of Almost Heaven—December, 1941 to May, 1942

Carl and the Wilsons were headed toward a joyous Christmas and New Year holiday season when December rolled around in 1941. Eddie had visited for Thanksgiving weekend, and Gurdy put on an amazing farm banquet complete with pumpkin pie, candied yams, turkey and stuffing, mincemeat pie, and other fare. They made the rare trip to church that Sunday.

Eddie's marks at university were high so far, and Maggie showed him how much she missed him, which put Eddie in the greatest of moods. Annabelle was well-settled with the Jacksons, and from what Carl could tell upon meeting them—inside their house—they had welcomed Annie with open arms, and she seemed to respond. Charlie was doing well at the Reverend's home, and learning the shoe repair craft for which he exhibited a great deal of enthusiasm, unusual for him. It was paying work he could master with sufficient skill to make a living.

Carl felt positive about his siblings' circumstances and about his own. Life was looking up for sure.

A little over a week later, the Japanese surprise attack upon Pearl Harbour and the Pacific Fleet worked to shatter much of the joy, and indirectly shaped the course of many of their lives well beyond the war, although they didn't see that far at the time. At one p.m. that Sunday, the radio was alive with reports, and that evening, when Gurdy and Grant turned on the radio there was nothing else but a series of news flashes. Everybody knew that if the reports were true, it would be war for the U.S., war on such a scale as had never been, even in the Civil War or World War One. The war instantly reached its tentacles into every nook and cranny of America, and Paragould was no exception. America had been brutally attacked in an unprovoked assault. The blood was up, temperatures were beyond boiling and at combustion level. Young men, older men, and those not yet men would rush to join or later would be drafted. But Carl was not yet at that point, and had much responsibility on the farm. He would never have passed lying about his age at that point even if he wanted to.

But it was different for Eddie. He longed to fly, had all the physical and optical qualifications, and was already motivated. But the Navy wasn't taking pilots at his age before the war. By March, the situation had changed, and if you were a high school graduate in the top fifty of your class, then you could qualify for enlistment and pilot training. Eddie went back to university at the beginning of the war for the U.S., but as soon as the policy was changed, he went to the nearest Naval Enlistment Office and applied, not telling his parents. With his outstanding academic record and area of studies, he was snapped up for Naval aviator training which took the rest of 1942 and into early 1943. He started pilot school and flight school in Pensacola, and gained his Naval aviator wings after successfully practicing landing on mock carriers on the Great Lakes. Eddie trained to pilot the new F6F Hellcat and he learned to love the performance and operational detail of the plane, and always took it to its climbing and maneuvering limits when the opportunities were presented. After the Great Lakes, he was assigned carrier duty on the USS Enterprise out of Hawaii, eager to test his newly developed piloting skills and help his country take back the initiative in the Pacific.

Grant and Gurdy loved their only child and were extremely proud of him. And although they were not happy about his choice to enlist and attempt to be a combat pilot, they nevertheless quietly supported his decision and never tried to make him feel any sense of betrayal. They realized the inevitability that war in Europe and the Asia/Pacific would engulf their little family one way or the other. As the date in May 1942 drew near for Eddie to report for basic training, Grant and Eddie, along with Carl, spent as many hours fishing in nearby waters, and talking about anything and everything when the farm work allowed. At first, Grant only wanted to bring Eddie along, which Carl understood, even though he was quietly conflicted.

But it was Eddie who convinced Grant to invite Carl to their fishing forays.

"Dad, we've all made Carl a right true fixture of this family and I know he is going to miss me and I, him. You and I can make our own time together to speak about things and say our farewells privately. But when I am gone to the Navy, I don't expect to be home much for a long time 'cause I have to give them six years unless, after the war, they're willing to send me to engineering school as an officer. I want to make sure Carl feels close to you, to us, 'cause you're not getting any younger and your heart ain't that robust anymore. He is a strong boy, bright, and wants to please you. Keep him here and be generous with him. If this war goes on long enough, Carl will be called, but you can cross that bridge if and when you come to it. Okay?"

"I see your point, son. But this farm is your inheritance, wherever you are and whatever you do. Someday, it will be up to you to decide who goes and who stays. Now, let's go fishin'!" Eddie could not imagine turning Carl out. With that, Grant told Eddie to fetch Carl from his room while he rounded up the fishing gear, which included long cane poles, casting rods, and reels, along with a bucket of worms in soil plus the tackle box.

Thus, these two basically principled men had quite inadvertently created a conundrum by deciding Carl's immediate future, while leaving his long-term future completely unresolved. Their attitude toward him was benign, yet Carl was really at rock bottom an asset, treated under the veneer of a first-class citizen. These positions and issues were never discussed directly with him, not because the two were trying to hide anything. Just the opposite. They saw their behavior toward him as righteous and honest—their moral obligation was to look out for him to a point and as they saw best. If Gurdy had weighed in, she would have espoused a different and more liberated view of Carl and his path in life. She knew from teaching him that Carl was capable of more and hungered for more.

Carl was oblivious to this reality. He was given every signal from Grant, Gurdy, and Eddie, that his life was with them, on the farm. *But what did that mean?* he thought. Gurdy had reopened education to Carl, and he craved more, yet, he really cared for the Wilsons and yearned to do right by them. Life on the farm pulled at him as well. After Eddie left for training, Carl began to imagine possibilities for himself; engineering, travel, working with wood, and other avocations, constantly dominated his daydreams. He also dreamed of playing some part in the war, but those thoughts were brief and infrequent. And at sixteen, some of his dreams involved girls. The secrets of his child exploitation at the hands of Worlick must always remain hidden, and he buried those awful memories as deeply as he could. That effort and energy would cost him in ways he could not yet imagine.

On their final fishing trip just two days before Eddie was to ship out, the three engaged in a far-ranging conversation about many topics. They intently watched their rods for any indication of a nibble or a bite, and if fishing was poor, then they would move over to a nearby small lake and try their luck with cane poles and minnows, in hopes of catching large perch or bass. But for now, their need to communicate outweighed the fact that fishing had been slow. After an hour of chatter about subjects as diverse as the price of corn, the war, politics—Democrats all—and other subjects, the talk turned to the recent killing of two members of the Southern Tenant Farmers Union.

One was a white union organizer, the other a black tenant farmer and organizer. The two men had worked together for improved conditions for field workers for several years.

Eddie brought the subject up. "What about the two STFU members shot in front of their homes last week?" he asked. "Right in front of their families, too." Carl sat in silence, waiting to see what Grant would say. He was the only one of them who had experienced the exploitation directly, and he never forgot what Charles had told him about plantation owners and other whites who would do anything, as Charles had emphasized, to keep blacks and whites from forming on common cause. Here was the proof of Daddy's insight.

"Well listen here, Eddie." Grant was interrupted by a slow and strong tug on his line, and without another word, he set the hook and in half a minute, had landed a catfish big enough to feed two people. "Only need one more like this one and Gurdy can fix up a mess of catfish and corn fritters!"

"So, what were you saying before the fish, Dad?" Eddie knew he might be uncorking a bottle of bile, but he couldn't help himself.

Grant was silent for a few moments as he cast his newly baited line into the current. "Niggers need to stay where they are, boy. What the hell, the only way white men and niggers gonna' work together is if they're both communists." Carl wasn't sure what a communist was, but decided to look it up on his own.

"Did these men deserve to be killed for that?" Eddie normally didn't take his father on regarding the issue of race, but now he was a man, shipping out to the Navy to fight half a world away and maybe never come back. And he did not like the dismal feel of segregated towns and cities. "I prefer to use the word Negro or 'black' when speaking about them, and didn't we fight a Civil War to free Negro slaves, and doesn't our country's founding statement say that all men are created equal?"

"What are you comin' at me for like this, Eddie? You've always known how I feel about them and minglin' with white folks on any level." He turned to Carl. "Niggers and poor white trash ain't got nothin' better to do than stir up trouble for farmers and landowners, Carl. You watch it or they'll be after everything you have."

'*But what do I have to lose?*' Carl asked himself. And he had been called 'white trash' often enough to know where society placed him. And yet, he never saw himself as such because the concept revulsed him.

Before Eddie could reply, Carl burst into the conversation. He didn't really know why but he felt compelled to speak. Something snapped in Carl upon hearing those words. He needed to defend his daddy, his Mom, and siblings, their friends and other field workers, and the many black men, women and children he had labored alongside during his childhood, until he came to the Wilsons' farm.

"I worked the fields since I was seven, first with my daddy, and then after he died, I got work on my own. Many days, I been out side by side with Negro families pickin' cotton, choppin' cotton and all. I always was treated kindly by them, and played with the boys and girls on rest breaks and after we got back to town. But then, we go our separate ways, them to theirs and me to mine. And wasn't much for me to ever go back to. Never questioned why it was that way, just always was. But I also never questioned that they have the same rights as we do.

You got poor white folks and poor black folks doin' the same shitty work for slave wages. Rock bottom, the only difference between me and them is the color of our skins. My daddy taught me that there's Presbyterians and Baptists, but they're both Christians. There's blacks and there's whites, but we're all humans. See what I mean?" Carl was satisfied with his fifteen-year-old's view of humanity expressed literally in black and white.

Grant looked at Carl in astonishment. He had never experienced Carl arguing a point with him, much less so emphatically and with such emotion. "Now, listen here boy, you are never to bring this up again or it will be the end of you on this farm, much as we have taken to you. Do you understand, Carl?" While Grant had genuine affection for Carl, he knew that Carl could be replaced and would tolerate no dissent on the issue of race.

Carl looked at Eddie, who remained silent and offered no support, and then to Grant, who was staring a hole through Carl. The boy had never seen Grant this angry, and Grant was angry with him! Then, Carl looked straight ahead and said, "I understand, sir. Already forgot it." In one moment, and for a reason that went against the grain for Carl, he saw clearly that a misstep on this issue would end his stay in paradise. His hurt ran deep.

Grant made a grunt of approval, and the conversation was over. Carl felt like a stranger for the remainder of the fishing and conversation as such ended that afternoon. His time with the Wilsons after that was never quite the same, as if tainted by some unseen pollution. Once again, he was brutally reminded that in his mid-twentieth century world in America, you were never really forgiven or accepted by the haves if you came from the have nots, and your opinions didn't carry the same weight as theirs. That went double in the South for many people because it put you in the same place as the blacks, and to such prejudiced people, both deserved to be there and stay there. Daddy had been right because two men with families to feed were now dead in common cause, killed by the same faceless men to whom Daddy had alluded years before. The justice system never held them to account. So now, a black mother and her children, and a white mother and her children, all lived on in fear and largely upon the kindness of others. But children never forget.

Carl believed there had to be a better world, and he looked to Eddie's example for some inspiration. *I want to make my mark in this life,* he thought as he lay gazing at the moon through his bedroom window one night. Formal education was all but beyond his reach, but learning was not and Gurdy had been steadfast in her mission to develop Carl's abilities in the three Rs. He began to think about how to use what he had learned and how and where to learn more. He was grateful to the Wilsons and had grown to love them as family, but that devotion was now filtered through a screen of disapproval from Grant, just sufficient enough to manifest itself in Grant's attitude toward Carl, which had become a bit more reserved and matter of fact.

That made Carl uneasy, especially after Eddie shipped out to the service. But he kept on with his life on the farm as before, somewhat wounded by the surprise of the intensity of Grant's reaction to his words on that last fishing day with Eddie. And he became an even more intense student of Gurdy's, a pattern she quickly realized but could only ascribe to youthful curiosity and energy. But now, Carl, at nearly sixteen and well-aware that he could never count on anyone else to see him through, simply wanted to cram as much 'learning' into his time as possible, because who knew what was down the road? And he would never think to dishonor the kindnesses shown to him by the Wilsons, or his pledge to Eddie to take care of his parents while he was off fighting the war. For the time being, he buried his distaste for Grant's bigotry out of sight, but the heaviness of that self-imposed burden only increased with time, and inevitably marred an otherwise happy existence.

Chapter 9
Battle Casualties 1943–1944

On the partly cloudy day of November 18, 1943, the carrier USS Enterprise was steaming toward the Gilbert Islands, some twenty-eight hundred miles northeast of Australia, as part of a Naval task force including cruisers, destroyers, troop transports with landing craft and tanks, marines, and soldiers. The goal would be to take two islands at one blow: Makin and Betio. Betio contained a newly built air-strip that could accommodate bombers, once taken, and then the Gilberts would become an offensive base of operations in the American drive to the Japanese homeland.

Eddie had just completed a pilot briefing in the ready room that morning. At dawn, on November nineteen, he would launch from the Enterprise along with other F6F Hellcats and bombers and torpedo planes to attack the ground forces and naval craft on Makin Island, and Betio in the Tarawa Atoll. If the skies were clear of Zeros, then the Hellcats were to turn away from their role as fighter escorts and launch strafing operations against the well-dug in Japanese forces. While the Hellcat was a slightly slower, stubbier craft than the faster, sexier Vought Corsair, it had better operational performance and was built to take on the Mitsubishi Zero. But it had the versatility to also perform as a ground attack craft. Eddie loved flying the Grumman, and as a student of aviation and a pilot, he appreciated the plane's versatility.

He spent much of the day studying the maps of the islands, checking on his plane's preparation for action, newly minted from Grumman, and engaging in pre-combat bravado with other pilots. But for one hour before dinner, Eddie sat in his bunk and wrote two letters, one to his parents and one to Maggie. To Grant and Gurdy he wrote allowable details of his life on the Enterprise, careful not to give away anything reflecting military operations or the impending battle. And, he asked if they were getting the support from Carl that they needed, reminding them of Carl's devotion to the family and the farm and to please give Carl his best. Eddie closed out with a promise to come home the first Stateside leave he could get. To Maggie, he pledged his undying love and the wish that when 'all of this is over,' he would return to marry her, finish his engineering degree, and raise a family with her in that order.

After dropping the letters off to the ship's Postmaster, where they joined the stream of thousands of letters and postcards that made their way across the Pacific every day through military security, and finally into local mailboxes in America, Eddie had a quick meal and retired to his bunk. His three a.m. wake up was not that far away, but he spent most of the night awake with pre-combat jitters and a recurring resolve to do his best no matter what.

Six hours after retiring for the night, Eddie was in the cockpit of his plane after taking off from the deck of the

Enterprise. He snapped to attention when he received a radio order from his wing commander. After taking off from the Enterprise and gaining the altitude sufficient to protect the bombers and torpedo planes from any Japanese fighters, the word came through that intelligence could detect no threat from any Zeros, so the Hellcats were ordered to slip in before the three bomber formations, and were to conduct ground strafing operations to remove potential enemy ground fire against the slower bombers, but they were to avoid damage to the airfield if at all possible.

As Eddie's wing began their strafing run along the beach, he heard a loud popping sound and the inside of the cockpit immediately filled with smoke. Somehow, exhaust gases were blown into the cockpit from the damage to his craft. Japanese ground fire had found its mark. His goggles were off due to the low-level run and his eyes hurt terribly, and he realized immediately that he was in trouble and unable to see properly. Then, his eyes began to burn. His only option was to crash land the plane, and hope it hit in the water instead of on land. He was too low for a parachute, but the Hellcat was slowed by his quick thinking with a combination of throttle and flap actions, and before he knew his real situation, he was jolted against his harness as harshly as a mule kick and then knew no more.

*

February 1944:

Things were somber at the Wilsons' farm. When Grant and Gurdy were informed that their son, Lt. Edward Grant Wilson, was shot down in action on 19 November, 1943, and lay in recovery at a Naval hospital in Hawaii, Grant hugged Gurdy and consoled her with "At least our boy will be coming home, and you'll see that everything will be fine, Mother." And with that, he kissed her on the forehead, put on his straw hat, and walked out of the kitchen door.

Gurdy was stunned by Grant's matter-of-fact response to the terrible news. Carl stared after Grant in wonder because it seemed that the aging farmer was in a very uncharacteristic trance, as if his nerves had been removed. But instead of following Grant outside, Carl put his arms around Gurdy's shoulders as she began to quietly weep, and he tried to comfort her as she grappled with the uncertainty of her son's situation.

"I know Eddie, Momma Gurdy, and I know if anyone can come out of this he will. I love him as my brother, Momma Gurdy, and he's my hero." He felt tears welling up but fought them back for Gurdy's sake. "I want to go into the Navy, too, and take it to those Japs!" He wanted revenge against an enemy he knew virtually nothing about, except what he gathered from the news. "Do you want me to tell Maggie? I know she's been callin' a lot since Eddie's letters stopped."

"Yes," she whispered through her tears. "But be a dear boy and go see to your daddy Grant. I fear something isn't right, and I don't want him to be alone. Please find him and see that he is okay." With that, she looked at Carl with pleading eyes. He couldn't refuse her and patted her on the shoulder and kissed her lightly on her head. Carl headed out the kitchen door without another word to find Grant.

Grant had taken the farm truck to the other side of the farm bordered by a large creek, where he had spent much time with Eddie when his son was a boy. It was their place, and when Carl joined the household, he opted to go to nearby St. Francis River for evening and night fishing. He, too, was a victim of uncertainty, but instead of finding joy in the fact that Eddie was alive, he felt overwhelming anxiety as thoughts and images of what might happen to their farm and to Eddie's dreams flooded his mind like an irresistible torrent.

Grant, bigot and racist though he was, was otherwise a gentle soul out of his emotional depth. As he stumbled through the creek-side brush with all of this swirling through his head, he suddenly felt his left shoulder to his left thigh go mostly dead and he collapsed to the ground.

He couldn't find his voice to scream out for help, with fear in his thoughts and no idea what was happening to him as the left side of his face collapsed. He suffered a massive stroke. As he lay there helpless and quivering on his right side, he felt hands gently caressing his head as a familiar voice whispered in his right ear.

"I'm here, Daddy Grant. I don't know what's happening to you, but Momma's okay so please don't worry. I've got to fetch a doctor and an ambulance 'cause you need a hospital quick! Just don't worry, we'll get you fixed up! I love you, Daddy Grant, stay with us." With that, Carl hopped into the truck and drove back to the house to phone the hospital in Paragould. He decided not to tell Gurdy anything until he had called the hospital for the ambulance, since she would soon have two crises to fret over.

Carl burst through the kitchen door five minutes later, ran straight to the phone, and dialed the operator with the urgent request that an ambulance was needed at the Wilson's farm, and he described Grant's condition as he had found him. The hospital told him it would take a good twenty to thirty minutes to reach Grant, and Carl would have to show them where he was, but in the meantime, he was to race back to Grant, cover him in a blanket, and talk to him to try to keep him awake. There wasn't much else he could do, as they said, until Grant could be cared for properly. Carl grabbed a blanket and recklessly drove in the shortest line across the fields to where Grant lay. He gently covered Grant and whispered in his right ear, "Stay with me, Daddy Grant, Momma sends her love—he lied— and the ambulance will be here soon." With his right hand, Grant squeezed Carl's hand. But fear had assaulted his mind, and the sudden inability to move anything on his left side confused him. Grant was in shock, and then there was the pain in his chest, enormous pressure. He felt himself slipping away into unconsciousness, and Carl pinched him hard on his right arm and this caused him to become a bit more alert. "So sorry, Daddy Grant, but they told me to keep you awake and I don't know what else to do." Carl was trying his best to be an adult, to stay calm, but it wasn't really working.

"Don't leave me, Daddy Grant! Please be all right. I just know you will." Carl hugged Grant, as he heard the siren of the ambulance in the distance. Gurdy directed the ambulance driver across the fields where Carl and Grant were huddled, and showed him how to take the tractor dirt road to them instead of the bumpy ride across the fields.

Grant's eyes were vacant, pointing to the sky, but he was still awake and could process some of the inputs from his surroundings. "You're still awake!" cried Carl. "They're here, Daddy Grant. You're gonna be fine, you'll see."

***

Grant Wilson passed away three weeks later. It was a week before Eddie was due back from recovery and his discharge from the Navy, being determined by Uncle Sam to be unfit for any further service. Without his corrective lenses, he was legally blind. The bullets that tore through his Hellcat's cockpit hadn't directly injured him, but had released chemicals in exhaust gas that had damaged his eyes forever. His broken collar bone and contusions were a temporary annoyance and would fully heal. As he sat on the edge of his hospital bed the afternoon before he was to be discharged, Eddie was informed of his father's death and just sat on the edge of his bed staring into a void created in his mind. Doubts and questions assaulted him as he sat in what appeared to others as a trance.

Would Maggie still love him, marry a man who could never reliably see without the aid of very thick corrective

155

lenses? Could he manage the farm? How would things go with Mom?

Could they afford to keep Carl? Will he ever become an engineer?

But angry eyes ultimately replaced the vacant stare. *'Why me? Better off if I'd died. I'll never fly again! I won't work the farm! Damn, I'll sell it and move Mom to town or wherever I find work. No! Must hold onto the farm, there's a future there like it or not.*

With Maggie coming to live with us as my wife, there'll be no room for Carl, especially when we have kids. He's gonna suck our resources in time and attention, and he is not family, as Dad pointed out!' As much as Eddie had taken to Carl, the boy now became the object of Eddie's anxiety and anger at his situation. In his angst, he fabricated reasons to eject Carl from the picture.

So as misplaced as it was, Eddie's anxiety had set him against the young man who viewed him as an older brother. Eddie resolved to make sure he would see to it that Carl's life on the Wilson farm was a dead end. *I have to call home, now,* he thought.

Carl had answered the long-distance call from San Francisco when Eddie called. "Eddie, so happy to hear your voice. I'm so sorry about your dad, he meant a lot to me and…" Eddie cut him off abruptly, "Put Mom on the phone." No hello, no expression of being glad to hear Carl's voice, and no questions about Mom or Dad or anything.

After a brief pause, Carl said, "Sure thing, Eddie." He called to Gurdy, as she was sitting in the parlor with a few friends who had called by to express their condolences and support as she grieved for her husband. But Carl wandered outside, his feelings hurt. He was looking forward to reuniting with Eddie, and he needed that connection now that Grant was suddenly taken out of their lives. He was seventeen now, a fully matured adult in the eyes of the society in which he lived, and not expected to have childish ways about him. But he certainly had no idea yet about how a man could return from war and combat as an emotional and psychological wreck, but physically be able to live a life… and where that paradox could lead.

Grant's funeral was delayed for two days to allow Eddie to return in time. Margaret was always on Eddie's arm, Eddie who hadn't said five words to Carl after he arrived. Carl was told to stand on the other side of the grave as the coffin was lowered into the ground, tears in his eyes, and a sense of loss that hadn't been matched since Daddy had died years ago. Carl desperately wanted to be included, but Gurdy seemed too deeply disturbed because of Grant's untimely death to mount any defense for him, or simply didn't care anymore.

But Carl had weathered much in his young life, and one thing he knew was that he was capable and smart, and wanted out of Paragould, somewhere where he wouldn't be looked down upon as the never-do-well offspring of worthless farm laborers, who who others said had the bad taste to die and leave him adrift. But he truly believed that somewhere he would have family and success and accomplishment. Carl envisioned his place in the world as a result of hard work and dedication, but at what? He thought, *I already know enough to pass my High School Equivalency thanks to Gurdy, but I got no money to speak of. I need a trade, a craft that I can afford to learn. And I want to get out of here!*

Carl wasn't dreaming of millions and a charmed life. He was dreaming of a steady income, a roof over his head, and food always on the table.

'*Join the Navy and See the World!*' the ad stated. That is exactly what he intended to do at seventeen, not wishing to wait for his eighteenth birthday several months later. So, Carl rode quietly in the truck as Eddie, Margaret, and Gurdy accompanied him to the farmhouse, where Carl instantly sprang up the stairs as the others stared blankly at him. People were gathering for the wake and bringing in food and drink for the afternoon. When he was sure that his saved cash was tucked into his pants, Carl packed his belongings, careful to leave all of Eddie's books, took one last look at the room that had been the safest place he had ever lived in, and went down the stairs to say good-bye.

He walked straight up to Eddie and Gurdy. "What are you doing, Carl?' Gurdy's voice trembled a bit but of course she knew what he was doing.

"Eddie, you've made it plain that the future on this farm and with this family doesn't include me," Eddie motioned as if to speak but Carl went on, "Please, I have made up my mind. Mom, Eddie, and dear Grant in Heaven, thank you for all you've done for me over the last couple of years, and I hope I gave as good as I received."

"Of course, you did, Carl!" Gurdy put her hand on Carl's shoulder in a loving touch.

But Eddie spoke to Carl as a stern boss would speak to a replaceable employee. "Things gotta change around here, Carl. And it's best for you and for all of us if you chart your own course in life. I'd like to give you a bit of money to help you on your way, it's only fair."

Carl knew that Eddie was hurting inside and simply said "No thanks, Eddie, let's just leave things as they are. And I wish you all the best with Maggie and the farm." Then, he quickly turned to Gurdy and gave her a big hug, whispering in her ear, "I can never repay you for what you have given me, and I will never forget you all my life!" He kissed her cheek, turned, and walked out the door to the astonishment of many of the guests, some of whom figured that Carl would always be the live-in farmhand.

There were murmurs and whispers of 'Just like those types' and 'You can never trust these itinerates!' and 'Poor white trash worse than niggers, no gratitude!' A couple of guests even suggested that he be searched.

He heard much of what was 'whispered' and as he left the house for good, he wished he were playing in the fields again with the black and white farm laborers and their children. He had learned valuable lessons for life, though the work was demanding and the money barely enough to feed him. Nevertheless, the guests' hypocrisies and conceits stung him like a slowly increasing number of hornet stings, until the pain in his mind caused him to start running down the road with his suitcase and shoulder bag to get away, get away, away… away.

Nobody offered him a ride.

Chapter 10
Carl and Dee—1944

Dafnie Nation had long since insisted on being called 'Dee' for short because she knew her name was uncommon in Northern Arkansas, to say the least. And when she checked, her given name was formally spelled Daphne, so she mistakenly believed that her name was a low-class attempt at cultural airs gone predictably off-target. That provided another reason to dwell in her seemingly bottomless pit of shame and self-loathing. Most people never noticed or cared about the spelling. But Dee she was, and Dee she would always be known by that handle to anyone with whom she chose to relate.

When she finished her eighth grade, Dee had gone a year before to live with her oldest sister, Edna, and her husband Alvin, and their two toddler daughters, Mary Lou and Linda, in Paragould. She had just turned fifteen in May 1944, at five foot three, a slim and pretty auburn-haired brunette with gray eyes. Dee was the last responsibility for Jack Nation, who longed to leave the farming life and move into town. While that was in the future, he welcomed the empty nest, and even now had no idea of the sinister actions of his brother.

Though Dee attracted the attention of older boys, she showed no interest in their crude or clumsy approaches and in any case, Dee was not looking to be strapped to anyone's carriage until she was out of her purgatory and settled elsewhere. The boys soon found out that Dee possessed the ability to dismiss anyone she didn't want in her orbit with various combinations of sarcasm, insult, and showing them her backside as she walked away.

"I want a real man, not a pimply-faced boy," she would stare with emotionless eyes. Or, "Go back to your Momma, she'll make a better girlfriend for you." Or more directly "You got nothin' I want, you pathetic turd." As she would abruptly turn and walk away, whether she had been going in that direction or not.

And that was how she dealt with those 'jokers,' as see deemed them.

She made it a point of avoiding being alone in public, but the girls who tried to make friends with her were ignored and soon stopped trying. Dee wanted out, wanted to go to California and get a real job which wouldn't be that hard now that the war was full on, even for a girl of fifteen. Nobody must know her secret, the secret that crushed her soul like deep sea waters and kept it from flying toward the happiness of some kind. Her older sisters had all married and two of them, Lee and Gay, had already moved away to California for wartime work, while their husbands, Preston and Earl, served in the Army. Edna and Alvin were talking a lot about California, and it looked like they were beginning to make plans to move there, where Alvin could find more work operating earth-moving equipment.

Alvin and Edna had already settled into a lifelong pattern of work, getting money, and being idle for months while they drank and gambled it away. The kids, of whom they would eventually have five—four girls and a boy—had to fend for themselves and Dee grew tired of watching the toddlers while their parents were busy cavorting. As time wore on after her fifteenth birthday, Dee grew more and more anxious to break free, but she had realized that she couldn't do it anytime soon, as she only made enough at her two part-time jobs in town to pay her share of household expenses, and occasionally bailing Alvin and Edna out when they blew through Alvin's considerable pay checks from his work in heavy equipment operations. Alvin was busy with his job from April to October, so Dee began to have more time on her hands since Edna was spending more time at home during these months. The thought of going to California with Edna's family did not appeal to her in the least.

On a warm evening in late June, Dee decided to take the bold step of going to the movies at the Collins Theater just to have something to do. *Lifeboat* was playing and she was interested in the story line; a German U-Boat sank an American merchant ship carrying passengers, and after pulling a sailor from the water it was discovered that he was a German sailor. To Dee, the ensuing drama would be irresistible. Alvin agreed to walk her there and Edna agreed to accompany her home when the show let out at eight-thirty p.m. They had, by now, realized that Dee was a loner who was not open to any suggestions about socializing with teenagers her own age.

"Here's an extra two dollars for snacks and such." Alvin was aware that Dee insisted on paying her way, but he felt sorry for Dee being alone and not having much to spend and, in any event, he was a generally kind-hearted man to a fault and that would not serve him or his family well over the years.

"I've my own money, Alvin. Don't need any extra." Dee was always suspicious of any display of kindness from man or boy. She saw the momentary disappointment on Alvin's face and quickly added, "But thank you very much for walking me safely to the theatre."

He offered her the two dollars with an outstretched hand, "Here, Dee. This is a gift, just wanted to help you out. I'm not asking you to do extra work around the house or run extra errands. Just a gift to use as you see fit. Besides, Edna thought it was a good idea when I told her I would fatten up your purse a bit." Alvin was making good money in these months, and wouldn't miss the two dollars.

That sealed it for Dee, and she expressed her gratitude as she took the two bills. If Edna knows, then Alvin isn't scheming for anything. But the truth is, she would never have taken the money if Alvin hadn't disclosed his discussion with Edna about his intentions. *Even a simpleton can scheme for the wrong purpose,* she thought.

In front of the ticket booth, Alvin said his goodbye and reminded Dee not to try to walk home alone and to wait for Edna in front of the theatre after the show. "I promise, Alvin! Won't go anywhere unless it's with Edna." With that, she turned to join the small line for ticket purchase.

The Collins was a modest attempt at Art Deco, a smallish theatre that held at the time one hundred seats. It had been put into service just two years before *The Jazz*

Singer brought sound to movies in 1927 and so had an organ pit. But in 1930 the place had been rigged with the first speaker system available for the 'talkies' and had only recently upgraded to a better sound system for more modern audio-visual technology. A movie like '*Lifeboat*' and the other movies of the day like '*Meet me in St. Louis*' and '*Gaslight*' demanded improved sound technology, even in a relative backwater like Paragould.

After purchasing a soda and popcorn in the lobby, Dee settled into a chair in the second to last row. She had only been to the movies three times in her life, including tonight, so it was still a new experience. It was mesmerizing. Dee was so intent on the experience that she didn't notice two slightly older boys ogling her from the back row, making hand gestures and wickedly laughing during their own secret exchanges in each other's ears. But the screen had totally captivated her from the opening of the weekly newsreel, which mainly consisted of the most recent successful actions of the American military in France—D-Day had been only two weeks earlier—and in the Pacific. Then came the cartoon, Bugs Bunny. Finally, the actual movie started. She didn't notice the two boys, smartly dressed for Paragould, edging closer behind her from the left. Dee didn't want to miss anything and only had eyes for the screen, waiting for the moment that people would be thrown together in the lifeboat. The two boys were really seventeen and the tall, thin boy with black hair called the other boy, slightly shorter and with brown hair, 'Steve.'

"Steve, what do we have here? A pretty girl all alone in this dark movie house. She must be lookin' for some fun. Are you lookin' for some fun, girlie?" At that, Dee froze and couldn't summon her usual bravado, couldn't even get out of her seat.

"Maybe she don't like us, Al," Steve whispered loudly in her ear. The nearest people were two rows toward the screen. "Maybe she's too shy to ask. What's your name, sweetheart?"

"None of your business!" She stood up at last, out of her torpor, and turned to them. "I don't have anything to do with dummies like you." She said this loudly enough that other moviegoers turned to *shhh* the kids. Dee took that moment to walk to the swinging double door of the lobby, but the boys were undeterred even by the glaring looks of people who had been interrupted. They followed Dee out, hoping she would exit the theater. There were a few people in the lobby at the refreshment bar and just entering, late to the show.

Al and Steve walked quickly up to their young prey, intent on forcing her to go outside with them as Al grabbed her by the arm. Dee looked at the staff for help, but they seemed intent on acting as if nothing was happening. The theatre manager was upstairs checking on the projection room.

"You're coming with us, girlie, we need an apology. We ain't dummies and can't be talked to like that by a girl, even a pretty one." Al was in no mood to show any mercy and clamped down hard on Dee's forearm. As he did so, he bent forward a bit and when he did, he suddenly found excruciating pain coming from the soft spot where the jawbone, the cheekbone and the skull come together. A strong hand had cupped in pressure on the right side of his head, and a rigid knuckle buried itself into the soft spot on the left side at the same instant. His head was pinned and the pressure on the nerve bundle hurt like hell. The pressure increased so that Al dared not try to turn around. Steve backed away as Al yelled, "Stop it whoever you are, and fight like a man!" A low and full-toned voice answered evenly. "She doesn't want to go with you and since you don't see that, it makes you a real dummy, Al."

"Carl, son of-a-bitch! Let me go and we'll call it quits and walk away. Okay?"

"You got to ask yourself, Al and Stevie, will it be worth it to carry on with me when I let you go? Well, my opinion is 'no.' Do you agree?" Carl knew how much it hurt Al because he had been on the receiving end of this move himself. He applied even more pressure.

"Okay. All right, all right! We agree." Carl let Al go, but he watched the two carefully as they backed away. "You can bet this ain't over, the two of you. You better watch your backs when you leave here, or anywhere else you go!" They could see the manager, who had been summoned by staff, enter the lobby and head toward them. He was a tall man in his thirties and sported a trim mustache. With that, the two turned and ran out of the theater and into the evening.

Carl stared at them until they were out of sight. The young man in the ticket booth gave Carl a thumbs up but nobody else paid attention. The manager said, "I don't want any trouble here, so take your fights outside!"

"No need to worry, sir. We were just going back to the second half of the show, right?" He looked at Dee with a smile and bright blue eyes and nodded his head, adding "Even if we have to sit apart 'cause we lost our seats."

At that, Dee nodded yes, and that was enough for the manager. "Well, enjoy the rest of the movie, kids. Those boys won't be back tonight." With that, he turned away with a slight and knowing smile.

The two went back into the darkened theater, the movie having resumed a minute before.

Carl made no move to touch Dee or hold her hand. He simply said, "Name's Carl Doe, that's D-O-E, and I'll sit a few chairs away from you just to make sure those two don't come back, if that's okay with you. Are you here all alone?" Carl had changed the spelling of his family name when he enlisted in the Navy, but not the sound of it. He longed for a clean break from this place and its memories, but he didn't want to disrespect the memory of his parents by abandoning the name. The Navy recruitment officer didn't care one way or the other.

"I am, and it's okay if you stay at least three chairs away and not behind me." Dee had been rattled by the boys and was glad of Carl's intervention, but not enough to trust him over any other boy or man at this point. They settled into seats in the dark, Dee wary of her surroundings. But her enjoyment in the movie slowly returned as she observed that Carl, sitting one row forward and to the right, was also interested in the movie and occasionally quickly glanced her way.

Dee had always carried with her the toxic emotional cocktail composed of shame, anger, fear, and mistrust. It was almost impossible for her to connect with others on a normal basis, and she was walking through life beneath a veneer of being 'stuck up' and more intelligent than others—which she often was—and not in need of anyone though deep inside she was hungry for love, attention, and real tenderness. But her ability to give the same was severely handicapped, though she secretly felt that she *wanted* to give as well as receive. Uncle Basil had ruined the childhood of a bright and inquisitive little girl and turned her into a walking emotional time bomb. Carl knew a challenge when he saw one, and though he had no idea yet what the challenge actually was, he felt a compelling attraction to Dee and was completely unaware that they had a shared history in child sexual exploitation: one through force, and one through treachery. He certainly had buried those experiences deep inside and his spirit remained unsinkable, but although Dee wore the results on her sleeve, you would have to guess what was wrong.

When *Lifeboat* was over and the lights came up, Carl got the nerve to ask Dee a question. "Is someone picking you up? I'd be happy to stand with you or walk you safely to your door if you prefer. And I didn't catch your name but now you've got mine."

Dee thought a few seconds before she answered. "I'm Dee Nation, Dee is short for Dafnie. My older sister, Edna, is gonna drive me home because I live with her and my brother-in-law, Alvin, and their two little girls. They're going to California soon." She didn't know why she blurted this last out, but it just came out without a thought. "If you want, we can see if my sister is out front." Another rather awkward pause ensued. "Thank you for helping me with those bullies, Carl."

"I know them, they're a couple of first-class jerks who've never had to work a day in their life. Me, I've joined the Navy and report to San Diego in a few weeks and I ain't never coming back. Gonna make something of myself and not gonna stick around this dead end of a town! The only things keeping me here are my brother, Charlie, and sister, Annabelle. But they're both being taken care of really well and can manage without me for now."

Walking slowly beside him, Dee gave Carl a sideways glance and saw a face bereft of guile, young and handsome and not showing the scars he carried inside. But she said nothing in return. As they exited the theatre doors, Dee spotted Edna waiting beside her 1936 Ford, as she waved from the exiting crowd. Edna simply walked around the car and got into the driver's seat.

"Say Dee, what are you doing tomorrow evening? I'd like to take you to a sit-down place for a bite to eat and maybe a little walk around downtown. Nothin' too special, but I know that I'm leaving soon for the West Coast, and I would like to get to know you better if you like."

Hands clasped together at her waist, Dee looked him in the eye for a few uncomfortable moments until Carl was about to say 'Well, all right, then goodnight!' when Dee smiled and said "Sure thing, Carl. I'd like that." And she gave him Alvin and Edna's address, which he wrote down on a small piece of paper from his pants pocket. "Pick you up at seven! Don't have a car but walking's fine." He hurriedly added, "I know how to drive but have been saving my money for when I leave for San Diego."

"It's okay, walking is just fine, Carl. See you then, Edna's getting impatient." And with that, she turned and walked away, not in her usual abrupt style but slowly and deliberately in an extra bit of hip-swerving communication to Carl. He watched the car drive away. Dee never looked back. Carl began walking down the street to the house where he boarded with four other men of varying ages, and yes, he felt levitation and elation all the way.

Dee liked the young man and knew he was not like most of the others. But he was also leaving town, and therefore, an additional point of interest was worth exploring on a date. Her instincts told her he wouldn't try anything. She went home and later in bed she wondered if in fact, her fortunes might be changing.

***

Carl had been working full-time at the mill just outside of town ever since he left the Wilsons' farm and had managed to save a few hundred dollars. Work was steadier than in Charles' day due to the war and better distribution of the hardwoods to the military and the markets. The current pay was much higher than in Charles' day. But mill work wasn't his future. He didn't know what that was but two and a half years in the Navy would help him answer that question and in the meantime would provide him with wages and training at a trade or some further educational opportunity. Although that exact path was unclear to him, he believed with all his heart that he would move up.

Hard work and a desire to increase his abilities drove Carl like a deep, smooth, and swiftly flowing river current with not much able to stand in its way. As a testament to Daddy Charles and to Gurdy, he spent much of his spare time studying, reading, and correcting his own vocabulary and language at the Green County Library in Paragould, which opened in 1936. Like a force of heavy gravity, books and magazines on materials, math and basic engineering drew him in though he often had to spend much time and ask many questions which resulted in him feeling frustrated because there was no mentor or teacher to guide him or correct him and he knew that his understandings were not complete. Yet, he progressed enough on his own to keep going.

Right now, without a high school diploma his options would be limited and he had resolved to get his equivalency, but getting out of Paragould was the first target he had to hit, and that had been solved through enlistment. Records of the time for people with his background were fuzzy and rules were bent because of the demand for military manpower, so he was able to convince the Navy he was eighteen, had no living family that were his responsibility, and was ready to serve his country. A couple of local adults vouched for his age, lying to give him an opportunity and anyhow he was to be eighteen within a week of reporting for duty.

But when you are seventeen and smitten, then practical considerations are pretty much tossed out the window. Carl was suddenly and inexplicably focused on Dee and his attraction to her. He had friends grown up from the feral packs that had roamed the area during the Great Depression, some of whom were already either in the services in the war effort or headed to jail. Because of the trajectory of his life, he hadn't made any friends with high school kids, boy or girl. They just didn't move in similar circles, having grown up in households they could rely upon and been educated at least to a high school level. A silent wall was put up when Carl was near such teenagers. It was a small town, and they all knew he had lived outside the 'norm.' Some of the boys went out of their way to taunt him with, "There goes poor white trash," or "Just another nigger lover," or "Ain't you in jail, yet?" But nobody picked a fight with him, and Carl did his best to show that their words never touched him which was not true. Win or lose, everyone knew they were going to get hurt. At that point, his reputation went before him. He was experienced and clever enough not to hang out near large groups of such boys.

As far as Carl was concerned, he simply thought that many people have a need to feel like they are better than others for whatever reason. But those peer attitudes toward him generated a lifelong mistrust of those educated 'others' and a disdain for shallow thinking about people. One thing motivated him above all other influences; Daddy had died trying to give a better future to his children and Carl was dead set upon making sure that happened for him. But that thing that motivated him was about to share the light with another motivation—the need to have a partner, a female partner, to share the journey. That motivation was ignited by his encounter with Dee.

Dee dressed in a red-dotted simple cotton dress with a white background and white collar, and waited for Carl to pick her up. Edna showed a great deal of indifference when Dee introduced Carl, who was as polite as you please. The two made an easy escape after telling Edna they were going to Katty's for dinner. After taking their seats at a table covered with a blue and white chequered pattern, and with several of the older dinner patrons grinning at their youth and freshness, Carl tried to draw Dee out.

"So how do you feel about staying here in Paragould, Dee?"

"You must be joking! Are you seriously wondering?" she spoke lightly, trying to keep from insulting Carl with her typical and spontaneous effort to verbally assault any boy who 'bothered' her.

"Well, yes, I am. I guess it's because I just did something that set me on a course to get out of the place where I was born and have lived all my life, and wondered how you felt about it."

"Truth is that I can't wait to get out of here. My sisters are in Los Angeles and San Diego working in the aircraft industry for the war, and I'd like to join them. Nothing is really holding me here. I must support myself so left school after eighth grade." *I want to escape,* she thought. *I want to get away from these people who ruined me.* But Dee would never let anything on like that to Carl. So, she said, "I'm tired of this place and want to see the world out there." This was also true.

With that began their exploration of each other's lives. Carl told Dee about his family, and what had happened to his parents and siblings, and generally about his life until enlisting and meeting Dee. He left out the abuse at the hands of Worlick. Dee told Carl about growing up on a small farm, losing her mother to childbirth when she was barely four, and eventually moving into town with Edna and Alvin when she was thirteen, leaving school. She said nothing about Basil and the years of abuse that robbed her of her childhood.

After an hour and a half of this conversation and the dinner, the two left Katty's to slowly walk back to Dee's home. They didn't say much during the walk and when they approached Edna's place, Dee turned to Carl and looking directly into his eyes said, "I've really enjoyed getting to know you, Carl, and hope to see you again." With that she planted a quick kiss on his cheek, an enormous step for her.

He wanted to take her in his arms, but controlled the urge and instead replied, "You will, Dee. Be sure of it. I am leaving for basic training soon and don't know when I will be back in town, but at least we have a couple of weeks to get to know each other better." He slowly reached for her right hand and softly held it in both hands, and she fought the urge to withdraw, a bit frightened to respond any other way. "Let's get together tomorrow after work, maybe about six o'clock?" She nodded a yes and turned to go into the house. Alvin was watching from the window and smiled.

"I'll see you in front of the hotel then," Carl called after her. On the way back to his boarding house, Carl whistled and practically skipped like a little boy full of energy and optimism and not a little bit of wonder at life.

The next two weeks presented a cornucopia of delight as the two explored each other, laughing and enjoying their time together. They awoke in each other the desire for closeness, and defenses broke down between them as they shared their innermost wishes for life involving family, work—'career' was not a word in their lexicon—and stability. Who could blame the two teenagers for such basic dreams? World War Two was fiercely waging, they were products of poverty, abuse, different forms of prejudice, and negativity, and the Great Depression. Life was uncertain, especially for the poor such as them. Many people in these circumstances just found someone and held on for dear life.

But unbeknown to Carl, Dee did not share his optimism about children. She secretly believed she would not be a worthy mother, but if Carl wanted children, then she would do her best, and he did want them eventually.

By the time Carl shipped out to basic training, the two were in heavy petting and exploration, but had not actually had sex. They each privately relieved their teenage sexual tension, yet vowed to each other to be together when Carl finished his basic in two months, wherever he was.

The Great Escape was on.

Chapter 11
The Great Escape—1944 to 1945

At the Camp Farragut Naval Base in Idaho, Carl received his basic training. Farragut served as a sort of overflow training facility for enlisted men, primarily for sailors destined for noncombat roles or support ships of one kind or another. Men destined for carriers, battleships, cruisers, destroyers, frigates, and submarines went elsewhere for basic and advanced training. The Great Lakes Naval Station in Illinois was the primary place of basic training and some advanced training for Naval recruits. Since the breakup of his family after Charles and Nellie passed, Carl had always found it difficult to find a home. Being part of a strong organization like the U.S. Navy provided options for Carl where he could at least have some choice—a new situation for him.

Toward the end of his eight weeks of basic, Carl was offered the chance to join the UDT—Underwater Demolition Teams—program, as he did well in his swimming and other physical demands of training. But when put to the test of swimming underwater without surfacing, and holding his breath for lengths of time, he couldn't meet the requirements because of his lung capacity, which had already been damaged by years of smoking. He was then offered training in one of the trades required on most ships, and he chose carpentry. Somehow, the allure of working with wood was strong in him, as it had been with Charles, and he instinctively knew that precision woodworking was a first step to greater things. The Navy also saw to it that Carl would be able to man an anti-aircraft gun crew or machine gun on whatever ship to which he was assigned to serve. And of course, he was required to swab the deck, polish the deck, clean the ship, and perform any duties required to keep the ship fit for service.

The lieutenant in charge of his basic training company wrote of him in his training report that '*Seaman Recruit Carl Doe is bright, eager, and gets along with his fellows. He will apply himself to any assigned task, is curious, and will ask questions if he is in doubt. Altogether, he should be a fine addition to the crew of any ship. His lack of formal education means that he will be best suited to a ship's trade position in addition to his general duties following orders aboard ship.*' Thus, Carl was pigeon-holed at the start of his Naval service. The system was big on valuing your status based on the limitations of your background and not on your potential. His commanding officer thought he was being benign to Carl, much as Grant had done on the farm. But in fact, he was prejudiced and relegated Carl to limitations in life, an accepted management practice of the time. Carl on the other hand saw nothing but opportunity in every door that opened to him. He refused to accept anything coming his way as a dead end. Carl had a choice and he chose ship's carpentry because that's what he wanted from among all ship's trades available.

I'll learn whatever I can about carpentry and use it as my way to other things, he thought. He continued to ignore the taunts about his 'white trash' heritage from some of the other recruits. He had been taunted all his life by the 'others.'

Much fun was had by recruits from other national regions at the expense of the 'Oakies' and 'Arkies' at basic training with derogatory comments on their accents often based upon incorrect assumptions about the difference between ignorance and stupidity. There were many jibes about marrying cousins or sisters. For the blacks in their segregated units, it was even worse; you were pre-destined to become a ship's cook or steward and regularly heard insults like 'midnight,' 'coon,' or worse. Commanding officers did not generally enforce rules against such derogatory labels but always drew the line at the 'N' word. No other service aspirations in the Navy were available to them, and Carl, being the weathervane that he was, did not hold with it but had his hands full trying to navigate his own future. The Army and the Army Air Corps were integrating black units into the service, but not mixed-race units. In that sense, the country's military hadn't really advanced in the eighty-two years since the fifty-fourth Massachusetts in the Civil War. As far as Carl was concerned, everyone wore the same uniform, and served in the same Navy and took the same risks. And he had to get back to Dee.

As November, 1944, rolled around, Dee received the latest of several letters from Carl, in which he expressed his longing to be with her, and how much he would miss her when he eventually shipped out. She was genuinely moved by affection for this different young man and did not fail to pick up on his plans for a brighter future. Dee had made her decision, and then resolved to see her father one last time.

Jack still farmed the same land near Delaplane and lived alone, but he had recently expressed his plans to move into town if he found suitable employment. Dee already knew that things with Carl were likely to come to a head and require serious decisions to be made. So, she resolved to see Jack at the farm since there was no telling when or if she would come to Paragould. She intended never to see him again after this.

It took a lot of willpower for Dee to return to the scene of the crime, where her childhood and future had been marred forever by her mother's and unborn brother's deaths, and by her uncle right under Jack's nose. But Dee was a stubborn girl and resolved to tell Jack what she was planning. Jack had a phone now, and Alvin agreed to take Dee out to the farm for a one-hour visit, to drop her off and pick her up while he found the nearest place to have a beer or two, and barring that he would just sit in the car and wait. Jack was a difficult man to talk to, and Alvin always took it personally.

On a Sunday in early November, they approached the farm in Alvin's car and saw that Jack's car was standing next to the small house. Being typical of tenant farmer and sharecropper farmhouses of the region, it stood on brick pilings. The car was the same Ford bequeathed as a wedding present from Ima's parents so many years before.

Dee felt a rise of anxiety in her stomach. She was resolute, nevertheless. '*Mommy died here; I died here. I will never see this place again!*' she vowed to herself.

When the car pulled up, Jack came out of the front door dressed in faded navy-blue overalls and his worn work boots, carrying his hat in his hand. Alvin rolled his window down and shouted "Morning Jack!" Jack simply nodded in acknowledgement, and then saw Dee opening the car door and stepping out, wearing the same dress that she had worn to dinner with Carl on their first date.

She looked straight at Jack and said in an even voice devoid of emotion, "Hi, Daddy. Alvin will be back in an hour. I have to talk to you today." Jack made a hand motion toward Alvin signaling for him to drive away. Alvin complied and he went in search of a beer to pass the time.

After a few silent moments, Jack turned to Dee and asked, "You in trouble? With child? Did they kick you out?"

"Why in God's name do you ask me that? And, why in God's name would you care, anyway?" Dee raised her voice steadily while asking these questions until it was evident that pure anger took the moment. Jack looked to the fields and did not meet her eyes.

"Did you come out here just to scream at me, girl? Or are we gonna talk? You got somethin' to say, don't ya?"

"I will not come back here again, Dad. There's two things I have to say to you, so you're gonna listen." Dee put emphasis on the last word as though it was something Jack never did. "I barely remember Momma, the only real memory I have of her is that she died in childbirth because she lived out here with you, with no phone and no medical care around. You didn't take care of her! It's your fault I never had a mother or a brother!"

Jack took a quick step toward Dee, who recoiled. Then, he caught himself and remained on the small porch. Dee stared, half defiant and half petrified. "Now listen here, Dee. Your Momma meant everything to me, and I ain't never recovered. All my daughters have left me and I am sick and tired of this life out here alone. I did everything I could as fast as I could to help Ima and the baby. Is that what you wanted to say, about your Momma and all?"

"No. First thing is, I met a young man named Carl Doe. We really like each other, and he is off training with the Navy. I'm leaving to anywhere from here. I intend to leave this cow turd of a place and go to wherever the Navy takes him. I know he's going to ask me to marry him when he comes back from his basic training next month. And there's nothin' you can do about it!"

"Suit yourself."

"I will. Even if he doesn't propose, I will leave this place and go West to join up with Lee or Gay. And Alvin and Edna are planning to go West soon as well."

"Is that it, then?"

"No." Dee looked around, took a deep breath, and turned her gaze upon Jack. His face showed confusion. Dee went on. "I'm telling you somethin' that nobody has heard from me before, and you are the only person I will *ever* tell." At this, Jack started to feel uncomfortable and sat on the edge of the porch, never taking his eyes off Dee. She continued.

"Barely a year after Momma died, Uncle Basil, *your brother*," she emphasized, "Made me do things in that house that a girl child should never have to do for a man. He took my childhood away, made me live with a terrible secret that clings to me like leprosy." Jack was wide-eyed, and his mouth was open, yet no words came out.

"You can deny it to yourself all you want, but he violated me for years and I finally got away from him, and from you. And now, I am gonna get away from here for the rest of my life."

Dee slowly spun around with her arms spread to express herself. "But now, you're gonna know what your own brother did to me, what you closed your eyes to all those years. I can't trust anyone, especially men, and I hate myself for giving in to him even though I was a little girl. A *little girl,* Daddy! And you didn't protect me."

Jack could see that Dee wasn't making this up. His own anger, perhaps at himself more than anything, swelled up like an instantly formed tornado on the near horizon. "I'm gonna kill Basil! He's always been a no-account son of a bitch!"

"That might make you feel better, being my late to the table Daddy. But it won't help me." She started to tear up as she backed away from Jack. "Don't come near me! I don't want your comfort. It's too late for that. There's one person who's proved that he cares about me, and I don't know if I love him or not. But I am going to hang on for dear life to find out if I can."

Jack could only stare at her in wonder.

"And you can go to hell, Daddy!" With that, she turned and walked the fifty yards to the road to wait for Alvin, wiping tears from her face. At least a small bit of her life's burden had been shed.

Jack slowly stood up and walked through the front door, gently closing the screen door and the latch door behind it.

Thirty minutes later, Alvin drove up and gathered Dee for the trip home. She said nothing and he asked nothing. It was one of the few tactful moments Alvin ever had. Heavy silence ruled the trip home.

In Jack's house, he stood leaning on the doorpost to his bedroom as tears welled up in his eyes. They were the first tears since Ima and the baby had died eleven years earlier. His mind went to a dark place. *'Basil. Why didn't I see it? Why didn't I die with the other boys in France? My friends. Better for everyone; for Ima and my son, for all the girls. What kind of life am I leading here on this goddamn farm? There's no peace. No peace.'*

***

Jack had first buried his depression and trauma after the war in his marriage to Ima. She was the only person with whom he had formed any kind of bond since returning from the war. He knew he wasn't a good father from the start. Ima had been the glue that held him to a semblance of a normal life, and he had never let the children into that circle. Now, the chickens had truly come home to roost.

Little Dee being sexually abused right under his nose was more than he could bear. At forty-six years old, Loran 'Jack' Nation finally broke. The stoic veneer completely dissolved.

He went to the corner of his bedroom where his twelve-gauge double-barrel shotgun was kept. Jack sat on the bed, tears starting to roll down his cheeks, but with hands calm and purposeful he reached into the drawer on the nightstand and took out two shells. In a smooth and practiced motion, he opened the gun, put the shells in place and set the shotgun stock down on the floor. Then, he slowly leaned a bit forward, placing the end of the barrels under his outstretched chin, eyes toward the ceiling and fingers poised. He cocked the hammers back. All it would take was a slight pressure on each trigger. Just one shell would do the job handily.

'I've wasted my life. I've let down my family. My family. I have grandchildren I've never met and Dafnie will probably be married with kids of her own. Where will I be? Dead and gone. What reason do I have to live?' He started to place his fingers on the triggers which surely would result in his entire head being dispersed in fragments and gore all over the bedroom.

Then, he pulled his fingers back and gently moved the barrels away before he uncocked the hammers and sat there for several minutes, a battle raging in his mind. Finally, a thought broke through his curtain of despair and self-loathing like the first rays of a bright and rising sun close upon the darkest of nights. *'Grandchildren, Ima's grandchildren. My grandchildren. Our grandchildren.*

Grandpa can be there for them or at least offer to be there for them. Maybe daughters will allow that, should allow that. And I want it!'

Jack resolved to carry on and change his life, finally move off the farm and to the town. He splashed cold water on his face and began planning the rest of his life. Basil was thankfully not nearby and lived in Tennessee. Jack vowed never to seek him out, but if Basil showed up then, he would damn well find a way to kill him for sure.

Dee had wanted to hurt her father, and had wanted to unload at least some of her burden. She succeeded in doing both, but it never would have occurred to her that Jack would seek self-redemption for his negligence and lack of care.

Soon, Carl would return to Paragould in early December for a break in service that would last through Christmas and just beyond New Year's Day. He was assigned to the newly minted attack transport ship USS Pickaway and was to report for duty in San Diego right after the new year began as a Seaman in Training for the ship's carpenter. After basic, he had been given one month of indoctrination into his upcoming training and responsibilities aboard the ship.

Carl and Dee had been in constant correspondence, and they planned to spend all their free time together. They would get to know each other better and plan their exit from Arkansas to California. The two hadn't figured on marriage yet but they shared an affection for each other and a vision of life in California until the war was over and Carl was clear of active duty.

On a cold and overcast afternoon in early December, the two met again at the train station.

Dee waited anxiously for Carl's train to pull into the station. She was dressed in a black and white dress with a faux vest and a tan overcoat that was a hand-me-down from Edna, who had helped Dee with her makeup so that she appeared several years older. Dee's nervousness was expressed through her short back-and-forth pacing on the platform. The train pulled into the station after a solid blowing of the steam whistle and much deceleration noise from the braking system. As Dee searched the exiting passengers, she spotted a sailor in his peacoat and white cap and instantly knew who it was three cars away.

The sailor shouldered his duffel bag, which held nearly his entire life's possessions, and began trotting toward her and she stepped up her pace. When they met, he dropped his bag and embraced Dee with a long hug. Then, he planted a passionate kiss on her lips as she offered her mouth in a surrender that was more pacifistic and calmer than passionate. Carl didn't know the difference and really didn't care. However, Dee's emotions at seeing Carl were true, and her embrace was more passionate than her kiss.

Carl was hooked for good.

"Let's go somewhere where we can talk in private. I missed you so much, Darling Dee!"

"I missed you as well, Carl." She buried her head in his peacoat and held on in the hug without end. As he finally took her by the hand to lead her away, he hoisted his kit bag and noticed several adult strangers smiling at these children in adult guise. His only reaction was to smile back at them and lead Dee off the platform. Proud of his uniform, proud of his girl, proud to be on top of the world.

"Let's go to Katty's for coffee and some pie. We can talk there. Won't be many people around," he said, as they walked hand in hand away from the station. Dee said nothing as she matched Carl's pace in her excitement and anticipation.

Mr. and Mrs. Katty had recently sold the business but had not yet abandoned it to the new owners. They were to take over the following week. When Carl and Dee entered the café, Bill saw them right away and called out to the kitchen, "Betty, come see what we have here! You'll never guess who just returned to town."

Betty came out of the kitchen wiping her hands on a towel and exclaimed, "Whoa, it's Carl Doe and his girl! All cleaned up are you, Carl? Looks like you've come good in the Navy. We're proud of you boy! What will it be for you and…"

"Dee," he answered, "Short for Dafnie. This is Dee Nation from near Delaplane. Yeah, she's my girl." He looked at Dee and she responded with a slight nod of yes.

"Honey, you might as well quit now. You're too good for the likes of him." But as Betty said this in a good-natured way so that everyone in the café could hear, she put her hand on Carl's shoulder and leaned in to say softly, "Real proud of you, Carl." He was so surprised that he had no response except to look back at Betty with gratitude in his eyes and a slightly red face.

The kids seated themselves and Betty asked what they wanted. "Just coffee and some apple or cherry pie, whatever you have, Betty."

"Well, it's on the house this time, Carl. Think of it as our contribution to the war effort! Where are you headed with the Navy?"

"Thanks, Betty. I'm posted to a ship going to the Pacific to support our attacks on Jap held territory. Reporting next month to San Diego. That's all I know," he said, and added with an arched brow, "And that's all I can say."

Betty smiled, "Well, you make sure you return in one piece to Dee and to all of us." Bill came over to shake Carl's hand and introduce himself to Dee. To Carl, he added a piece of advice, "It can be a negative world out there, Carl. Keep your head down and stay true to your dreams." He turned to face Dee. "He came here years ago with nothing in his pockets and nowhere to go. And now he's off to fight for his country and it looks like he has someone to fight for!" Dee didn't know what to say and looked wide-eyed at Bill.

Carl continued to grow red with embarrassment as Bill put a hand on his shoulder and then walked away toward other customers who needed his attention. "They like you, Carl," observed Dee.

"Well, the first time I was here you wouldn't know it," he said.

"Maybe you grew on them like you're growing on me," she said, smiling coyly.

The one thing about Carl that bordered on annoyance for her was that he was often too serious. She felt that she had enough of that for the two of them. "I really hope I am, Dee." was his response instead of something akin to, 'Like a bad habit.' That would have evoked some rare laughter from Dee. She yearned for spontaneity but didn't know how to generate it herself. More baggage from her past.

The pie and coffee came out quickly, and by the time coffee refills arrived, the two ended their moments of silence and began to discuss the future.

They agreed that neither of them wished to remain in Paragould or even in the area. Dee understood Carl's difficult circumstances and when he explained his time with Worlick and Dorothy, he disclosed nothing other than Worlick's drinking and the habitual beatings received from him. Dee for her part, disclosed the trauma of losing her mother at such an early age and the indifference of her sisters and Jack. Her sisters were older and had sought escape through marriage. Dee had really wanted to finish high school, but life had intervened.

"I know I'm only fifteen. But I will go anywhere with you, Honey." The use of that word toward him caused Carl to feel a euphoria he could barely contain. Terms of endearment toward him were totally unfamiliar since his parents had passed, except for expressive and innocent little Annie who was now fourteen. Dee continued, "I want to be there when you return from your duty at sea. I want us to get to know each other, and if what we have is real, then we can see about making things permanent when all this war stuff is over. I'm old enough to make my own decisions, and right now, I decide I want to be with you wherever you go."

"I think you know how I feel, Dee. Darling Dee. I will never force anything on you. But I can't lie, my heart tells me that we have something special going and it's tough enough for that to last over time and distance. You have sisters in Southern California workin' in the aircraft industry. Maybe they can help you get a job there, and between the two of us, we can manage enough money to see us through this war. We're winning against the Japs and the Nazis, and things are picking up steam, so I don't see the war lasting all that much longer. Maybe one or two years. I have plans, Dee. They're not certain yet, but I know that I will better myself and break out of this half-heaven, half-hell we live in here. I hope you can share it with me and put tough times in the past."

Dee stared at him for a few seconds, then said, "Please get me out of here now, Carl. I don't want to be separated from you anymore except when you're away on the ship. There's nothing for me here and I want a future clear of this place."

"All right, then, Honey. It's settled. We're away from here!" The two left Katty's arm in arm and Carl dropped Dee at Edna's, planted a kiss on her lips which was more ardently returned than before, and proceeded to the boarding house where he had arranged to spend his leave.

As he let go of Dee, he said "We've got less than thirty days to clear out if we are to go together. Get hold of your sisters and I'll take care of your train ticket. We must leave for the two-day trip to L.A. on 3rd of January, then I'm on to San Diego. You've got to have things arranged with one of your sisters before we leave, as I won't have time to help you get settled in L.A."

"I'm there with you, Honey." That was all the motivation that Carl needed from thereon.

The couple spent the next three weeks busy making arrangements and getting ready for Christmas. In the time permitted due to Dee's two part-time jobs, the two spent hours on long walks and smooching. They hardly noticed anyone in public, as those falling in love will do. Dee arranged by phone to stay with Gay, who was living alone since her husband Earl was away in Europe. Lee's husband had turned out to be a heavy drinker and had hit her on more than one occasion. She had just given birth to her first child, a daughter they named Donna, and the father was being dishonorably discharged for repetitive drunk and disorderly behavior, and would soon have to find work since Lee had to take care of the baby. So Gay was the safer of the options for Dee, although Lee offered to take her in as well.

Just before Christmas, Carl asked Dee to accompany him to his visits with Charlie and Annabelle. He wanted to show off his girl to the only people left whom he really cared about.

And he didn't know when or if he would ever see them again. He bought for Charlie a model ship, and he purchased the book 'Little Women' for Annabelle, as their Christmas presents.

"Are you sure they'll like me?" asked Dee.

"Well Charlie is different, Dee. He doesn't say much, and you never really know what he might be thinking. But he's pretty smart about some things and is practicing the trade of shoe repair, makin' a living with the help of the Reverend and his family, bless 'em. Just don't expect too much talk from him. As for Annabelle, she's real smart and is doing well in school, ninth grade. Her second foster family is adopting her, real nice people the Jacksons are, and they take good care of her. I've always checked in on her over the years. We're very close and I want you to like her, hope you do."

Dee uncontrollably felt pangs of anxiety over Carl's request. '*His sister is younger than me and already ahead in school. She can never know about me, never.*' She didn't know how she would handle the situation, and she wanted to be okay with Carl's brother and sister. But the demons within began to exact their toll in doubt and self-loathing.

Two days before Christmas, they paid each of Carl's siblings a visit, first to Charlie and then to Annabelle. The shoe repair operation was run by the church and Charlie was paid for his work and lived with the pastor's family. Over the years, they had coaxed a level of response from him, and he began to communicate in an autistic fashion. Charlie had been seventeen when he was finally settled into their home, resulting from community pressure on Worlick, who had lost his grip on his castle after Carl left.

It happened in 1940, just days after the baseball bat affair. Worlick was coming off a drunk and was furious. He beat Dorothy, who finally grew a bit of spine and ran to Pastor Redman to complain. In a long conversation with the Pastor and his wife, Dorothy recounted through her tears some of the horrors of living with her husband, but never discussed her forced prostitution. People in town were not blind to that anyway. And after all, you can't live in a pariah household in a small town and hold such secrets from everyone. Carl's escape had given her a small seed of incentive and she needed help to make it grow.

"I can't go back there, he'll most likely kill me," she sobbed. "And I've no money to run and anyway I'm afraid he'll find me. And Charlie can't do for himself. He needs lookin' after by good Christian people."

To Pastor Redman, this was a call to evangelical arms. "Don't you worry, Dorothy. He has a husband's rights, but not the right to beat you and Charlie, and deprive you of a decent life. You stay here for now and let me talk to a couple of the other reverends and we'll go see Worlick. We can discuss what to do with Charlie, who is not Worlick's son. Everyone around here knows that Worlick don't work at anything except the bottle and the cards. Things got to change, and it's our Christian duty to see to it that it's done." Dorothy gratefully accepted that she should remain in the Pastor's house for a while, feeling some degree of safety. Nobody seemed to be bothered that 'Christian duty' had been absent for years.

Charlie had always taken his beatings in silence. Not because he willed it so. Because he wasn't capable of crying and only silently recoiled at the pain inflicted, which usually enraged Worlick even more. Charlie's habit when being near anyone who suddenly moved, was to instantly shrug his shoulders and protect his head, quickly shrinking from them.

People just hadn't figured out where that habit came from, and ascribed it to Charlie's peculiar condition.

At that moment, Dorothy was gone to who knows where and Carl had humiliated him. So Worlick took it out on Charlie, who was sitting on the porch lost in his own world. Worlick rushed up behind him, grabbed him by the collar, and dragged him in his fury into the front yard. A clear view of this action was had by many neighbors and passers-by.

"You silent son-of-a-bitch! Say something! Where's your sister?" Worlick began to savagely beat Charlie with punches to the back of his head and kicks to his back. Charlie beat his hands uselessly against the attack, and Worlick violently shove him to the ground. The beating was draining Worlick of his energy, and he paused, breathing heavily and trying to gather himself for another onslaught. As he did so, he looked up and swiveled his head. At least ten or twelve people were staring at him and began yelling for him to stop.

"Leave the boy alone!"

"What the hell are you doing, Worlick?"

"We'll take care of you for sure." A few men started to approach from down the street.

"Stay back and mind your own business!" he warned them. But he knew in his gut, coward that he was, that his days as lord and master of the downtrodden were coming to a close.

Charlie lay shaking, bruised and hurting on the ground before Worlick. "Okay, okay." And with that, Worlick turned and ran into the house.

Several pairs of hands reached for Charlie. One man said softly, "Don't worry, son, we'll take you somewhere safe." Charlie finally broke his silence.

"Good, good. Want to go, want to go. Where's my sister? Where's my brother? Where's my sister? Where's my brother?" he kept repeating as he was gently inspected for damage and taken away to the reverend's home, where he would eventually be taken into their family.

A group of three local clergy intervened with Worlick and Dorothy. After days of meetings and discussions, it was determined that Worlick wanted to change his ways and accept Jesus as his savior in the Church of Christ. Dorothy was reluctantly persuaded to give life with her husband a second go, if he would forego beating her and if he continued to be employed and support his family. In the end, Worlick's consequence for his horrible behavior in life was really his loss of that life. What he ultimately gained years later was responsibility, children, and a degree of self-respect. Dorothy gained freedom within the confines of her marriage. Worlick eventually believed in his own redemption. Carl never believed it for a second, and never spent even a moment in the presence of the newly minted Christian couple.

So, on this December morning in 1944, Carl and Dee left Charlie to his happy existence after Carl presented him with the model ship. Charlie responded with, "Carl's ship, his ship. Carl's ship, Carl's ship." He paused. "My brother.

Thank you. I will keep it always." With that, he looked down at the ground and said no more. It didn't go unnoticed by Carl that Dee hadn't said anything but hello and goodbye to Charlie, but he knew that if you weren't used to it, then communicating with Charlie would be awkward.

They went to the Jacksons' home to see Annie, who ran down the porch steps and jumped into Carl's arms. "Big brother, how I've missed you. You must tell me all about the Navy and things." In a trend that she could never control, Dee went within herself and looked at anyone who expressed affection for Carl or friendship with him as a threat of some kind.

"And who's this?" Annie asked with a smile, because she knew already from Carl's letter.

"This is Dafnie Nation. Dee to all who know her. Dee, this is my dear little sister, Annabelle." To Carl, this was the most important introduction of all because these two were the two most dear people in his life.

"Very pleased to meet you, Dee." Annie extended her hands, and Dee said as she took Annie's hands in her own,

"Please to meet you, too," in a monotone.

And when Annie kissed her on the cheeks in greeting and said "I can't wait for us to get to know each other," Dee offered her cheeks without a reciprocal kiss and said,

"Me, too."

The Jacksons were kind, open, and hospitable. The young lovers were offered coffee, cookies, and other snacks near the Christmas tree. Carl complimented them on the excellent care and love that Annie was receiving and complimented Annie on her achievements in school and choir. Much was made of Carl's service in the Navy, and when the Jacksons, without guile, asked of Dee what her plans were, she told them that she was going to live with her sister in Southern California and work in the aircraft industry. In truth she felt like a 'bump on a log' as the saying goes. It was a feeling she tried to escape all of her life when in social settings, with only limited success.

At the end of the hour-long visit, Carl and Dee were escorted to the front walkway and Carl asked Dee to wait a moment so he could say goodbye to Annie, who waited on the porch.

Dee watched him walk away and turned to look at the street rather than toward the porch.

"What's wrong, Carl? Is Dee shy?" she whispered so that Dee couldn't hear.

"Yeah, she's shy and withdrawn sometimes around other people. She'll loosen up. And she loves me, Annie. And you know I'm not shy."

"Well, that's the main thing, Big Brother! I hope and pray that everything works out for you two. Be careful, Carl, I can't imagine a world without you in it. Thanks for the book, I've got to read it anyway next year for school, so I'll be ahead of things." She hugged him hard and kissed him on the forehead with his head in both her hands. "Love you forever, Carl. My Big Brother!" With that, she turned and ran into the house with tears starting to run down her cheeks, not looking back so that Carl wouldn't feel bad.

"I love you, too, dear little Annie," he said even though she couldn't hear. But she knew.

When he turned toward Dee, he saw that she was facing the opposite direction. She turned around to face him and quickly embraced Carl so hard that he was a bit shocked. "I love you, Honey. You're so good with your brother and sister. And I know you'll be good to me."

"Of course, I will, Dee. I love you, too. Always." Here was a puzzle to be put on the shelf and assembled another day.

Two weeks later they made their way by train to the West Coast.

Chapter 12
No limits? 1945–1948

With Dee quickly tucked away in Gay's apartment near Burbank, Carl left the next day to report for duty aboard the U.S.S. Pickaway. Gay's place was quiet since she and Earl had no children yet. He was in the Army serving domestically at Ft. Benning in Georgia in support of the training programs for infantry. The Army considered Earl too laconic to ship overseas in a combat role. She worked in the Burbank Lockheed factory delivering small parts and supplies to the assembly lines for production of the P-38 Lightning and sometimes for the B17s. Ten-hour shifts were common.

Gay was the one sister who took after her mother Ima in looks. Her broad and open features, thick lips, and short brown hair would have told anyone that she was Ima's daughter. But she did not have Ima's quick wit and was taller than her mother by two inches. She never had a bad word to say about anyone and was happy to share the apartment with Dee, which she hoped would relieve her boredom when not on the job.

When Carl left the next morning after dropping Dee off and sleeping on the couch, Gay remarked, "He's nice, Dee. You're lucky, but you're a bit young to marry. What's the plan?"

"I need to get a job, save some money, and be here for Carl when he returns from duty. I'm not lookin' to kick my heels up in the meantime, Gay, just want to spend time with my sisters and work so I can save some money for when this war is over."

With the burden she carried in her mind, Dee had an aversion to doing the things that most young people do, mingling at gatherings, socializing, and exploring being an adult. Her relationship with Carl was about as far as she dared to go. He was gregarious in nature and optimistic, full of energy for life, and needing the approval of others for jobs well done.

"Well," answered Gay, "Getting a job is the easy part. Keeping your man-bosses and coworkers out of your panties is a different matter, especially if they know you're married or have a beau off fighting the war." She paused to let that sink in. "They all assume that you want the kind of company they think you're used to."

"Well, Carl and I haven't done it yet. I'm sure we will when we are married. I don't see that happening until I'm a couple of years older," she proclaimed with her nose slightly elevated, and eyes partly closed. Gay would have been the next target in line for Basil if Dee hadn't been available to be his victim. In her adolescent mind, Dee thought '*My sisters should see that I am doing everything the right way and not giving myself up to anyone before it's sensible to do so.*' The realities of her feelings for Carl, her hormonal urges just now being naturally freed for expression, and circumstances would cause Dee to revise her plans a bit when the time came. Now, she changed the subject to her most pressing issue.

"So how do I land a job like yours?" she asked.

"I'll show you the ropes. There's work everywhere if you want it," Gay smiled, and the two plotted for hours how to get a fifteen-year-old girl to work in the defense industries around Los Angeles or in San Diego.

***

The rolling seas east of New Caledonia hosted a convoy of nine ships, including a cruiser, two destroyers, five attack transports full of marines and the ships' crews, plus a fuel ship. Carl stood on the main deck of the *Pickaway* after his training session learning how to fashion different sizes of buttresses to shore up various weak points in the ship's hull in case of damage. In truth, he had already mastered this part of the ship's carpenter craft and was a bit bored. He had recently built a couple of customized desks for officers on board, and his growing expertise did not go unnoticed by the X.O.—executive officer—and with his recommendation Carl was elevated to Petty Officer third Class after only eight months serving on the ship. He had studied his responsibilities and requirements and was eager to do more.

The flotilla was to join up with other Naval forces to prepare for the invasion of Japan, and the date was the fifteenth of August, 1945. On the sixth and ninth of that month, the two atomic bombs had been dropped on Hiroshima and Nagasaki, respectively. There had been

201

much speculation and even betting on when the invasion would take place, but the sudden appearance of the weapon of mass destruction changed the calculus for the Americans and the Japanese.

As Carl stared at the partially cloudy late afternoon sky, he heard whooping and shouting from below deck. One of the Seaman Trainees under him burst through the nearby door shouting, "It's over! Over! The Japs have surrendered! They're gonna sign an unconditional surrender to that goddamn army wingnut MacArthur. Word is that it'll be on the Mighty Mo so the Navy will host it all." Carl began to smile.

"You're not shittin' me, are you, Herschel? I'll tie you down and make you listen to opera music if you are!"

By now the whole ship was coming alive with the buzz and sailors and marines were flooding onto the deck. On the loudspeaker the Captain's voice came over the system loud and clear. "It's official, men. To all the crew of the *Pickaway,* congratulations on a job well done. And to the marines in our care, congratulations on your ultimate and peaceful return home! But we don't know if all the enemy subs have the word, and our convoy will observe battle readiness until we get the all-clear from Admiral Nimitz himself. Do your best to enjoy the moment. Write your wives, sweethearts, family, and friends. We won't be going home until ordered to do so. Dismissed!"

Herschel remarked, "Tomorrow morning, it will be orders from old 'assholes and elbows' to scrub the deck. But hey, that's gonna end soon for sure!"

Carl's head began to swim. He hadn't seen Dee in nine months, but they wrote a steady stream of letters. She was working for Douglas Aircraft sorting bolts and other parts and stocking the supply room for hardware supplies. "Hey, Carl, let's see if we can talk to some of the boys at chow." Chow was at eighteen hundred hours for enlisted men.

"Sure thing, Herschel. But we have two hours until then. Guess what I'm gonna do?"

"Let me see," he put his index finger under his chin in mock contemplation, "Uh, you're writing a letter? Could that be it?"

"Very funny, but yeah, you nailed it. Brilliant as usual. You'll go far Herschel!" Carl slapped Herschel on the back and was rewarded with a look that conveyed "Up your ass, Carl." With that, Carl went to his bunk space to fetch a pencil and paper to write a letter to Dee.

When he settled into his bunk, he placed the paper over a hardback book he had acquired in Hawaii titled *Principles of Trigonometry,* and after a few moments began to write.

'August 15, 1945
Dearest Darling Dee,

It's no military secret, the Japanese have unconditionally surrendered. With Germany and Italy gone, and now the Japanese, that means no more war! That means I can come home to you. I long for you, for your touch, for your smile, and for your love for me. I never had someone stick to me like you have. It makes me want to dance with you forever, as if I can dance! We're young and have our whole lives ahead of us. I want to spend it loving you, and ultimately our children, if we're allowed. Dee, I want you so badly and long for your sweet embrace. I want us to have everything with each other now that this damn war is over.

I intend to make something of myself and thank God that Congress and the President, may he rest in peace, saw fit to give us servicemen a helping hand by making the Servicemen's Readjustment Act law. My Daddy didn't get that kind of help in time because the New Deal came too late for him, and for us, his family. I remember that he hoped to join one of the conservation corps camps for work. But as I understand it, the Act provides for cash support to train at a trade or to go to college. It also will help us to buy a house someday because the Act provides loan guarantees. With this help, and me being a hard worker and good learner, we can make it, Dee!

We love each other. We can have a fine life together, Dee. Think about what you want. I know what I want. I'll be out of the Navy in a year, but I'm due for a month's leave early next year.

Will let you know when as soon as I do. Got to go now or I'll miss evening chow, which ain't much to miss!

All my love,
Honey'

When Dee read this letter, her first reaction was relief. It seemed like the madness of the war would leave the two of them relatively unscathed, when there were so many who would have to pick up the broken pieces of their lives and move on. She was completely bored by the routine tasks of delivering parts and supplies to the assembly floor, and really never considered a career at anything, not because she wasn't smart, but because she needed the kind of protection that Carl could provide—emotional and financial support—because she instinctively knew that she couldn't stand on her own and the extent of damage to her was beyond herself to manage.

There were no services or programs in her day to help, and the working-class attitude toward psychologists and counsellors was such that if you even discussed it or thought about it, you were somehow inferior because you were expected to deal with your own problems whatever they were. And while the next thirty years would see a sea change in such attitudes in American society, it would be too late for Carl and Dee.

Carl, a young man full of optimism and drive, longed so much for the family that fate took from him and never replaced. But he also would not stop until he had achieved some as yet unknowable attainment in life. An unidentified but powerful urge to create simmered within him as magma and gases slowly, yet inexorably, build up to a volcanic eruption that cannot be forestalled forever. The ghosts of Charles and Nellie came in and out of his dream conversations over the years. He basically saw America as a country that rewarded the industrious, the capable and the honest. He did not include 'the connected' in his calculus because that was a concept unknown to him. His family disappeared, his friend Cheeks disappeared, the

Wilsons disappeared. Carl was a young man without a network of any kind except the Navy and what the GI Bill could provide. Dee was his network. There were many who unlike him had endured the horrors of combat on land, at sea and in the air. From the poor and lower class such as Carl, many hard men emerged after the war, and it was fortunate for America and for the rest of the world that America experienced an unparalleled economic boom and middle-class growth where such men often found a comfortable predictability that kept them in check. Carl was not one of those.

Dee was a teenager carrying a huge weight of self-loathing and anger, desperate to have someone she could trust to take care of her. She possessed high intelligence not matched by drive or ambition. Inside her mind, she simply believed that she didn't deserve it. Anything and anybody that protected her, had to be defended from the outside world, a world that would never understand or forgive her, so she imagined. Uncle Basil had planted a cancerous tumor that ravaged her mind.

The two needed each other, but from the beginning those needs were not clearly identified between the two of them. Two kids had been tossed upon the complicated shores of life with no appreciation of what lay ahead.

Shortly after the Japanese signed the surrender, Carl continued to improve his ship's carpentry skills and counted the days until his scheduled leave Stateside, when he would reunite with Dee, now sixteen and much wiser in the ways of fending off unwanted advances from much older men. As late December approached, he began to practice asking Dee to marry him, awkwardly on one knee, with a variety of short and heavy-on-content speeches.

They started with words like "Since I've known you" or "I realized how much I miss you" or "When two people meet like we have" or "I knew when we met." The entire lot of these alternate beginnings to his proposal were forgotten when Dee ran into his arms outside the Naval dock in San Diego and kissed him and hugged him so hard that he couldn't believe it.

He blurted "Marry me, Dee!" That was his speech.

"Yes, I will, Carl. I will, I will," she whispered into his ear, and for the first time in their relationship, she felt real longing for him, to touch him and for him to touch her. She was safe, and she knew that he would never hurt her. She felt a freedom that she had never known, the freedom to explore sexually, with tenderness and feeling. He responded with a heightened sense of expectation and a desire to please Dee. They were now really in love and ready to make a go of it with each other.

"I've got until the end of February, nearly two months, before my next posting to the Missouri, and then discharge in August. Let's get married before I go back to the Navy, Dee." Her answer was to press her hips into Carl and stare at him directly with an unmistakable invitation. "We can do anything we want until wedding day," she said in a husky tone.

He smiled. "Aye, Captain. Full speed ahead!"

"Hold it, sailor! Captain wants slow speed *gradually* increased to flank speed! Understood?" she arched her left eyebrow.

"Copy that, ma'am." And away they went in search of a room, to linger in San Diego for another day before returning to Gay's place in L.A., where they would stay until Carl shipped out again.

They found a small hotel near the water and registered as Mr. and Mrs. Doe, which brought a grin to the proprietor's face because Doe was a legal alias. He had seen them come and go, married, unmarried, business transactions and more, since his hotel was not far from the Naval base. *These kids are young,* he thought. *But earnest.* He didn't ask. *What the hell,* he thought. *Who am I to stand in the way of a sailor and his girl?* He took the cash and sent them to a room with a limited view of the sea and as they went to the stairs, he muttered to himself,

"Ain't young love grand?" then went back to reading the sports page of the newspaper.

When they arrived at the door to their room, Dee turned and looked into Carl's eyes. "We're as good as married, aren't we, Honey?"

"We'll get the rings and make it official, Dee, within the month and before I ship out. You are the one for me, always." He kissed her tenderly and felt the sexual tension increase. "But today is our day, and I am carrying you across the threshold!" With that, he dropped his duffel and scooped her up in his arms. *She is so light,* he thought, and he wasn't wrong there. Dee was a petite five foot three inches and weighed all of one hundred pounds. He carried her into the room, grabbed his duffel, closed the door, and thus began their dance.

Dee had some experience from her childhood ordeal, Carl had none with girls. She wanted to give Carl pleasure, and at first, hesitated, but as he proceeded with gentle attention, Dee discarded her reservations and gave herself to Carl if not with passion, then with surrender. Carl had no way to gauge the difference. He was too wrapped up in his need for her, and his joy at finding someone who wanted him to read any subtleties into the situation. Dee was able to convince Carl that this was her first time, and that contrary to legend, women didn't always bleed when deflowered. It didn't matter anyhow because Carl wanted to believe it with all his heart.

They spent the rest of the day and evening making love, talking softly about the future and how they would explain themselves to Gay and Lee. The next morning, they would have to take the train to Los Angeles as Dee must return to work on a job that was already being wound down.

After another month went by, they were married by a judge at a civil ceremony in Los Angeles, she nearly seventeen and he nineteen, with Gay and Lee in attendance as witnesses on the fourth of February, 1946. Two weeks later, Carl shipped out to the USS Missouri battleship. There was no war on anymore, and Carl used the time to increase his skills in ships carpentry. The Missouri was a much, much larger ship than the Pickaway. For six months, Carl learned in a more comprehensive shop and increased skills in technical woodwork with what to him was an incredible array of tools and instruments. He loved the work and vowed to use it as a pathway to the economic and work stability that had eluded members of his family in the 20th Century. Upon discharge in August, he enlisted in the Naval Reserves which meant two or three weeks a year away from Dee, with pay. He also passed his high school equivalency and went on to take advantage of the training benefits of the GI Bill, by working for Nash Cabinets in St. Louis, where he and Dee decided to plant themselves to raise a family. Her sisters and their husbands, except for Edna, who had migrated to California, also lived in the greater St. Louis area, and that gave Dee some comfort. Carl and Dee moved into the ground floor of a rented two-storey brick house in St. Louis with Brooklyn-style front steps. It was early 1947.

When Carl reported to Nash Cabinets, the owner, Cary Nash, knew a hard worker when he saw one. The place was a mess, a fire hazard by any modern standards but at the time there was no oversight on safety, no requirement for taking sawdust and chemicals out of the air. Aboard ship, Carl had dabbled in rudimentary furniture for officer quarters and through his self-taught basic trigonometry and geometry he had already mastered the design and execution of precision curves and symmetries. He possessed an artistic eye coupled with technical drive.

"You'll be a good cabinet maker, steady work, Carl, and we'll talk about wages when the government money runs out. Welcome to Nash Cabinets!"

"Thank you, Mr. Nash. Glad to be here." But he thought at the same time, *No way I'm staying a cabinet maker. I'm not letting anyone set my limits for me. I'll do whatever it takes to move on and up. No limits! Right now,*

I've got to pay the bills. He also knew that Nash told him that his government supported pay was $1.50 per hour, and after two years they would discuss an increase. He assumed that Carl wouldn't know that in fact he should have been paid $1.90 per hour. Overtime rates did not apply, he was told. Carl decided that mastering precision wood working, use of hand and power tools for all aspects of the job, and at applying finishes to the product were useful skills to acquire, and he intended to do just that. *Always add to the kitbag,* he thought.

These were the days before lighter materials and mass production hit the cabinetry and furniture markets. The quality of the work including dovetail joints and carefully applied finishes in lacquer and selected stains was generally maintained in the industry and became a near-religious observance for Carl.

The thing was, he had no clear idea what moving on and up would mean. Only a rather vague premonition draped his vision. At this time in his life, there were no limits in his mind, only advantages in possibilities and opportunities. '*Maybe I can't get an engineering degree, but I'll show them what I can do!*'

So, much to Dee's chagrin he proceeded to spend extra hours accelerating his skills and knowledge. It wasn't long before she began to complain to him that he was being taken advantage of by Nash Cabinets, and it was foolish to give them so much time for so little money. Dee had retreated to her relationships with her sisters Lee and Gay, and never tried to get work. She had her own safety zone in life, always strangely nervous even around her sisters.

When New Year's Eve rang in 1948, Carl and Dee had a get together with Lee and her new husband Preston and Lee's daughter Donna, and with Gay and Earl who were as yet childless. Many beers were consumed, and after singing Auld Lang Sine, Carl and Dee went back to their place and made a baby. He was twenty-one and she was eighteen.

Chapter 13
What You Carry and What You Overcome,
1948–1952

Mr. Nash thought he had it pretty good, indeed. He was able to work Carl like two or three people. The boy's production was off the charts, and Nash was free to exploit his government-sponsored 'trainee' while skimming a bit for his company. If he had bothered to know what Carl was really thinking, then he would have wondered who was using whom.

Carl was turning twenty-one when he started at Nash. His Arkansas accent had not yet disappeared into his Midwestern accent, and to Nash he was a simple country boy who would work hard to keep his pay check coming, especially since his wife was now pregnant. Carl and Dee, Lee, Gay, and their husbands were a tiny part of the migration of millions of hitherto poor whites and blacks from the cotton belt states to the job centers of the time in St. Louis, Chicago, Minneapolis, Detroit and all over the Midwest of the United States. And the rest of the outward migration, which had begun in the Dust Bowl 1930s and carried into the Post War years, moved to the West Coast, mostly to California.

Dee's two sisters settled in and around the St. Louis area, so contact among them and their families was frequent. Lee had recently started dating a man named Preston who was thirty years old and had been an infantry support in Patton's third Army when they 'liberated' Buchenwald. That infamous testament to the monstrosity of which humans are capable sent the prejudiced, stoic, and hard-bitten Preston into instant panic. He never recovered from what he witnessed, though he buried it deep inside, and covered himself with the constant veneer of racial and religious prejudice always. He and Carl never hit it off. Lee was a kind, sensitive and generous person and Carl could never figure out what made the two tic. Maybe it was the fact that Preston ran road repair machinery to fix or build asphalt roads in the region and that work put him away half the time.

As for Gay's husband, Earl, he was so laconic that Carl thought the man had had his nerves removed. Carl sized him up as a nice man who preferred life to be simple. He had no work or skill ambition, preferring to consider his work on loading docks with hand trucks sufficient to provide a steady if modest income. For many from the poor and working classes of the 1930s and 1940s, they preferred stability over achievement. And who could blame them? But Carl was driven. His drive to be something, somebody of achievement and creativity would never be quenched by settling into a slot that society said you were destined to stay in.

He wouldn't have been able to put words to it at the time. It just was an undefined energy that drove him to an as yet undefined future.

As the six of them were sitting in Carl and Dee's apartment one Sunday afternoon in May, Lee asked a simple but loaded question of Dee. "Carl's at work so much. Doesn't that bother you?"

Dee just stared back at her.

"I mean, you being pregnant and all." Lee had not really intended any mischief with her question.

"Mind your own business, Lee. Carl's just trying to get ahead and I'm fine." Then, she raised her face and looked up. "He's not going to make cabinets and counters all his life!" But there was tension in her voice and her sisters knew enough not to say anything else on the matter.

After everyone left, Dee reproached Carl.

"You get paid for forty hours a week, but you work sixty or more, and if I didn't have my sisters nearby then I would be lonely. Why do you have to work so much? I didn't want to be pregnant for a couple of years more, and I don't know what kind of mother I'll make…"

He put his arm around her shoulders. She pushed him off. "Dee, you'll make a fine mother."

There was pleading in his tone, and her voice became bitter in response, "How can you know that? You don't know anything. All you know is work, work, work! And there's no money to show for it. I'm left sitting here afraid, not afraid of having a baby but afraid of what comes after. Don't you understand that?"

"I'm trying to, Honey. I just thought that we're building a future together, and right now, please understand that this job is only temporary. Once I've learned all there is to know and do, I'm moving on to a better job and more money. I've got to do that, for us." He looked at her belly, now showing the pregnancy. "For all of us," he added.

Dee let him put his arm around her as they walked to the bedroom for a nap. She didn't say anything, and Carl misread this as acquiescence. It was anything but that.

As Carl lay sleeping in the late afternoon of that warm spring day, Dee's mind was racing.

'He's a good man, I know. But what about me? I didn't really want children, don't have any job skills. I just want to hide, to hide so nobody can find me. I spend my days reading, making the meals for us, cleaning the apartment. Why do I feel like I'm in prison? Where would I go if I got out? I have to be normal. Nobody must know about me. And I do care for Carl. He's so good to me, and I feel terrible the way I talk to him sometimes. He's only trying to make a better life for us. I'll do better. I'll be the best Mom and wife that I can be, I promise!' She grabbed some sleep after a few minutes passed. The baby hadn't started the hard kicking yet.

As Dee's pregnancy progressed into the third trimester, she settled down and took on a more peaceful aura. Her sisters spent as much time with her as possible, and Carl did not let up on his hours at work. Dee stopped complaining about his hours, and when she wasn't doing chores or cooking, she read magazine articles about successful birthing and child rearing. She also started bonding with her unborn baby, often talking to him/her and promising to be a good mother to him/her.

For a young woman who grew up on a farm, she felt that their little apartment would not do at all. One night after they had gone to bed, Dee laid a hand softly on Carl's shoulder. He was facing away from her on his side and at her touch his eyes instantly opened wide. "You okay, Dee? Is everything all right?" He rolled over to face her.

"I'm okay. We're okay. Don't worry, please." She let a few seconds go by before continuing. "I was wondering about having our own place, Honey. Somewhere that gives our baby a chance to play outside as he or she grows."

"I'd like that, Dee. But right now, I'm not makin' that much, and we can barely afford the rent on this place. If somethin' happens, then we've only got enough saved to help with baby expenses. I mean, having the baby. There's no room for using the money for a down payment on a house. I plan on using the GI Bill loan guaranty when we've saved a bit more money in a year or two, and I'm making better pay. We should make do right here until then." He thought the matter was addressed and started to roll over. She caught him by the shoulder again.

"Listen to me, Carl. If there's a way for us to have our own place, big enough for a young family, we should take it. I don't want to have our baby in this tiny place." Dee thought that a change of location would do her good and she wanted a place they could call their own. She knew that Carl wouldn't deny her anything within his power to provide. She had just turned nineteen, and wanted what she wanted, needed what she needed. Anything to move her away from her shame.

"Dee, most people start out like this and work their way up in life. Please show a bit more patience!" Carl's calculus was that his wife would show some reason.

"I'm not talkin' about other people. I'm talkin' about ME!" She raised her voice and continued. "I feel like you don't care about what I say." Carl's expression was that of a wounded child. She knew that she had hit him in the right spot. She had an uncontrollable urge to hurt him, and yet, the moment it was done she regretted it. She loved him as much as she could love and trust anyone in this world. "I'm sorry, Carl, I didn't mean that. It's just the pregnancy." She reached for his hand, and they embraced quietly and for several moments. But now, she had another reason to be ashamed, and a mental and emotional tug of war thereafter ensued… all grounded in Uncle Basil's actions and Jack's ignorance.

But Carl, much as he needed to advance his knowledge and skills, also needed his family, and Dee in particular, to love and to love him. His youthful optimism about family and work gradually morphed into a combination of dogged determination for a career mixed with an ongoing capitulation to trade for happiness with family.

The next morning, after a fitful sleep, Carl looked into Dee's eyes as they lay in bed as he put his hand on her cheek and said, "It's okay, Honey. I'll get the paperwork going on the VA loan guaranty and we'll find something we can afford for little or no down money. It may take some time, perhaps a year, but I'll do it."

Dee hugged him and replied, "Thank you, darling. When we have our own place, with our own baby, you'll see how good that will be." She planted a quick kiss on his forehead, and with that, she got up and proceeded to make his breakfast while he got ready for work. She realized that the one thing she could never change about Carl, was his dedication to self-education and improving his skills. *'But he is right, that is how we get ahead,'* she reasoned. However, Dee always felt the strong pull of her secret self-loathing and mistrust of others against the more forthright desire she had to help her husband to help their family. This internal conflict was not perceived clearly by Carl, and Dee also could not understand it for what it was.

Toward the end of Dee's pregnancy, Carl made good on his promise and started the process of obtaining a loan guaranty for ninety percent of the price of a home. By July, he had worked at Nash Cabinets well over a year, and told Mr. Nash that he was due a raise and couldn't sustain his growing family on $1.50 per hour at forty hours per week, pointing out that he produced for the company and deserved the raise. After keeping Carl in suspense for a week, he agreed to a raise to $1.80 per hour. This allowed Carl to qualify to purchase a house with a maximum value of three thousand dollars. Carl and Dee went looking, followed the ads and talked to realtors, finally settling on an old brick house on Benton Street in an area that would be slated for urban renewal within five years, although Carl had no such knowledge at the time. The price was two thousand and eight hundred dollars. They moved into the house just after the baby was born.

Near midnight on a late September night, a baby boy was delivered to Dee and Carl at St. Mary's Hospital. Dee was exhausted from nine hours of labor, birthing a baby boy at over nine pounds. As per the custom of the time, Carl waited in the area reserved for fathers and relatives to be told of the results, and was only able to see the baby and mother when both were in the maternity ward bed.

Dee was exhausted to be sure. She had already refused to nurse the baby from her own body and had opted for warm milk formula in a bottle. The formula was a mixture of cow's milk, water, and carbohydrate additive. Avoiding breast feeding kept the infant and mother from bonding in that special way that breast-fed infants generally have with their mothers, and it was not yet commonly known that immune systems were generally stronger in breast-fed babies. The phrase 'Mother's Milk is Best' had not yet caught on.

Carl was shown into the room, which contained four maternity beds and an ample curtain screen for vision privacy but hardly for noise. It was four in the morning, and their new son was about to be fed as the nurse brought him into the room on the heels of Dad. Carl stared in wonder at the bundled infant until he was handed over to Dee, who slowly sat up to hold him and receive the prepared formula from the nurse. "There you are, darling. Your beautiful and healthy baby boy! May you be a blessing to each other in God's eyes." The nurse was a Catholic Hospital Sister, and even though Carl and Dee were definitely not Catholic, neither of them minded this fact.

"Thank you, Sister," said Carl, and he leaned over to kiss Dee as the Sister walked out. "How are you doing, Honey?"

"How do you think I'm doing, Carl? So many hours of labor, and a really big baby, and my body will never be the same!" Carl's enthusiasm was undeterred.

"He's a strong looking boy. What shall we name him? Maybe something from each side of our families?"

Dee looked up from her feeding infant, "I love him already. We've got to make sure he has a proper education, Carl. I want to teach him to read and write before he goes to school. But I don't know much about mothering." Dee felt genuine love, but had serious doubts about being a good mother.

"I know you'll do fine, Dee. You're starting at the right place which is love. The rest will follow naturally." He saw the doubt on her face. "What about Wesley Loran Doe? Names from both of his grandfathers." Inside, Dee abhorred the thought of using any of Jack's names, given or family. But she couldn't think of a good reason to object without discussing the reason with Carl. "You know, it seems a shame that I never got to meet him. That's got to change. Wesley needs a grandfather in his life, doesn't he?"

Dee's eyes shot daggers at Carl. "My dad is not good grandfather material! Why do you think I don't have anything to do with him? He ignored me all my life before and after my mother died." She was getting too close to blurt out the truth, and hastily added in a more conciliatory tone, "Well, if you insist, we will try but only when Wesley is a year old or more." This was said more to keep him off her back on the issue and to buy time.

"Agreed, Dee. We're moving into our new house and have a new baby, and we have to settle into our lives with another mouth to feed! But I would like for our son and his grandfather to meet before our son is walking and talking and starts to have memories of his own. Is that okay with you?" He looked at Dee with honesty and a bit of pleading in his tone. Such a happy event was being spoiled and he wasn't sure why.

Of course, Dee's worst nightmare was that Jack would trip up and disclose her secret. Her abuse as a child wasn't her fault, but she was adamant that it was something that absolutely couldn't be shared with anyone. '*I must have a 'Come to Jesus's talk with Dad before this all gets too cozy.*' Use Wesley as leverage to keep Jack quiet on the subject, she figured. And that's what she would do.

They moved into the house on Benton Street in October, and furnished it with second-hand furniture, some of which Carl was able to enhance with his skills. But it soon became apparent that while Carl was very attentive to mother and baby when he was around, he wasn't around all that much because of long hours at work. Dee sank into a post-partem depression, going through the motions of cooking, cleaning, and caring for the baby with little to no enthusiasm. Contact with her two sisters nearly ceased. Carl was not blind to this, but at twenty-two years old, he was not equipped to deal with it. He continued to work long hours for the extra bit of money provided by his employer, but it was soon evident that no further adjustments were to be made on pay.

The couple and their infant moved into the old brick house in a neighborhood pockmarked with empty lots and visible dilapidation. But thanks to the GI Bill, it was theirs. Clothes were washed with a washing board, cooking was electric on a small stove and oven, and the pipes froze in winter. It was a two-story house with a narrow and steep stairwell, dating back to the post-Civil War years. In the basement was a small coal furnace to heat the house and it always needed tending.

One Saturday evening, a year after Wesley's birth, Carl took an extra-long time to walk to the store for a few necessities. He needed to think. Of course, he mistakenly assumed that the real cause of Dee's problems was his long hours at work, trying to build a future. The secret held by Dee was taking its toll. '*I'll talk to Gay and Lee and see if they can visit Dee to cheer her up. And next year, we can invite Jack to visit his grandson. But what do I do about work? We can't afford a step down, only a step up. Anyway, I won't have it!*'

Carl knew that he wanted to expand his skills by working with a range of materials such as fiberglass, metals, plastics. Shaping them and combining them with his growing expertise in wood and finishes was where his creative drive and craft interests lay. But where to do that? And how to move up? He vowed to begin researching employers in the greater St. Louis area and to bring Dee out of her slump, as he saw it. By the beginning of 1950, the stage had been set for improving things at home and giving direction to Carl for his next move.

When Carl approached Gay and Lee about visiting Dee, they were concerned about her and vowed to pay regular visits and to get her out of the house. Wesley was turning two years old soon, and was able to be walked in a stroller though he had already taken first independent steps at just under one year. And Dee was pregnant with their second child, so the pressure to make more money ate at Carl's enthusiasm. He was proud of his growing family and couldn't figure out why Dee didn't express her own enthusiasm more often. It was a question that he simply wasn't equipped to ask.

He investigated alternative career and training paths and the aircraft industry, which had been and continued to be robust in the St. Louis area, offered just the right kind of opportunity. McDonnell Aircraft Corporation was a large employer and had facilities located at Lambert Field and elsewhere. Their booming mainstay was the fighter jet market and Carl learned that the company accepted promising young talent to learn work in the mock-up and modelling phase of aircraft development. The tools and materials, and the techniques, that he would be exposed to would surely help him to elevate his career, he reckoned.

When he discussed it with Dee, he found that anything that promised more money and a better standard of living was good with her, adding that she would be so proud of him if he was to move up like that. Of course, that was all the moral support Carl needed. But he didn't know anyone at McDonnell so he would have to make a frontal assault.

He spent three weeks putting together his application and stressed his love of working with wood and desire to work with other materials, assuring the company that he would be a fast learner and a reliable worker who would always be ready to go above and beyond.

He was turned down. No reason was given. When he asked the personnel office about it the answer he got was "We have dozens of qualified applicants for each position." As was his style and character, he simply began designing a different approach to achieve his goal—to become an aviation industry mock-up technician. Mock-up was done by hand in those days, with the application of basic geometry and trig and the knowledge of precision instruments and how to use them effectively. It was labor-intensive. *This can all be learned,* he thought. So as his daughter Gwen was born in 1950, close upon the heels of his rejection by McDonnell, Carl began learning what instruments and techniques he would need to know so that he could qualify for entry level employment and training. The money would be better than the sweatshop in which he labored so many hours per week, including many weekend days.

The three couples started spending more time together as weekend work allowed at each other's places over the following months and this seemed to cheer Dee up a bit. They would play cards, talk about Truman, the Korean war, the price of baby formula, and just about anything but themselves while consuming a case of beer. One afternoon, as little Gwen slept the sleep of a baby in the next room, Wesley toddled into the room from where he had been playing with some toys on the floor, and without anyone noticing, he began to mimic the adults by hoisting the beer bottles one by one and draining the last drops left behind by the adults in each. After succeeding in draining twelve or thirteen bottles, half the case, he plopped onto his butt. Dee and the others turned to look at him and could see he was a bit tipsy.

"Goddamn! He's gonna make a real Marine," said Preston in his gravelly voice.

"Oh my God," laughed Lee. "Wesley's gonna be an alcoholic!" She kept laughing and the toddler smiled. Carl got up. Silently and gently, he picked up Wesley, who promptly peed so that it ran down his little leg and made a significant puddle on the floor. Dee was not amused that her son, albeit a two-year old, had raided the beer bottles.

"I don't think it's funny. What's so funny about a two-year old drunk?" She took Wesley from Carl's hands and scolded him into the next room where she changed his soiled clothes.

That scared him a bit but he didn't cry.

"He's still a baby, Dee." Carl reminded her, but her mood was totally soured.

The group began to go bowling each week, which was the one outside entertainment they could afford. The kids now included Wesley, Gwen, and Danny, who was Gay's first child, and well as Donna, when she wasn't visiting her natural father. They all provided a children's gallery and needed constant attention from the three sisters.

As Thanksgiving and Christmas approached, Carl reached out to Jack by telephone. He decided discussing it with Dee would not be effective, and he was determined to unite his children with their only living grandparent. Jack was now fifty-two, living in Paragould and working full-time as a deputy sheriff. It had not been hard for Carl to locate him in the phonebook.

"Jack, this is Carl your son-in-law."

"Is something wrong?"

"Well, the only thing wrong is that you and your grandchildren haven't met!"

Carl couldn't have known, but his response had triggered a tidal wave of emotion in Jack, who remembered his episode with the shotgun and his vow to be a grandfather. His eyes started to tear up, but his voice was unbroken.

"You know that Dee and I aren't speaking. Did she tell you why?" he asked in an even voice.

"No, she never told me and I never pried after it was clear to me that she would retreat inside herself whenever the subject came up, so I stopped asking."

"Does she know that you're calling me?

"No. But I want our kids to know their grandpa. Three out of four passed many years ago. You're it, Jack. Want to be a family?"

There was a pause and then Jack laid out his condition. "I'll be happy, very happy, to be a grandfather to your children and to her sisters' children if they'll let me. But I have to hear it from Dee, and you'll have to tell her you called me. If she gives me a 'yes' on the phone, I'll be up there directly. I reckon that's the best I can do."

Carl was now on the spot and there was only one thing he could do. "Yes, Jack, I'll tell Dee and plead with her to let you into our lives, or she has to tell me what it is between you two. You're not going to, are you?"

"I won't, even if pig shit turns pink. And I ain't never ever seen pink pig shit. What are they, boy or girl or both? How old are they?"

"Wesley Loran, middle name in your honor, is two, and Gwendolen Gay is six months old."

Jack, who had long since given up on the existence of God, thought '*There is a God. I have a grandson! I can be a grandfather to their kids!*' Jack remembered himself and said, "Just remember what I told you. She must invite me in, or I don't make a move much as I'd like to." He bore his own secret of the shotgun and his despair.

"Fair enough, Jack. Christmas is coming soon and there can't be a better time to get together. I'll talk to Dee right away." His positive tone did not betray the trepidation in his heart.

"Well, I'm not going anywhere. She knows how to reach me. And thanks for the news, Carl." With that, he hung up, always a man of few words and hidden emotions. Carl was left to ponder how to broach the subject with Dee, who was worn with the care of a baby and toddler and clearly bothered by something. Carl, after so many years in the wilderness with no family support and no guideposts on much of human behavior, simply wanted everything to be okay. He began to smoke two packs of cigarettes per day in worry that it would be so.

Christmas Day, 1950, saw a real family settling at the crumbling brick house on Benton Street. Everything seemed to be cooperating. A light snow provided a White Christmas. Carl had picked a six-foot tree from a tree lot for half a day's pay and grumbled all the way home, carrying the tree because he had no car. But the selection of store-bought and homemade tree ornaments, strung popcorn, glitter 'icicles' and lights provided ample cheer in their small living room. Jack had contributed to the cost of decorations and doted on his grandchildren, particularly on Wesley. They were his penance for being a failure as a father. Dee barely tolerated his presence.

This reunion remained tense between Dee and Jack, and they never resolved the issue between them as long as they lived. Being around each other for the sake of the children simply meant that they had to tolerate each other's presence. Their emotional dysfunction blinded them to the effects this ultimately had on the kids, and upon Carl. Dee had become too comfortable in her self-loathing and victimization bubble, and Jack hadn't apologized or said 'I love you' to anyone, save Ima, since he was a child himself. It was a perfect recipe for a sustained armed truce, and eventually, everyone saw it for the charade it was. But Jack's enthusiasm for bouncing his grandchildren on his knee and buying them toys and sweets was real. That was obvious. Dee's desire to see her children happy at such a young age was also real. It was enough for Carl to reduce his stress level down to a pack a day.

Jack also spent time with Gay and Lee and their children when he visited St. Louis every six months during the next two years, as he was able to get enough time off from his part-time deputy sheriff's job, basically the town's jailer, so that he could visit. In the summer visits he and Carl, and sometimes Preston or Earl, even went to a few of the National League Cardinals games at the old Sportsman's Park which the team had rented from the American League St. Louis Browns. It was still in the era of the smell of freshly cut grass, rusting iron pillars, hot dogs, popcorn, and beer with a whiff of sweaty cowhide in the air. All the trappings of Heaven for those who loved the game.

Two years came and went. Christmas of 1952 arrived. Jack had just arisen from his bed on the couch at Benton Street on a frosty day after Christmas and Dee showed up by herself with a coffee in hand for each of them. She sat down after handing Jack his coffee, to which he nodded his head in thanks, and looked levelly at him as if she saw something beyond his position.

"This is the last Christmas you'll have in our home. We'll bring the children to see you in Paragould or wherever it is you will be. I'm not letting Paragould or the farm into my house anymore, but I'll let my family into your neighborhood when it's convenient for us. Sorry, but that's the way it is." There was no apology in her voice.

"You mean when it's convenient for you. What's Carl got to say about it?"

"He doesn't have a say. It's my decision and the only way you and the kids get to see each other." Jack simply shook his head from side to side slowly in disapproval, then arose to prepare for leaving. "I'll take the first train or bus I can catch for home."

"Aren't you gonna spend your last day here with the kids?"

"Won't stay where I'm not wanted, especially by my own kin. I'll be out of here in thirty minutes. You can visit when you want to." He proceeded to collect his things and head for the bathroom. "Don't say anything more, Dee. Said enough already. I'm through letting you pin things on me. You don't know what it takes to farm forty acres as a tenant and provide for four daughters all alone. You think I could be everywhere? See everything? You had enough to eat, a roof over your head, schoolin', sisters, and clothes on your back. So shut up about things you don't know about."

Dee had a look of consternation on her face bordering on worry, as she quickly retreated up the stairs without a word. Jack let himself out twenty minutes later. Dee wondered what she would tell Carl and Wesley. Gwen was still a toddler. Carl stirred at the uncharacteristically late hour of six-thirty but it was still a seven thirty a.m. work call at Nash's.

"Where's Jack?"

"He had to leave all of a sudden, wouldn't say why." She busied herself by starting breakfast.

"Are you ever gonna tell me what's between you and him? I'm your husband, Dee, you shouldn't hold back on something important! I need to understand. And what will we say to the kids?"

"We're here and he's there. I don't want him in our life here. Sometimes, he can have us in his life there! Or are you too much of a moron to understand that?"

Carl picked up his lunchbox and Thermos of coffee, put on his coat and made for the door.

"What I understand is that I'm going now, and what is it that I'm supposed to understand?" With that, he walked out the back door and slammed it hard. Dee jumped, startled by the ferocity of the door slamming.

Chapter 14
Breakout, 1952–1953

November 4th, 1952, was election Tuesday, and Carl was proud to cast his first ever vote in a national election. He wanted to instill a love of country and democracy in his young son, who at the age of four, knew something big was going on as Carl walked hand in hand with Wesley down the crowded streets to the polling station a few blocks away. He asked his father what voting was and why was it happening now?

"Everybody who's old enough can vote, meaning I get to tell America who I want to be president of this country. It's my right to vote the way I want to vote, for whatever man I chose to be the next President of the United States. That's something to fight for, son. We're a democracy, which means every adult has the right to vote." Carl knew that practically speaking not everybody had the access to voting that he had. But his four-year-old son didn't need to know about it just yet. It would be over a decade before Congress would pass a law to implement the principles defined in the Constitution thus enabling all eligible adults to exercise their right to vote. Even so, perfect execution of the principle was never completely attained as the individual states were able to run amuck if they so choose.

"How many men get to run for President?"

"Two, one Republican and one Democrat. They're the two groups who each put up a candidate every four years and tonight's the night to vote."

"What happens if one of the men doesn't win?"

"Nothing, but they can always try again."

"Can we get some candy on the way home?" The boy's priorities were well-defined.

"We'll see, Wesley, we'll see. Be patient, this is very important for your dad, and I want you to remember this night and especially when you learn what it means when you are older." In truth, Wesley never forgot that night, the only time in Carl's life that he voted for the Republican presidential candidate, retired General of the Army and Supreme Commander of Allied Forces in Europe in WWII, who had been wooed by both parties. Wesley at four figured that if it was important to his dad, then it was important and that was enough for him.

His dad's enthusiasm was embraced by the little boy. In his four-year-old's mind, his child's intuition told him that candy would be part of it.

After the election, Carl took a different approach to McDonnell Aircraft. The company was continuing to hire for its expanding work force and advertised training on the job as well as with select courses. Carl decided to write a short argument for why he should be hired to work in mock up where he could contribute from the outset while learning the skills and trad necessary to become 'the best' such technician they could have. He stressed his drive to get his high school equivalency, study the basic geometry and trigonometry that would be useful to his understanding of what the engineers required, and his now considerable skills handling wood as a material. "I see my future as being proficient with multiple materials such as plastics, metals, and fiberglass." This approach landed him an interview in late January of 1953, in the same week that Dwight Eisenhower was sworn in as the thirty-fourth President of the United States. Always present in his thoughts, was the drive to make a better life for his family, to provide a more normal path forward for everyone: Dee, Wesley, and Gwen. Carl triple-checked his writing, or rather his printing, to make sure that he wouldn't be embarrassed by a misspelled word or incorrect grammar. His attachment to his application did the trick.

McDonnell was a growing company, and in the process of expanding the total of their facilities including their administrative offices. At twenty-six, Carl was still young enough to be considered for the type of company grooming program being offered. He had to convince his interviewers that he wanted what McDonnell afforded him in professional training and job security, and in return, he would give the company his all to help it to be successful. The alternative would in his mind require relocation to California or possibly Texas to work in the same industry with one of McDonnell's competitors such as Lockheed.

He entered the cramped offices where the interview was to take place. They had hastily been erected during WWII, and were now undergoing expansion. The Cold War with the Soviets and the Korean War involving China acted as accelerants to the defense industry in America.

The arms race was on. Get ahead, stay ahead. Carl's interview was with two men. George Mills was the assistant personnel manager. Craig Halley had been sent by the airplane mock up department to participate, which was unusual. But the bold self-advertisement by Carl had drawn him into this meeting, and he wanted to evaluate the young man face to face. In the digital age, someone with Carl's background and education would have been weeded out by the 'system.' It's doubtful that human eyes would even see his application.

Mills was astute enough to know initiative when he saw it and had passed Carl's letter attachment and application form to Halley. If an applicant met basic requirements, then he would look for any indication that would distinguish him from the others. Halley had worked twenty-two years as an engineer managing mock-ups of various craft in aircraft development programs at three different companies, and had barely slept between 1940 and 1945. Mock-ups were essentially perfectly scaled models from miniature up to full-size. They provide what is termed 'high fidelity' practice and training environments for designers, pilots, technicians, and others, by employing mathematics and skilled tooling and manipulation of a range of materials. Carl knew that this was the technician slot where he would find a good fit to be productive and learn a lot.

When the three men sat down at a modest table with the two interviewers directly across from Carl, they saw on his face a sincerity without desperation. They also saw confidence but not cockiness. "Good morning, Mr. Doe. May we call you Carl?" Carl nodded a yes.

"Good morning, gentlemen and thank you for the opportunity to interview with you." Carl displayed a friendly smile and the three stood up to shake hands. After seating, the questions began.

Halley took the reins. "We've read your attached letter, Carl. Why do you want to work in mock-up at McDonnell?"

"Mr. Halley, I could tell you about my need to support my family or the desire to make more money. Both of these reasons are true, but the reason that I want to work at McDonnell is to learn about and become expert in using and shaping different materials for specific purposes.

There's nowhere better to do that than McDonnell. I know something about using wood and applying finishes, but I have much to learn about the other materials and I'm excited about that."

"Are you able to work extra hours if needed? We do pay overtime for all time worked over forty hours per week," added Mills.

"Just point me in the right direction and I'll get it done whatever it takes." With this, Carl laid his hands on the table, palms down and fingers slightly spread, a signal that said '*I've nothing to hide and what you see is what you get.*'

"You've a good service record and nearly five years as a cabinet maker and wood worker. We'll check with your current employer to verify your employment record, but I have to tell you George, Carl can start as soon as you can process him." He turned to face Carl and said, "If you accept the terms of employment to be given by George here, then you're in the training program for nine months and we'll see after that if you go permanent. Now, if you'll excuse me, I must return to the shop. Have to stay on schedule for the latest fighter jet!" He stood as did Carl and shook hands, then left the room.

Carl was about to levitate, but kept his calm enough to let Mills continue, who then said,

"Carl, I believe you will be a fine addition to the work force here at McDonnell. Here is a sheet that describes the general conditions of your employment for the position of mock-up technician trainee, which is as Craig told you a nine-month term. If you successfully complete the training, you will begin work with the position of Mock-Up Technician one, and with good work and behavior you can move up to higher levels with more demanding work and higher pay. However, the Company reserves the right to cancel your training program if you are seen to be unfit to proceed. The trainee pay is $2.60 per hour, and the odds of overtime during the training period are slim. Later is a different story. Can you live with those terms? This will all be in writing if you come back tomorrow to read and sign the employment papers."

Carl fairly jumped out of his chair to shake Mills' hand. "My answer is yes! Thank you for the opportunity, Mr. Mills. I won't let you down."

"It's not me you have to worry about letting down. It's Craig Halley, who's taken an instant shine to you. And *he* has to make old man McDonnell happy. Come back tomorrow at eleven a.m. and we'll do the paperwork then. Plan on spending a couple of hours here for preemployment processing. You'll start in two weeks, but mind you, we have to contact your current employer at Nash Cabinets to verify your record before we do all of that. I'll have my secretary get onto it right away." With that, he said, "Job well done, Carl. Craig knows his horseflesh, so to speak. The fact that this interview took so little time proves that you made an impression… and now you need to follow it up!" With that, he turned and left.

On the bus ride and walk home, Carl's head was full of competing needs. He would have to get a car, no doubt about it. Maybe they could move closer to work. Wesley was to start kindergarten in September. Gwen had just started talking at two and a half. Dee was always on him about time at work and more money. Well, here was more money per hour, and a forty-hour work week for at least the next nine months.

After some discussion with Dee, who reacted to the news by hugging Carl but saying nothing, it was decided to buy a used car and to delay Wesley's school until after New Year. This meant only half a year for kindergarten but that didn't trouble either of them because Dee, following in Ima's footsteps, had been teaching Wesley the beginning of reading and writing from the age of three. It was the most enjoyable part of being a mother for her, and a close bond between the two emerged as a result, however temporary that proved to be. Over and again, he heard from Dee that he would be the first of all the sisters' families to go to university and that set in his little boy's mind a critical goal, which he also bounced off of his aunts and uncles. He didn't really know what university was at that age, just like he didn't really understand why people voted in elections but if it was important to Mom and Dad, then it must be important. Dee had lit the fire of learning in Wesley, before she once more sank into the oblivion of self-loathing and despair. Sadly, those actions never resurfaced once Wesley started his school years.

But Carl had snared a real job opportunity that promised to aid him in his aspiration to become part of the American Middle Class. And he felt certain that he was going to make the most of it. When he reported for his first day of on-the-job-training at McDonnell, he saw Daddy Charles and Momma Nellie in his mind, as we walked across the employee parking lot. They were smiling at him. He stopped in his tracks and closed his eyes and relaxed for a moment to feel a wave of elation and love flow through him as had never happened to him.

It's gonna be all right, Momma and Daddy. The images dissolved and he opened his eyes.

The future beckoned.

Chapter 15
The Big Company and the American Dream
1953–1959

As the child's song goes, *"Old MacDonald had a farm…"* in this case, *"Old McDonnell had a firm…"* James McDonnell, known as Mac, had studied physics at Princeton and Aeronautical Engineering at M.I.T. He was also a pilot. Ultimately, his entrepreneurial drive led him to build one of the pre-eminent military and civilian aircraft companies of the Twentieth Century. His vision was transformative from 'aircraft' to 'aerospace.' The irony would not have been lost on Carl that the two of them had grown up in North and Central Arkansas, and that while Carl's parents worked the fields as cotton pickers, Mac's parents owned the cotton fields and a couple of mercantile stores. He served the McDonnells' interests as his father had done before him, and as he had done as a child. After a rocky start in the days of The Great Depression, Mac's company was now firmly ensconced as a major aircraft developer and manufacturer for all branches of the military except the Coast Guard.

And Carl was thoroughly enjoying his training with the company, unaware of the McDonnells' exploitation of his family.

"I can't believe how many resources are there!" He exclaimed to Dee one day after work/training. In a rare disclosure he added, "I can see myself someday as a real craftsman and artist at what I do." At twenty-seven, he remained full of youthful exuberance and optimism. But Carl was always motivated by what he could do above the consideration of money. In his mind, if he did good work and gained great skills, then the money would be there. Life had not taught him differently at that point. Perhaps, the ghosts of Charles and Nellie that lived in his mind had something to do with that. His aspiration wasn't rags to riches. It was rags to self-respect.

The company pushed the envelope in jet propulsion fighter aircraft, missile technology and attempted rotary craft development but in that it never succeeded. It was a company of ideas, always seeking the next level in speed, power, armament, versatility, and overall performance. In the case of missiles; ground to air, air to ground, and radar jamming. Carl's can-do temperament was suited for an innovative corporate culture, where ideas percolated up and where the will existed to experiment. That is, if you were an engineer or scientist. Technicians and skilled workers often had suggestions or ideas that were derided and then brought forward as the brainchild of engineers or supervisors. Suggestions and ideas from staff at his level were welcomed but rarely rewarded even with recognition. At Carl's level, you weren't connected in the way that allowed you to deserve it.

Building a full-scale mock-up of a fighter jet was no small feat of engineering and technical application through highly skilled techniques and effective selection of materials. The benefits of doing this were immense for pilot training and design refinement. These benefits included but were not limited to; ergonomics of the pilot environment and in some cases the navigator/weapons system officer, the instrumentation array itself, the optimization of pilot view from the cockpit, wind tunnel analysis to test the plane's aerodynamics before committing a test pilot to fly a prototype, and many more.

Carl had often dreamed of flying, wondering what it would really be like to pilot a craft. But that was never to be. However, the next best thing as far as he was concerned was to work with people who were innovative in producing machines for flight while at the same time, he garnered much knowledge and expertise in shaping materials to meet technical specifications. It was a blend of art and technology. Precision machine tools and micro-hand tools were mastered by him in two years of intensive on-the-job training, and at the end of that time, he received an array of tools and instruments from McDonnell that would aid him in any mock-up assignment in which he might be required to participate.

Dee noticed Carl's growing confidence and commitment to his craft. Her happiness was tied to his success to a great degree. And while she was an involved mother when the children were pre-school, and without conscious intent on her part, a screen emerged between her and her children as they matured. She began to emotionally withdraw from everyone, and this led to misplaced communications. When her son at age six decided to play an April Fool joke on her by serving her morning coffee, he put salt instead of sugar as he thought it would be funny. Dee did not share in the humor and screamed at him at the top of her voice.

"I'LL BRAIN YOU IF YOU EVER DO SOMETHING LIKE THAT AGAIN!" Her son felt like a criminal for pulling off a practical joke. He was sent in fear to his room for the rest of the day, wondering if he would ever really be 'brained' and Carl was asked to take the belt to him when he returned from work. While he didn't want to do it, Dee had to be placated or there would be hell to pay. She had still not calmed down from the morning. So, Wesley learned at an early age that his mother had no sense of humor, and that you could get severely punished for something in which you had nothing but good intentions, in this case, to share a laugh and move on to a real coffee for Mom. A different lesson should have been learned. He also learned that his daddy would do things that he didn't want to do to keep the peace with Mom.

It was a punishment that Carl took no pleasure in, nor did he really think there was a crime. But he was working so hard to get ahead and he was tired, and he had no real experience with dealing with child-rearing. His weakness was Dee. He wanted so much to please her and feel her pride in him. To his credit, he only took the belt to Wesley three times, but each time was at Dee's insistence, and two of those times Wesley knew he had done something wrong where a 'Go to your room without dinner' would have been a more commensurate punishment. Gwen, a quiet and malleable little girl, never received such punishment, and learned early not to follow her brother's lead in Dee's house.

Carl and Dee bought their first car, a green 1950 Plymouth sedan. Used cars held very little value in Missouri, and thus were more affordable. The Plymouth would service the family and allow Carl a more efficient means of getting to work. In 1954, the family sold the house on Benton Street and moved up to a 1940s bungalow with a front and back yard. Carl had just completed his nine months of initial training and was offered permanent employment as a mock-up technician.

It was a small three-bedroom house with one bathroom and a modest kitchen. Most importantly, there was a fenced-in back yard and that allowed for the family's first puppy, a black Cocker Spaniel named Cookie. For nearly two years, the Does stayed put. Wesley was already in his second school and in first grade and was beginning to experience his role as the 'new kid' in school. It meant being subjected to the inevitable intimidations and fights that ensued when he came to a new school, which happened ten times in grades one through twelve. As a result of the constant moving, his lasting friendships were with books, stories, and movies.

"I know we'll be happy here, Carl." Dee purred shortly after the move. "School's a short walk for Wesley, and there's a big yard for the kids to play in. They're already pestering us for a dog. We've got to get some new furniture and I want a washing machine for the laundry. And a professional portrait photograph of the kids." Dee had turned herself out in full make-up and dress to add to the image of an up-and-coming middle-class family. Carl was happy that Dee was happy.

"I'm making enough money for us to afford instalment purchases for the furniture and washing machine at Sears, so we can get to that right away. We should have Lee and Gay and their families over for a weekend visit, picnic meal in the yard. What do ya say?" He moved to put his arm around her waist.

"I don't think we'll be having them over here. We can keep going to Lee's or Gay's for visits and the kids can see their cousins then."

"We ought to have them for a visit once and a while. We're already going one way to Jack's in Paragould, and it's a long drive there and back. The kids will notice and wonder. Why don't we invite our relatives here?"

Dee pushed his hand away and said as she raised her voice, "Because I don't want them here! I don't need them here. It's enough that I go to see them. I don't want to talk about it!" And with that, she went to busy herself in the kitchen as the children came out of Wesley's room to see about lunch. Carl just stood there, perplexed and a bit hurt. He thought, this isn't right, not how it should be. But Carl had no idea how to fix things except to give in for everyone's sake, including Dee's. Every time that Carl discussed his work colleagues and budding friendships at work, Dee would see in his stories a threat to herself. As years passed, Carl knew instinctively that it was strange that Dee didn't develop any outside interests or cultivate even befriending neighbors who came to their door to welcome them to the neighborhoods. Except for shopping, doctor visits, and family outings, Dee didn't have any interactions with people. The frequent moves, always based upon Dee's severely expressed dissatisfaction with a place or the people in it, didn't help.

Carl knew that something was wrong, that Dee was never happy for long with any place to which they moved. In the years between 1950 and 1970, the family moved eleven times, more than once it was twice in one year. Dee and Carl succeeded in providing for their children, but never attained any locational stability until 1964, in California. Once Carl entered the Very Big Company in 1953 and began his real climb in expertise, the constant moving started. Through it all, he remained steadfast in his pursuit of excellence in his craft, because he knew it was the only way that his children would have opportunities never available to him or his brothers and sisters. And certainly not to his parents.

Professionally, Carl was in the right place at the right time. McDonnell Aircraft MA had two jet fighters successfully in service when he joined the company: the F2H Banshee and the F3H Demon. MA focused upon craft that could take off and land on aircraft carrier decks and be stored below deck efficiently and safely, but also maintain the kind of versatility for air to air and air to ground combat. Those features also made the jets attractive for the Air Force and Marines. In 1953, Carl's first assignment was to assist in mock-up work on the F101 Voodoo, which was designed as a long-range bomber escort for the emerging Strategic Air Command. Like the other MA fighter jet designs, the engines were under the fuselage which allowed for greater speed and thrust. Carl was required to learn how to use metals and micro-tools to make the smaller mock ups, and power tools, larger drills, and chisels to shape fiberglass, wood, and plastics to make the full-scale mock ups. Grinders, polishers, microtools and grades of sandpaper were employed for the small-scale mock ups that sat in display areas or on desks. Each mock-up was completely custom built.

Whenever Carl expressed an interest in expanding his knowledge and skills into a new area of work, MA responded with support. His drive, abilities, and enthusiasm for new challenges did not go unnoticed by management, and well into the development of the F4 II Phantom in the mid to late-fifties, he was ensconced in the technician hierarchy as a 'go to' figure for difficult assignments. The Cold war with the Soviet Union showed no signs of abating, and MA's development of versatile, high performance jet fighters gained the company a sufficient degree of respect and even admiration from the government and the military.

MA's attraction to the best and brightest aerospace engineers and designers was strong and competitive with the likes of Lockheed and Grumman.

A third and final child had been born to Carl and Dee in 1957, and he was a boy, Christopher Terry Doe. His was the only name of their children not associated with the families of Carl and Dee. By this time, Dee had become anti-social to all, save her nuclear family, and increasingly spoke of a desire to return to California to live the rest of their lives there. This excited the children, who were by then quite used to avoiding calling anywhere 'home' so that the allure of the Golden State was strong. But the needs of putting food on the table, sustaining three children, and continuing to grow in his unfinished career path impelled Carl to frustrate those discussions about California, which in turn frustrated Dee. The result was constant tension, and everyone felt it in their own way.

The F4 II Phantom had just been flown for the first time in 1958, and all signs were that it would be a big hit in the military markets. Carl received two class promotions and several raises in the years between 1953 and 1959, and by the end of that period, he was personally ready for a new challenge. One Sunday afternoon in 1958, he was fishing on the Missouri River with his son, Wesley. Much was on his mind, and as was his habit with his many fishing trips with his son throughout his life, Carl first concentrated upon the relaxation and escape of the fishing and the outdoors. After an initial period of largely quiet time, he usually tried to pass on to Wesley as much fatherly wisdom as he could muster at the age of thirty-three.

Much of it was grounded in Carl's memories of Grandpa Charles and the Wilsons. But Carl had always held back information about his real childhood until this day, when he deemed that his son would be ready to absorb more.

While sitting on a driftwood log the day after his tenth birthday side by side with his dad, Wesley watched the end of his new spinning rod as he waited for another bite. The Missouri River was half a mile wide at this point, and the brown waters flowed powerfully and steadily toward their merger with the Mississippi twenty miles eastward. This would be their last trip of the season on the Missouri because they would have to wait to fish these waters until the spring flooding abated seven months later. Carl's son sensed that the quiet time of the trip had been adequately observed.

"In this week's Weekly Reader at school, we learned about the Russians' space program. We don't have one yet, do we, Daddy?"

"Not really, Wesley, but we're working on it. There's lots of smart people working on it so don't worry about that." They both looked out onto the river's waters as they spoke.

"Well, I hope we do, and I hope we send men up there. I read the universe is so big, even our galaxy with the stars we can see, that we could never find out everything that's out there. I wish it was night and we could see the stars right now!"

"Never say never, Wesley. We only find out what we can do when we agree to say *never say never.* Don't forget that, ever." He put his hand briefly on Wesley's shoulder.

"Could you fly a plane into space?"

"No, because first there's no atmosphere thick enough to support the aerodynamics of winged aircraft. Second, the plane's cockpit would not protect you from the cold vacuum of space which is what's out there when you escape the Earth's atmosphere. Third, there isn't a plane around or on the drawing boards that would have the power to escape Earth's gravity and return. Follow?"

"Yes, Dad." But he didn't understand fully most of the details of these concepts. "So how are they gonna put someone in space?"

"Rockets. Powerful rockets to take someone up there. But bringing them back is tricky and whatever craft is designed and used will have to withstand pressure, re-entry heat and other issues that airplanes don't have to bother with in the atmosphere of this planet." Their eyes never left the river during the conversation.

But today, Wesley had something else on his mind. "What happened after Grandma Nellie died? Where did you go? Who looked after you?" Carl had previously lied about his age when he was made an orphan. He wasn't sure why, but he told the story to his children that he was orphaned at seven, when in fact, he was completely orphaned at eleven. He also omitted the fact that he changed the spelling of his name from Dough to Doe when he entered the Navy. For reasons known only to him, Carl never disclosed the real spelling of his family name to anyone after he changed it.

"Nobody at first." He answered curtly. "I lived with my sister Dorothy and her husband, Worlick, until I was eleven, then struck out on my own because I couldn't get along with Worlick." He intentionally mixed the years up thus throwing an intentioned fog into his son's mind. DNA had only recently been discovered and graphed in the double helix, so nobody at the time really knew how much it could reveal.

"How come? And what about your sister?" Carl had opened a can of worms, and Wesley was about to peer inside. The danger that Carl felt at that moment was palpable and drew a harsh response.

"That's all I will say about it. Stop asking, Wesley! Don't ask me about that again." He said this as he turned his face toward Wesley, who looked confused but obeyed his father on this.

Carl read the hurt in his son's face and immediately switched the subject in a genial tone, "You've caught a nice mudcat, good work, son! Let's see if we can get another two to make dinner. Even better, let's see if we can get one of those channel cats before we go home."

"Okay, Daddy," a relieved Wesley replied. "But what happened after Dorothy and Worlick? When you left them where did you go?" Questions were swirling around in his head, the kind that eventually must have an answer.

"Well, the only people that I could call Mom and Dad again took me in on their farm. Gant and Gurdy. I loved them and they taught me a lot." He didn't mention their son, leaving he impression that the two were childless.

"How long did you stay with them?" Wesley was reassured by the story.

"About four years."

"Is our family name really Doe? Everyone makes fun of it at school as they say it is not a real name." Wesley had been meaning to bring this up for some time and figured the time was right.

"My dad was an orphan and when he was a boy, he was taken in by an old woman named Dough, and he took her last name, so I don't really know what our family name is, and neither did my father." He correctly spelled the name D-O-U-G-H and that was the only time he did so.

"Oh." Wesley was left feeling thoroughly unsatisfied by this information. To him, the recounting of his father's childhood was filled with "I can't remember," or, "It was so long ago and nobody has any records." He knew not to press his dad further, and went back to concentrating on the fishing.

A month later, the newly formed National Aeronautics and Space Administration announced the Mercury manned mission, and the beginning of their effort to recruit astronauts for the missions that would include sub-orbital and orbital flights and full recovery of the craft and the astronauts. A month later, MA was awarded the contract for building the Mercury Capsule at their plant in St. Louis. The next day, Carl was called into the office of the head of the company's mock-up department.

"How would you like to work on the space capsule in mock-up, Carl?" he was asked. "It will be your only assignment for the next four or five years, and we'll be overseen by NASA all the way."

Without hesitation, Carl replied "You bet, sir. What I really mean is *Hell Yeah!* I'm all in if you want me."

"Well, since I just told you I want you, you're all in! We're hitting the ground running, and a full-scale mock-up of the initial design is required by the end of March. Long hours are certain. This is just the beginning. Is that a problem?" The answer was an emphatic head shake from side to side.

Carl Doe, cotton-picker, abused child, orphan, feral kid, and self-educated white trash castaway, had just entered the space age. Cheeks would have been proud.

Chapter 16
One of Four Hundred Thousand, 1958–1962

It has been noted by several chroniclers of the space race between the Soviet Union and the United States, that the U.S. effort at manned space flight ranging from Project Mercury to the Apollo missions to the moon a decade later involved four hundred thousand men and women working as a gigantic team. Carl had become one of the four hundred thousand. President John F. Kennedy in his inaugural address of January 20, 1961, knew that the Mercury program was advancing and would soon launch an astronaut. He clearly stated the vision and challenge to use the momentum of the moment to call for placing a man on the moon by the end of the decade, and returning him safely to Earth. The four hundred thousand plus a lot of money made that happen.

In the following weeks before Christmas, 1958, Carl and his teammates underwent a crash course in the initial design of the Mercury Capsule, which included functionality of the design and ergonomics of the instrumentation, and the pilot's very limited operating space. Then, the production engineers and their NASA monitors explained their thoughts about materials, both inside and outside of the capsule, during several presentations given to a mixed audience of engineers and technicians. At the last presentation before New Year, Carl raised his hand to ask a question of the Chief Production Engineer, a man in his late fifties with steely gray sweptback hair and a hawkish gaze.

"Will we be required to do some of our fabrication and fitting inside the mock-up?" he asked.

"What's your name, son?"

"Carl Doe, sir." He stood up as he said his name and there were a couple of low-level laughs from the crowd.

"That's a good question, Carl. Our plan is to avoid fabrication inside the mock -up and to fabricate and shape all parts and components, including the pilot's, er, the astronaut's seat in the workshop to be installed in the mock-up. I hear that you're particularly skilled with wood, copper, and brass. I look forward to your input as we progress." This pleased Carl and he swelled with pride to hear this from the top production engineer in charge of everything including mock-ups. His peers were watching. *'Get a grip on yourself! It's what you do that counts.'* He was well-aware that engineers, especially program directors, didn't usually ask for the opinions of technicians.

Later that day, after work and at dinner, he was sitting at the table with Dee and the three children. He suddenly wore a grin as he looked down at his plate.

"What's so funny, Carl?" asked Dee. "Fried chicken not good enough tonight?"

"It's not that, Dee. I was just thinking about something that happened at work today."

"What happened, Daddy?" Wesley wanted to know. "Somethin' funny?"

"Just something that makes me feel good when I think about it, Wesley. The head of production for the Mercury Capsule Program singled me out for a compliment in front of my co-workers. He didn't have to do that. I'm surprised he knows who I am."

"He probably wants something from you, to do more work for less money or have you snitch on your brothers." Dee's tone of voice conveyed the surety of one who has made up their mind, without a hint of either conjecture or evidence.

"It's not like that." Carl was stunned. "He wouldn't have even said anything if I hadn't asked him a work-related question at his presentation."

"You'd just believe whatever they say, you're so gullible sometimes." The instant Dee said this, she regretted it. She didn't know why she lashed out or demeaned people, especially her family. It was always a knee-jerk reaction. The kids were confused, none of them old enough to say anything directly or ask their mother what she meant.

"Sometimes, Dee, people actually say what they mean, and aren't always trying to gain some advantage over you. I've worked hard to get to this point, and I've got to give it all I've got and learn as much as I can. That's how we get ahead, Honey. I never got ahead by playing politics or by doing someone else in and never will." He spoke patiently, as if explaining himself would solve the problem.

"You don't give a damn what I say or think!" In front of the children, she got up noisily and carried her plate to the sink. Wesley and Gwen knew to follow her. One would wash and one would dry. They had been taught to perform this chore after dinner the year prior. If you dropped a dish or glass and it broke, you were not forgiven. Carl slowly finished his dinner and left for the TV.

When the kids were in bed at eight-thirty, Dee came up behind Carl and put her arms around his neck as she whispered in his ear, "I'm proud of you, Honey. I didn't mean to say I wasn't."

"I know, Dee. It's important that the kids know that, too."

"Why aren't you angry with me? You should be. You never get upset, no matter what I do. I wonder if you care."

"Maybe you and I should speak more about what I do at work. You'll understand what's happening. But not in front of the kids, just us."

"All right. The kids are in bed, already asleep. Let's start now. I want to know everything." She knew that Carl wouldn't embellish or mislead, he would give her straight talk. "Just don't talk down to me."

"Dee, Honey, you're far too smart for that. And if I go slow and deliberate, it's just because that's how I do it with everybody, because I always want to get it right."

"Let's get started, then!" Dee's spirits were lifted. It was a chance to escape her boredom and negative thoughts, even if just for a little while. They coped with their problems by diverting themselves to something positive, which in turn left problems unsolved and issues unattended.

Carl worked with total commitment on the mock-up team to complete a full-scale model of the capsule for the required reveal to the NASA team in late March, 1959. The team was in a rush and the mock-up astronaut seat had become a materials issue. Everyone understood that eventually, the seat would have to be custom fitted for each astronaut but for purposes of evaluating progress, a perfectly contoured seat had to be completed on time.

In February, the technicians working on fiberglass seating were having issues of contouring the seat to specifications. Carl approached his supervisor and suggested he be given a try at using wood for the mock-up, because it could easily be shaped to technical specs in sections and form the basis for a moulded seat, which was the ultimate use. Jack, his supervisor, was a mother hen to his team members.

"Hey Jack! I've been thinking that," he was cut off before he could finish. But Jack smiled as he interrupted.

"We're in trouble now," he smiled, "Carl's been thinking again! What's on your mind boy?"

"I know that fiberglass has its uses and a great future as a core material, but this job can't be done in time using the techniques available right now. I believe that in fairly short order we could fabricate a contoured wood seat with laminated sections, to meet the curve requirements in the drawings and stay on time for March 17. We can do that without learning any new tooling techniques."

"Okay. Now that you've opened your pie hole, walk me through a step by step how you think we can do this in three weeks and install it in the mock-up."

"Well, happy to do that Jack, but let me get some paper and pencil." Carl fetched paper and pencil and explained, with drawings, how that would be done and how many people it would take. Most important, he mapped out a work schedule that would allow three techs to get it done in two weeks. Jack saw that he had clearly given this a lot of thought. "It's a mock-up, right? Nobody's gonna make an astronaut seat out of wood to send into space, but we can shape the seat to the requirements of each astronaut very quickly and accurately with wood to go on to use that for a mould or as a model for other materials."

"You may have something, Carl. Let's see the Director of Mock-up right away and see what he decides. If it's a go, then you're going to work on it."

The Director was suitably impressed and ordered a three-man team to begin work at once to select the hardwood, heat bonding, and final shaping. "But be warned," he cautioned, "The results must be just right mathematically and technically. Now, get to it and good luck!" Two weeks later, the oak seat in four sections bonded with heat and epoxy was delivered for installation in the mock-up of the capsule. The Director was pleased and gave the credit to Carl's supervisor, who in turn apologized to Carl. It was commonly known that the solution to the time and materials on the seat was at Carl's initiative, and his co-workers generally patted him on the back. But at that time in America's workplace, credit did not always go where credit was due. Carl continued to consider himself a well-paid peon, but nevertheless a peon.

That was the point in his life at which he committed to the goal of ultimately working for himself once the kids were out of high school, and would no longer be at the risk of any potential business failure and his family would be less reliant upon steady income. *Ten years,* he thought.

In April, NASA announced their selection of the Original 7, America's first men in space. It was on for real now. The Mock-Up Inspection Board toured and reviewed the full-scale mock-up as scheduled in March and the outcome was a list of desired improvements in the functionality of the cockpit concerning instrumentation array, astronaut environment, and escape or egress. Over the next three years, there would be many Mercury meetings of the Inspection Board at the MA facilities and many interactions with the individual astronauts on the part of the mock-up team.

At the end of 1959, the family moved to a farmhouse a couple of miles outside of St. Charles, a suburb of St. Louis that sits across the Missouri River. In those days it was still a small town surrounded by farms and country estates. The two-storey white farmhouse with a full basement and small barn was no longer a functioning farm home. The family rented the house with a nearby creek where the kids caught crayfish and perch, petted horses and the imported Brahma cattle, and ran in nearby cornfields. Wesley and Gwen rode a school bus for the two miles into town, while Chris the toddler stayed with Dee. All considered, it was the high point in their childhood. With the additional income from Carl, they were able to buy antique oak dining and other furniture that Carl refinished for Dee. An upscale auto, a Chrysler Saratoga, was acquired to replace the 1956 Plymouth station wagon.

But now in his mind, Carl knew that he was reaching the peak of what he would be allowed to do in the space program at MA and that there really wouldn't be any further mountains to climb. An artistic and creative siren sang in his head, and he began to follow it on a long road, with a sense of responsibility and a well of common sense accompanying him on the journey. It was during this time at the white farmhouse that he began to expand his work outside of MA, to include word of mouth business on the side as a furniture refinisher and antique restorer. It was a beginning.

After he acquired an old compressor and spray apparatus, Carl kept busy about twenty hours a week in addition to his Mercury Project work. His first major job was to rebuild and refinish an oak pump organ built in the 1880s. From there, he went on to rebuilding and refinishing antique dining sets, beds, chairs, tables and other items up to two hundred years old. He kept his fees low for trade reasons, which made Dee upset.

"I don't understand, Carl. You could be charging thirty or forty per cent more for such good work and it takes your free time away from us." Her tone was always as if he had done something wrong or even something stupid.

Carl's responses became less defensive and more dismissive. "I've got to finish this work," or, "If we're going to California someday, we'll need a bigger nest egg." And then, he would simply walk away to work at MA or in the barn with the restoration work.

Dee's self-isolation form the world was only breached in controlled visits to relatives, including Jack in Paragould. The kids loved visiting him and now that he had his own forty acres thirty minutes' drive on gravel county roads from Paragould, they couldn't wait to spend time there. Twenty acres of hardwoods and twenty acres of corn was like catnip to them. Gwen loved feeding the chickens and playing outside when it wasn't too cold, and if she had to sit by the pot-bellied stove as wood burned, Jack would take her on his knee and rock with her in the chair. As a bonus for twelve-year-old Wesley, Jack taught him how to shoot a twenty-gauge shotgun and hunt quail, rabbit, and squirrel. That's when Wesley found out that he didn't like the feeling he had after he hit the target animal, and thus he never became a hunter. Dee relented to the visits but never warmed.

In May, 1960, Carl took Wesley on a two-day fishing trip to the Busch outdoor reserve that was open to the public for camping, hunting, and fishing in its many lakes and ponds. It was vast, one hour from St. Charles, and gave them plenty of space to be alone. After setting up their gear and sleeping arrangements in the car, Carl built a fire and they sat for a while looking at the stars and the half-moon and listening to the sounds of night. Frogs were making their croaking calls and many species of birds were making their various noises as they settled into their evening. Owls hooted to round out the symphony of the setting sun which had just disappeared over the horizon.

"Dad?" Wesley had a question. "Do you think we'll get our astronauts into space?"

"We will, for sure. It's just a matter of time. Better to do it right and do it best. You understand?"

"I think so. You always try to do your best, that's what you tell us in Little League. It's just that so much is happening. Russians saying they're gonna bury us. Atomic bombs. Negroes getting sicked on by dogs in the streets. I just was wondering how we manage to do the rest, like putting men in space."

"Well, your country, the good ol' USA, isn't perfect for sure. But if it weren't for us, the world would be in much worse shape. And remember, we get to choose our leaders based upon the majority of votes. Don't forget that President Eisenhour ordered integration of the schools and backed it up. We voted him in, and he did his job on that point. There's other things I'm not so happy about." While majority victory wasn't always true because of the role of the Electoral College, it was a principal belief that Carl would not yield upon. "And he was re-elected in 1956."

"Did you vote for him again?"

"No, I voted for the Democrat, Adlai Stevenson."

"Why?"

"Because Ike is a Republican, and Republicans are always for the rich man."

"So why did you vote for him before, Dad?"

"Well, Wesley, everyone makes mistakes. Mine was believing he would be a different Republican when it came to the common man, and he was such an effective leader in the war. But that wasn't the case, and I had my blinders on. Now, Senator Kennedy might be the Democrats' candidate. We'll know after August. I like what he stands for, even though he's a millionaire! And he's young to be President of the United States. But he proved what kind of man he is when he risked his life to care for his injured crew on PT109. How a man acts when things go wrong is much more important than how they behave when swimmin' in success and money. And just about anybody would be better than Tricky Dick."

"Yeah, I saw him on T.V. when they did a report about his torpedo boat and what happened." In Wesley's boy mind, the image of self-sacrifice and heroism was irresistible as the awe in his tone presented. "He's also talkin' about doing better on Civil Rights and I've been seeing a lot about that, too."

Carl suddenly remembered his daddy's words of warning long ago just off the cotton fields in Northern Arkansas. But now the times felt different. "It's a new age now, Wesley. The right ideas are coming forward. But be mindful that it will be a struggle for all of us to get to the place that we're supposed to be. People will be hurt, killed. But a society where all have equal opportunity and respect and are equally dealt with under law is worth it."

"I believe that, too." Wesley at the age of twelve was already interested in the issue of oppression and had begun to read '*The Rise and Fall of the Third Reich*' by William Shirer. He could hardly put it down unless he made one of his frequent reference visits to the dictionary.

"Nobody is free unless everyone is free. That's where America needs to go." That was to be Carl's final word on the subject. His son had other ideas.

"Yeah, but why would you sick dogs on people in the streets if we are so free?"

"Like I said, son, we aren't perfect but most of us are trying to live up to *all men are created equal,* and should have the same rights. But there are always men who want to keep others down, and some of them want to keep the Negroes down more than anything, because they're holding on to their need to feel superior. So, you'll see that those men will do just about ANYTHING, and I mean anything to make sure that whites and blacks can't live on an equal footing."

"Why do you hate Worlick so much, Dad? Why didn't Dorothy stand up for you as her younger brother? And why can't we see my aunts and uncles?" Wesley's voice wasn't angry or accusatory. He was genuinely curious.

"Worlick was a bully who lived off my hard work as a boy and treated my brother Charlie very badly. He beat anybody who didn't do exactly as he said." Carl looked away and made a half-sad and half/angry face that his son couldn't see. "Now, you're not to ask me anything more about it. Ever!"

Wesley grew quiet and tried to concentrate on his fishing for the rest of the trip. He tried his best to hide his frustration.

As Christmas of 1960 approached, shortly after Kennedy's victory in the presidential election, a buffet Christmas Party was held for the Mock-Up Team, management, NASA representatives and the Original Seven. It was held in the hall where three different mockups of the Mercury Space Capsule were displayed. It was possible to enter and sit in two of the models. The astronauts were given preference to take a seat in the mock-ups and they milled around in quiet discussion and occasional laughter at quips meant only for their ears.

This lasted half an hour.

Meanwhile, the rest of the crowd slowly gravitated each to their own familiar cohort.

However, the program director over loudspeaker encouraged people to mingle. "This is a team effort and a team celebration! Not a gathering of tribes." There was laughter in response to this, including the astronauts. "So, mingle and get to know something about your other team members! Thank you everybody, and Merry Christmas and Happy New Year to you all!"

Carl had worked with each of the astronauts and quickly realized one thing after meeting all seven. They were a bunch of over-achievers on career paths in their respective branches of the military and were highly competitive with each other to be 'first,' but once a decision would be made, they would all stand behind and support whoever was chosen for a mission.

When it came to his work, there were those in the group who listened and those who listened and also asked. The latter group included Shepard, Glenn, and Carpenter. It was also Carl's job to listen to their questions and take note of their suggestions on the hundreds of work issues related to making the craft as operational and efficient as possible. And the seat was paramount. Each astronaut's weight and measurements were the guide to a custom seat fitting that was critical for each astronaut and Carl was instrumental in making that happen in addition to all of his other project mock-up duties.

As he sipped a cola, Carl heard a familiar voice behind him. "Okay, Carl. Who's got the fattest ass among us? We're taking bets and you're the reliable source on the spot!" Gordon Cooper put his hand on Carl's shoulder with an *it's up to you* while nodding his head.

"We know who has the fattest head," said John Glenn as he walked toward the two and pointed at Cooper.

"Been lookin' in the mirror, John?" retorted Cooper. Seeing a cluster forming around Carl, two more astronauts joined the discussion; Grissom and Carpenter.

They all pleaded with Carl with mock sincerity that they just had to know as their honor could not be satisfied any other way. Carl held up his hand, a bit embarrassed by the attention as others in the crowd noticed the group growing around him.

"Gentlemen! Please, this information is a state secret and if I tell you, then they'll have to kill me. The knowledge of the biggest ass in the astronaut corps is that serious!"

They all laughed as Glenn said, "Guys, I think we have the makings of a politician here!"

Carl couldn't think of anything to say except, "Really, it's a great honor to be able to contribute something to the space program and to you guys. I'm not risking it all like you, and I want any of you who go up there to come back safely to your families. Excuse me." He walked away toward a couple of his mock-up teammates. Glenn just smiled and didn't say anything.

"Humble is as humble does," said Carpenter.

"Hmmm, now we know who has the biggest ass, Scott. The test pilot from so much sitting," quipped Cooper, and they dispersed to go on to other mingling.

A bit later, all seven astronauts were seated at a long table with stacks of color photographs of themselves in full NASA astronaut attire, each to autograph their photos to anyone present who wanted one. Carl hit the station of each astronaut and asked for an additional signature on a blank piece of paper, so that he could give it to Wesley as a Christmas present. When he came to Glenn, he was asked by the astronaut, "Can you spare a couple of minutes, Carl, before you go home? I know it's been a long day. I'll come and find you if that's okay."

Carl had no idea what Glenn could have in mind, but he couldn't deny the request out of respect for him. "No problem, John. I'll be nearby." Formalities of rank or even the use of Mr. had long since fallen by the wayside between front-line workers and astronauts. Carl collected his autographed photos and piece of paper and wandered nearby to talk to Martin and Jasper, two mock-up colleagues, and engaged in idle conversation with them. Soon, out of the corner of his eye, he saw Glenn rise from his chair and signal to Carl that it was clear for them to talk. People were starting to leave so the crowd was thinning out as Glenn motioned Carl to a spot along the wall.

"I don't want to keep you from your family, Carl. Thanks for agreeing to speak to me. Now, I don't mean to pry and if you think I'm off base, just tell me. I'm a Marine and I appreciate directness."

"I'm okay, John. I'll let you know if you're off base with me. But happy to do what I can. You've always been a straight shooter with me, and we've had a good working relationship."

Carl didn't know where this was going and tried his best to hide his growing anxiety about this talk.

"This may sound a bit corny, but I would like you to tell me in your own words what motivates you to work so hard and do so well at it besides a pay check. That's for starters."

"When you come from nothing, and where everyone expects you to end up dead or in jail, you either succumb to that image or you fight for something else. If you fight, you allow yourself to have your own dreams and goals. You do the best you can, and nobody can take that from you; what you know and what you do." Glenn stared at Carl and slightly nodded his head but said nothing.

Carl went on, "To be honest, John, the kind of work I do here is as close as I could get without a university degree. Those are options I never had a real chance to take. I love learning more and more about materials and shaping them for use. But there's a need I have to be more creative, and I believe I have found it."

"Outside of McDonnell?"

"Beyond this work. I can't tell you what that is right now, but there's a strong pull. And," he was interrupted.

"Your family comes first!" Glenn popped in.

"Yeah, you're right. A man has responsibilities first."

"Yes, he does, but that doesn't mean he can't pursue his dream, Carl. Thank you for agreeing to indulge my curiosity. May you and your family have a great Christmas!" With that, he shook Carl's hand and walked back to join his mates, who were once again readying a drinking crew among the astronauts and derided Glenn with laughter about his abstinence. Carl had no idea, but John Glenn had just performed his first political research and would eventually be a three-term U.S. Senator after failing twice in that effort, and would also become a failed presidential candidate.

It was a frosty evening when Carl arrived at the farmhouse. The orbital mission of John Glenn was fourteen months away, Alan Shepard's sub-orbital mission was five months away.

'When the orbital mission comes, I will have learned all I can here. That's when we go to California. That's where my business will be someday.' He walked the short distance in the freezing air to the house, his mind made up.

Dee was at the door. "I thought you'd be home two hours ago. Have you eaten? How was it?" she let him kiss her lightly on the cheek.

"It was good, Dee. I brought some things for us to keep." He reached into his twelve-inch envelope and pulled out two autographed pictures of John Glenn and Alan Shepard.

"Where are the others? Aren't there seven?"

"Got them all right here," and he pulled the paper with all seven autographs from the envelope. "I'll give this to Wesley so someday he can remember what a great effort his dad was a part of."

"So how much longer is Project Mercury tying us up here in St. Charles?" Carl's radar detected hostile craft on the horizon.

"Could be another two or three years, but I'm only gonna' stay until the first orbital flight, then we go to California."

Dee gave him a hug and asked, "Promise me?" She looked hard into his eyes.

"I promise, Dee. Until then, we will keep going as we are. If I'm gonna' be hired by an aerospace company in California, then I need some more experience at McDonnell first. How are the kids? I brought something home for Wesley."

"They're in bed. Carl, I can't stand it out here anymore. I want to move into town. Wesley and GG would stay in the same school. It's driving me batty out here."

"This is a great place for the kids, even for Chris at his age. We need to hold on for only another year or so and then move to California. But you know that it helps if I have job interviews lined up. And there's more aerospace in Southern California." Carl was pleading a case and wasn't sure if he was being heard.

"I want out of here now!" Carl knew the signs. Dee had been lethargic lately, not talkative.

She cut back on the complexities of meals and wasn't really engaged with the children. Carl had a panic feeling that everything they had worked for could come crashing down if they made the wrong move now.

"All right, we'll see what we can do about it." He surrendered as he always did in order to buy peace at home, not realizing that so many moves drained finances, energy, and left the kids without any ties outside the family. He simply tried to make everybody happy in the only way he knew how, since the two of them had little to no experience with a normal family life and never put Dee's childhood exploitation on the table so it could be dealt with. He lit a cigarette, sat down at the kitchen table and said, "I've got to wake Wesley for a few mintues and then I'll come to bed."

Dee walked over to Carl and placed her hand gently on his shoulder. "All right, Honey. I'll be in bed." And she walked out of the kitchen not feeling triumphant, rather feeling sorry that she had to put Carl through these episodes and therefore not feeling very good about herself.

Carl finished his cigarette and picked up his folder as he proceeded to Wesley's bedroom. He turned on the ceiling light and gently shook his son, who was sound asleep. "Wake up, Wesley. Wake up."

"What's up, Dad? What time is it?" He rubbed his eyes and blinked to open them in the light.

"It's not late, only ten o'clock. But it's time for me to give you something." He pulled the small white sheet of paper from the folder and unfolded it. Wesley couldn't imagine why such a small piece of paper could be so important at ten p.m. on a school night. He took the paper in his hands and read the list of signatures and instantly knew it was special.

"The seven astronauts, all on one sheet of paper! Wow! It's mine?"

"Yes, having these seven signatures of our first men in space is special. I was able to collect them this evening at the Christmas party. It's yours and I hope you know how important it is. Put it in your drawer and keep it safe."

"Thanks, Dad! This is amazing. You really work with them!"

"Now, go back to sleep after you put this up. We can talk tomorrow but you must make the school bus in the morning." Carl got up to leave for bed. There were no hugs or physical contact, but the love and care between Carl and his son were for the moment palpable in the space between them.

"Thanks again, Dad." Carl only nodded in recognition as he walked out. He had other things pressing on his mind and his family had uncharted waters to navigate. One of four hundred thousand was soon to leave the team to follow his twin dreams to create with wood and sustain his family.

Chapter 17
Cosmos, 1982 and Beyond

"*Cosmos* often simply means 'universe.' But the word is generally used to suggest an orderly or harmonious universe, as it was originally used by Pythagoras in the 6th century B.C. Thus, a religious mystic may help put us in touch with the cosmos, and so may a physicist."—*Merriam Webster Dictionary.*

Carl, at fifty-six, lay in bed waiting for the next day when an ambulance would carry him from his home high on a bluff overlooking Beaver Lake to the hospital in Fayetteville, Arkansas. His thoracic cancer had been detected through a mild heart attack the prior September, and despite chemo and radiation therapies he was now firmly in Stage three, where his lymphatic system had been invaded by the disease. It was April, and he knew that this was a battle he would not win.

Dee, now a trim and partially graying fifty-four, came into the bedroom with soup and a bowl of fruit. "I managed to get Brutus settled with a new owner. I wish I hadn't pushed you to buy that damned Doberman. I just wanted us to have more security out here where we're a bit isolated. Here, you should have some soup and fruit." She placed the bed tray on his lap. Carl was able to feed himself, though he was unsure how long that would last.

"Yeah, well, I was against it, you know. But then I thought, well, Brutus would keep you company during this time, but he isn't the companion type." He coughed slightly even though he kept his voice at a soft level all the time now.

Dee raised her voice, "You don't have to rub it in, Carl." Her face instantly turned to a hurt look, then to an angry face, "You knew in California that you were sick, didn't you? Why did you keep it from me?"

"You want me to feel guilty for dying, Dee? Why now? Can't you just support me as best you can while this fucking cancer does its dirty work? Our kids are all in California." He paused to cough softly. "Wesley is the only one that has come to visit since the heart attack. Now, he's gone silent because all you could do was insult his wife and then wouldn't apologize. Then, you wanted him to apologize to you! He made a decision to stand by his wife and I made a decision to stand by mine by calling him to reconsider and apologize to you, which he refused to do."

"Why are you taking up with him on this?"

"I understand his decision, Dee. What I don't understand is why it all got to that point!"

He coughed again and Dee said nothing. "I'm tired and I just want to rest now." He shoved the food away and turned his head.

"What am I going to do without you, Carl. I'm alone here. I know my sisters will visit from time to time, but I can't stay here."

"You wanted to move to this remote place, and I wanted to give that to you. One last time," he said without facing her. "I was to design and build custom furniture part-time for as long as I could, and you would be happy in the country here."

"For as long as you could! Then, you knew something was wrong. I tried and tried to get you to give up smoking, but you always found a way and didn't care what I wanted, which is *you*; healthy and the two of us where we want to be for our golden years."

"Dee, smoking is only part of it. Asbestos fibers, plutonium, and breathing in toxic chemicals in the spray booth for years all added their effects. I'm not apologizing for anything to anyone. I won't even apologize for loving you all these years. Now, let's remember us as a couple who've raised good children and who've been dealt a few bad hands. I've got to sleep now, Dee."

She didn't know how to respond as she was just now coming to grips with Carl's likely death. She left the room in silence. Carl was exhausted and drifted off to sleep.

On the prior September 2, Carl and Wesley had their last fishing trip together at Half Moon Bay in California, where they went out for the day on a party boat to catch whatever the ocean would yield up. Carl and Dee were moving three days later to Arkansas, and their plans sounded good to the children, with the exception that the move would take them far away from their four grandchildren: two from Wesley and two from Chris.

Wesley hadn't seen Carl for two months. Carl had been busy selling his business, Doe's Custom Craft in Livermore, and his house and select belongings. But the two each felt that they needed this one last trip before the move because nobody could know when they could get together next. They arrived by separate cars as Wesley lived in the Sunset District of San Francisco and Carl came from Livermore.

Wesley greeted his father as Carl stepped from his pick-up in the parking lot, upslope from the pier and the store where arrangements were made. "Hi, Dad! Here we are at Dark Hundred. I need some coffee."

"You're right there! Let's find some." And then, they walked side by side to the building. After coffee and donuts, and collecting the deep-sea gear for the day, they boarded the boat along with over twenty other anglers and set sail in the dark as the first rays of the sun slowly emerged from the Pacific horizon over calm waters.

It was an eventful day from a fishing standpoint as they hauled one and a half potato sacks of rockfish and soles from the shallow depths. Wesley noticed that his dad was having occasional trouble with the gear and didn't have his hooks in the water as constantly as on other trips. He was also uncharacteristically quiet. When the fishing was over, the boat returned at two p.m. and they had their fish cleaned and wrapped at the pier.

"We're moving in two days, so you take all the fish. I wouldn't know what to do with mine."

After loading the fish into Wesley's car, Carl started to say his goodbyes, but Wesley said, "I'll walk you to your truck, Dad. We're not gonna' see each other for a while."

"You don't have to do that."

"I want to, Dad. You've done so much for me, for us, and it's the least I can do to say a proper goodbye."

"Okay, Wesley." Carl smiled slightly and nodded his head uphill toward his truck.

As they walked, Carl started to wheeze and breathe heavily. It was a slight slope, and Wesley had never seen his father in this condition. He was instantly alarmed. "Dad, this isn't good. When was your last physical?"

"About six months ago, and everything was okay."

"Well, it doesn't sound okay. Promise me you'll have this looked into, maybe someone needs to check your heart." He put his arm around Carl's shoulders. "I love you, Dad. I want you to see your grandchildren grow up. And I want to see you enjoy your semiretirement you so richly deserve." This made Carl a bit red in the face. "So please take care of yourself and get to the doctor!"

"I will, I promise. Good-bye, Wesley, and give your little rascals a hug from Grandpa!" With that he got into his pick-up, started the engine, and drove away. Wesley was a bit dumbfounded by the abruptness of Carl's departure and he couldn't see the tears forming in his father's eyes as he drove away. He didn't realize that Carl thought he was actually saying goodbye for good, and didn't want a fuss made of it.

Everyone got the news of Carl's heart attacks in September and October, and by November, his cancer was diagnosed as already advanced to Stage two. Upon hearing the news from his father over the phone, as Dee had stubbornly refused to speak with any of their children, Wesley immediately hatched a plan to travel to his parents' home in Arkansas. He held little hope that if he waited further, he would be able to have a real visit instead of a bedside vigil. And he wanted a real visit. He booked a flight into Kansas City with a connector to Fayetteville for a five-day visit which was all he could get away from his new job in Alameda. His wife Jacqui stayed back with his four and two-year old children. She was fully supportive of his trip.

Jacky was a thirty-three-year-old Sephardic beauty that Wesley had met in university and married later in 1970. While she had been soundly rebuffed and shunned by Dee in spite of her sincere efforts to connect, she always got along with Carl, who had a talent for getting along with everyone. The two seemed to like each other. "You've got to be with your father now, Honey. You don't know when or if you will see him again. I will handle things here, not to worry." She hugged her husband for reassurance, and he hugged her back.

"It's a curse, apparently, of our family. I only knew one of my grandparents, Jack Nation. And it looks like our kids are only gonna know one as well, my mother, since your parents passed away years ago. She's a bitter woman, God knows why, and very hard to get along with but I will not argue with her for Dad's sake while I'm there."

"Get them each a Christmas present, Wes, not a goodbye present. You'll be there before Christmas and back here for Channukah."

"Good advice, Honey. I'll think on what to get them."

For a couple of days, he pondered what to get his dad. Carl had always been difficult to shop for. Fishing or outdoor gear was a no go. He gave thought to Carl's life and interests outside of work and family and realized that his dad had unfulfilled interests in space exploration and science. Wesley had enthusiastically watched the recent series 'Cosmos' hosted by Carl Sagan, the renowned astronomer from Cornell University. It had 1980 state of the art special effects, details of the struggles and insights of scientists from ancient times to the present, and illustrations of the magnificent scope and beauty of featured elements of Cosmos. One final message was clear. Backed by spectral and other analyses of exploding stars, or nova, and by employing the physics and mathematics of matter in the vastness of space, Sagan concluded, "Thus, we are all star stuff." In essence, we are here and alive on this planet because the deaths of stars have seeded and continue to seed the universe with the elements necessary for the formation of new stars, planets, and the potential for life. Wesley wanted Carl to believe this as an unspoken gift to his dying father, but only if he realized it through his own self-exploration of the recent book by Sagan, and his collaborators by the same title which included most of the information in the series as well as the impressive artwork.

Meanwhile, as Carl and Dee prepared for the arrival of their son, tensions were high in the Doe house. Carl had completed his first round of chemotherapy and was to be measured and marked for radiation therapy to begin while Wesley was visiting. He required more sleep than usual and was severely fatigued for long stretches of time.

But his mind remained active and curious.

Carl was no longer driving, and Dee transported him to the hospital for his sessions, which would be three times per week for six weeks. Wesley, they knew, would insist upon driving Carl during his visit. It was hard for Dee to realize that they would host their son in their home even though he hadn't apologized to her, in fact didn't know what to apologize for.

Wesley arrived on the turboprop on a Sunday two weeks before Christmas, and was to stay until Friday afternoon. After what to Wesley was a warmer than expected greeting, Carl and Dee walked him around the mini estate. The house had two fireplaces, there was a dog run behind a chain link fence, a garage, and a building for Carl's shop. The plan had been to commission designs and build them for shipment to customers around the country, but Carl never got the chance to continue such work because the cancer was seeing to it that Carl's passion was left behind in his old business in California.

After a dinner of baked pork chops, sauteed apples, and sauerkraut, the three sat for a chat and it was agreed that Wesley would drive Carl to his sessions that week and if Carl was up for it, he would show Wesley around the area. When Wesley and Carl were alone, Wesley pulled his Christmas present for Carl from his bag just as Carl went into a coughing fit that was obviously painful.

"It's okay, Wesley," he panted and raised his hand. After a few moments he calmed down. "You'll get used to it."

"No, I won't, Dad. I've never seen you like this. You've always been so strong and purposeful and I can see that you are weakened and have lost weight. I need to get used to that and it's not easy."

"I didn't get cancer to make you feel good or bad, Wesley, it just happened. And now I could use a smoke."

"Are you kidding, Dad? What the hell? Are you so eager to leave your family behind? What about Mom? What about Allie and Josh? What about me?"

"Listen, Wesley," Carl started to say something but ended up coughing again for nearly a minute. Wesley could only stare in disbelief, afraid for his father, wanting to get out of here with him to anywhere that involved sitting side by side with their fishing rods in hand. Finally, Carl continued.

"I've done the work I wanted to do, raised my family as best I could and never chased other women or took to drink or gambling. Smoking has been my vice. I'll be damned if I am going to apologize for it! Besides, there's plutonium, fiberglass, asbestos, and lacquer spray not to mention ammonia and paint remover. Cigarettes may be the least of the damage. I don't want to hear anymore about it! I get enough from your mother."

"She's just afraid of losing you, Dad. We all are."

"I love you, son. Never doubt that."

"I know, Dad. Your way of saying it is by doing something about it. Kind of like me taking seven months to help you start your business. My way of showing you how important you have been to me. And I think it's something you would've done."

Carl said nothing in return and for a long moment there was silence between them. Then, Carl opened his present and remarked, "It's a big book, lots of pictures. Does it say anything important?" He smiled.

"Yeah, it does. But I want you to find out if you believe in what it says in the end, which is based upon science. I know that you can read it while you're going through the next weeks of radiation therapy." In answer, Carl looked serious and grabbed the book, then began turning pages slowly.

For the rest of the visit, father and son spent much time together. They looked at the photographs of Carl's grandchildren, and of the family together at Carl and Dee's California home.

They discussed many things, some trivial and inconsequential and some that were deep and meaningful. In Wesley's eyes, death hovered over his dad, unseen but palpably present. He knew in his heart this was it and while that realization settled firmly in his mind, he was nevertheless completely happy to have had these few days uninterrupted and while Carl possessed all of his mental faculties and most of his mobility. On the day of his departure, Dee prepared soup and sandwiches for lunch and they sat around the table not saying much. Dee's patience was now running thin, but the day before she had taken Wesley shopping for the kids, and the result was a bag full of toys. As she cleaned up in the kitchen and then went into the bedroom to freshen up, Carl and Wesley had a last chance to speak alone before heading for the Fayetteville airport for the connector flight to Kansas City.

"Dad, I wish the kids could've spend more time with you. They're so young. And I wish we had more time together." He said this slowly, tentatively, not knowing what the reaction would be but determined to express the sentiment.

"I'm going to tell you something, and you have to keep it to yourself and only to you. Can you promise me that?" Carl stared into Wesley's eyes for any sign of sincerity and intent.

"Of course, Dad. If you tell me something in confidence, I swear that I wouldn't even share it with Jacky." Carl did not detect any lack of resolve on his son's part to keep an important secret.

"You've rightfully asked questions about my childhood years, trying to fill in the information gaps. Just understand that some things are too painful to relive. But when you're facing death, things change. I mean, I don't want to hold onto some things that I've kept inside all my life."

"I think I understand. We may never have the chance to talk face to face after this. I need peace, too, Dad. What is it you want to tell me?"

"I was… mistreated. Dorothy was mistreated and Charlie was mistreated. All of us by Worlick. He put Dorothy on the street." Wesley knew what he meant by that. "And he beat Charlie and me and made us do all kinds of hard work. He is a bastard of the first order and I wish I'd killed him. That's what happened to me after Mom died. And I hate Dorothy for what she allowed to happen, maybe it wasn't her fault. Never talk about this to anyone!" He began to cough and wheezed for a few moments. Carl could not bring himself to give over the whole truth. He diplomatically let his son fill in the blanks.

"I promise."

"Well, good then. Let me tell you more about Daddy Charles and Mother Nellie and little Annabelle." Wesley listened with full attention, never interrupting his father, for a full thirty minutes. The only interruption was the sporadic coughing and wheezing, but Carl was being very precise in his memories. "I lied when I told you so many times that I couldn't remember them as they were and my life with them. I'm sorry for that. There's so much I wanted to run from after becoming an orphan and I had to have something to run to, if get my drift."

Dee came into the room. "It's time we go to the airport. Wesley, are your things ready?"

After saying their goodbyes at the airport, Carl and Wesley each experienced the suddenness of the bottom dropping out, in knowledge of the finality of their parting.

Dee loved her son, but she didn't like him nor his wife, so her love was not unconditional.

In January, 1982, Carl read Cosmos. In February, he deteriorated and started having vivid dreams that Dee thought were nightmares but in fact constituted an approach by Carl's subconscious to leaving this world during the slowly dissolving vapor of life. It may be that the reassuring thrust of the book *Cosmos* provided Carl's spirit a way to cope. Nobody could ever know but him.

He was asleep, heavily drugged. Out of the blackness suddenly appeared the white room at MA where the final mock-up of Friendship seven was being assembled. Carl watched as the technicians and engineers busied themselves in their white jumpsuits and caps. Nobody seemed to notice him. Then, he received a tap on the shoulder.

"Hey there, Carl." He spun around to see Astronaut Glenn smiling his All-American smile.

"Hi yourself, John. Where am I?"

"You are in a dream, for sure. I couldn't wait to go up there and circle the Earth, to see what it's like." Glenn looked up at the ceiling in wonder and as Carl did so the ceiling dissolved into a night sky full of stars with no moon. It was brilliant and astonishing.

"I want to thank you for all of your help, you and your teammates."

"You're welcome, John. But you knew… or know… it's risky."

"Carl, you can't bullshit a bullshitter. Don't forget I'm a politician now!" He smiled again and said, "If there's one thing a cotton-pickin' cotton picker knows about, it's risk! Bye, Carl, they're all out there waiting for you, all part of the Cosmos." Before Carl could say anything, Glenn vanished as did the dream, but Carl awoke crying

"Wait! Wait! So much to talk about! Don't leave me alone!" Dee assumed it was a nightmare or at least an unpleasant dream. Glenn was alive in the real world, as Carl knew.

A week later, Carl was in the hospital for observation and testing to determine future medications. Once more heavily drugged, he fell into a deep sleep. His dream appeared and he instantly knew where he was, at the edge of a field laying on his back with a long blade of grass in his teeth, chewing as he surveyed the stars above. A half-moon graced the night sky. He sensed someone next to him.

"Where the hell you been, boy?" It was Cheeks as he was that night they feasted upon crawdads. "I been waitin' a fair while. No Carl!" He elbowed Carl in disapproval.

"I came as soon as I could, you idiot! Been busy."

"I know all about that, stupid! Earth to space boy! Earth to space boy! Been trackin' you all along. At least one of us got to hell out of here. I'm just stuck like a vegetable with that nice reverend and his family. Wish to hell I hadn't tried to ride the rails that time."

"I've missed you, Cheeks. I thought we'd be friends forever. You saved my life, remember?"

"Yeah, I remember, tadpole. But here, I didn't go anywhere. Been with you all along, you were just too stupid to know! But I'm here because you remember me now. And don't worry. Not Worlick, nor those bastards that threw you into the deep water nor anyone else is going to hurt you… out there." Cheeks pointed to the heavens. "You'll just laugh at them, promise! By the way, great work on the spacecraft." He emphasized the last word. "Space boy," he said in admiration. "My friend, the space boy." He dissolved into nothingness as did the dreamscape.

Again, Carl awoke with the cry, "Don't leave me! Cheeks, come back!" The nurses on duty assumed he had experienced a nightmare.

By April, Carl was clearly presenting with a significant weight loss and occasionally palsied hands and neck. But his mind remained sharp and he was determined to put up a show of fierce resistance for Dee's benefit, but he had long ago decided that his current journey was his last in this life, and was gradually becoming comfortable that his end was near. *'Just so much damned pain!'* Carl was struggling to breathe, which caused him much pain and discomfort and for the first time in his life he became cranky and difficult to deal with. It took the cancer gnawing away at his insides without letup for him to change his colors.

During his final weeks spent at home, he had another dream.

Annie as a five-year-old little girl appeared on a tree-lined pathway. They were walking hand in hand slowly, as if they had all the time in the world. Again in this dream, it was night and the sky was full of stars, though slightly diminished as a starscape due to the full moon.

Annie broke the silence. "You promised me you'd come and take me away from the Nooners, but you never did. I hated that place and only wanted to be with my family, with you." She looked up at him with an accusatory expression, part sad and part angry.

But she didn't let go of Carl's hand.

Seconds elapsed. Finally, Carl drew a deep breath—this was, after all, a dream—and looked down into Annie's upturned face, full of freckles and reddish curly hair. "Annie, I never forgot my promise, but in truth I knew that I couldn't make it happen. I didn't want to add to your sadness and I always felt terrible about promising you something I couldn't deliver." He squeezed her hand and smiled a loving smile.

"I forgive you, brother. I really do." Her voice now turned into the voice of the grown Annabelle but her body remained that of a child. He was astonished and shocked into silence.

She continued in the mature voice. "We all had our difficulties; you, me, Charlie, Dorothy, and Martha. You've got to forgive everyone, Carl. It's the only way. Dorothy was a child bride to a bully and a pervert. She came good in the end and raised a family. Charlie is blameless. Martha is someone we never knew. And you, God! You had the hardest road of all and look what you've done and the life you carved out for you your family. And you gave me the absolute greatest Christmas present ever! Just remember, big brother, we all have our demons and foils in our lives. But love is forever, the only thing we take with us. I'll miss you, but will have my time later to explore the Cosmos with you and the others."

"Oh, Annie!" He cried, as he stooped to hug her, but she vanished as did his surroundings and all he saw was blackness. And then, he awoke with the immediate cry of, "Annie, dearest sister, don't go! I'll never see you if you go." Then, he began to weep the dry-eyed weeping of an advanced cancer victim until his mind convinced him that his dreams were messages meant for him and him alone, from people who were always with him in one way or another. His inner Cosmic light switched on and he silently thanked Wesley for providing the circuitry through Carl Sagan's book.

By May, Carl had to be moved via wheelchair. His walking days were over. There were no longer any treatments, just pain management and the drugs used to make him sleep soundly did just that, but the effect was to put him in a trancelike state during the waking periods. Dee did her best to make him comfortable and pledged to volunteer for hospice work for terminally ill patients outside the hospital, a movement that was gaining steam in the greater patient care community.

One night in May, Carl found himself in a field of grass on a moonlit night. In the distance, a short walk ahead, there was a group of people holding what looked like a night picnic, sitting around a blanket. One of them, a woman, waved to him to come over and join the group. There were six of them: four men and two women. And one of the men was African-American. As Carl approached on foot, it became clear to him who was there: Maynard from the hotel, Eddie, Grant, Gurdy, Nellie, and Charles Wesley Dough. Nobody was eating or drinking, just chatting and looking out over the river or up at the moon and stars.

In his matter of fact and even tone, Maynard spoke first, "Well, Carl, I see that you got your little doll to sis. She like it?" He raised one eyebrow.

"My God. You're the man at the hotel who took pity on me that Christmas Eve! Wait a minute, wait. I never saw you again, and never knew your name. but you know mine." There was a bit of wonder in his voice.

"You're pretty slow for a NASA space technician, boy. Haven't you figured it out that everyone here knows you. We're all lookin' at you, kid. You are us and we are you. But fair enough, I'm Maynard."

"Then you know that my little sister Annie loved the doll, still has it after all these years. And I'm grateful forever, sir. But right now, I need to speak to my two sets of parents if you don't mind." Carl extended his hand and Maynard took it, smiled, and then vanished. Carl turned toward Grant and Gurdy, while looking at his parents to whom he said, "Mom, Dad, I am saving you for last so please don't disappear!"

"That's not up to us, my dear little man," said Nellie. When she said this, Charles smiled and nodded his head in agreement. "But please go ahead. We're not going anywhere."

They all appeared as he remembered them. Charles was not sickly, nor was Nellie. Grant and Gurdy looked exactly like they did when he first saw them at the café that fateful morning. Eddie's eyesight was perfect but strangely he had his flight suit on.

"I grew to love you like a son," said Gurdy, as she put her arm around Grant. "You never misplaced our trust in you. I just wish we would have sent you to school, proper."

"It's okay, Momma Gurdy, you kept me on the road to learning and I found my way, was lucky to have found you and the boys." He gestured to Grant and Eddie.

"You know, Carl," said Grant, "Death is the beginning of something wonderful. I left my hatred and bitterness behind, unburdened. I'm glad to see that you have lived a life free of hate and bitterness. Lord knows that's a miracle in itself. And your life has had such meaning. Loving a woman who never thought she deserved it, accomplishing so much in your craft and artistry, and raising three good children. And, a bit of good fishing to boot!" They both put their hands on his shoulder but before he could embrace them, they vanished. He turned to Eddie.

"I'm still not used to that, Eddie…" But Eddie cut him off.

"Carl, I know what you've done with your life and God knows I have been sorry about what I said and did to drive you away. But you managed to turn lemons into lemonade, my brother. Things worked out well for Maggie and me, and our two kids. Just remember, sometimes we hurt the ones we love because we don't believe we can be what they need anymore. Brothers forever!" And with that, Eddie vanished before Carl could respond.

"Wise words, Carl," said Charles.

"But why am I talking to everyone who's ever really believed in me. I was so stupid 'cause I thought in my pride I did it all alone. But nobody ever really accomplishes anything without others."

"And who believed in you when everyone was telling you what your limits should be?" asked Nellie.

"Dee."

"And?" she persisted. Carl gave this some thought behind a furrowed brow.

"Wesley, he always cheered me on but I didn't appreciate the support he was showing. He helped me to get my business off the ground and I never thanked him for that. Carl suddenly had a blank stare until Charles interrupted him.

"We've always been part of you, my boy. We can no longer be sorry nor have feelings of guilt. Remember what Clyde Barrow said to us as he sneered his way to his death?

"Cotton-pickin cotton pickers? He's not part of you and you're not part of him, the parts that go on into infinity, in this Cosmos. Neither is Worlick. You've hidden your abuse in shame all your life, never talked to anyone about it and that effort cost you connections with the people who love and support you the most."

"You know that?" Carl began to tremble.

"We all know it. Like the man said, we are you and you are us. We're all headed together to wherever we go when you die, son."

Carl couldn't help himself as he moved toward his parents, who were smiling at him. He reached out with both arms only to see them vanish as had the others. Again, he awoke in a drugged stupor and all he could do was groan and move his hands.

By the beginning of June, he was in the hospital full time. All the medical staff could do was to try to make his last days as comfortable as possible. Dee was camped in his room most of the time, sleeping or reading. There were occasional moments of lucidity from Carl, but they were infrequent and unpredictable. Sometimes he would murmur the word 'cosmos' over and over without opening his eyes. Dee had no idea why. But one night in mid-June Carl had another dream, as vivid as the others with only one person in it.

He was outside of a cinema house. And it was in Paragould with 1930s and 1940s cars parked on the street, but no people could be seen. It was night. A young woman emerged from the theatre and Carl instantly knew that it was Dee as a fifteen-year-old girl in a polka dot dress. He gazed at the approaching figure in wonder. When she spoke, it was with the voice of Dee as she was at fifty-four years old.

"I've got something to tell you, Honey."

"I've got something to tell you too, Dee."

She paused in her steps instantly and asked, "What is it, Carl? We can have no secrets now, can we?" She moved forward as if to touch his arm and he recoiled.

"No, Dee. When I touch people in these dreams, they disappear and they don't come back. I know that you're here with me so that we can say goodbye to each other. I won't be here much longer. I'm joining the Cosmos."

"Is that what you've got to tell me? Your secret?" She seemed disappointed.

"No, Dee. I am telling you now that I was sexually abused and exploited, often beaten, when I was a boy by my brother-in-law Worlick, as was Dorothy and Charlie. I've carried this with me all my life and I know now what that has cost me." He waited for her to absorb this information.

"Well, why didn't we know this a long time ago? Carl, we were two kids thrown together by poverty, abuse, and war."

"Dee, I know you have been unhappy often, but I could never get passed the barriers you put up, nor you mine. I'm dropping mine now, at last. Will you drop yours as well?" He looked into her eyes and said, "I've never stopped loving you, and maybe I could have figured out a way to bring more happiness to you."

"Carl, listen to me. There's nothing you could have done that you didn't do. You've been a loving husband, a good father and provider, and I'm the one with the secret. I love you and we'll be together again, out there." She swept her arm around to take in the surroundings and the sky. Then, she rushed to hug him before he could react, and she vanished as the others had vanished.

"I guess that's it for me," he said to nobody and then left his dream, never to return as he descended into a drug induced coma in the hospital from which he would never awake. In his mind there appeared snippets of visions but they flashed in and out without making an impression. Sometimes, he could hear Dee's voice, and then his daughter Gwen's. She had arrived from California to be at his bedside in vigil.

In mid-morning in early July, Carl's eighty-five-pound body gave up this life. He sensed a release, pleasant and peaceful, as he felt himself drifting upward with no goal in sight, just a peaceful sensation. He could see the world below, much as Alan Shepard and John Glenn had done in their capsules, and he felt the pull of the stars beyond. And suddenly, all the people that were dead and gone appeared before him, smiling. Carl drifted in silence to the waiting throng and then everything faded away. *Peace,* he thought. *Finally, peace.* The immense and many-colored expanse of the Cosmos gently pulled him away from Earth toward the uncharted. And he knew no more in this life.

www.ingramcontent.com/pod-product-compliance
Lightning Source LLC
Chambersburg PA
CBHW051132190726
48290CB00006B/1813